THEIR FIRST NIGHT TOGETHER . . .

"Ingrid?"

Max's call was soft. The cabin was so quiet. So *still*.
Annie tried to batter down the horrid images that kept
rising in her mind's eye. Ingrid would have rushed to them,
if she were there. If she were able.

The screen door was closed, but beyond it, Ingrid's front
door was ajar.

Annie would never forget the scene that flashed into
view: Max leaning forward in a crouch, his fists balled,
ready to attack; the familiar shabby gentility of Ingrid's
living room, petit point cushions on the cheerful chintz
sofa, linen drapes in cobalt blue with a design of white
shasta daisies, and, in the center of the room, staring
sightlessly up at the stippled plaster ceiling, the body
spread-eagled on the blue-and-grey hooked rug.

HONEYMOON WITH L~~O~~VE
Murder

Carolyn G. Hart

BANTAM BOOKS
NEW YORK • TORONTO • LONDON • SYDNEY • AUCKLAND

HONEYMOON WITH MURDER

A Bantam Crime Line Book / January 1989

CRIME LINE and the portrayal of a boxed "cl" are trademarks of Bantam Books, a
division of Random House, Inc.

ISBN 0-553-27608-5

Published simultaneously in the United States and Canada

Bantam Books are published by Bantam Books, a division of Random
House, Inc. Its trademark, consisting of the words "Bantam Books" and
the portrayal of a rooster, is Registered in U.S. Patent and trademark
Office and in other countries. Marca Registrada. Bantam Books, 1540
Broadway, New York, New York 10036.

PRINTED IN THE UNITED STATES OF AMERICA

OPM   25 24 23 22 21 20 19 18 17 16

To Kate,
Editor Par Excellence

ONE

Jesse Penrick didn't miss much on his solitary nocturnal rambles. Lights at an odd hour. A visitor never before seen. An unfamiliar car.

It was the car that attracted him in the ghostly hour just before dawn. The car and the window lighted at such an unusually, for this cabin, early hour. Jesse sidled between the oleander and the exterior wall to peer through the smudged window. He liked looking in from the darkness, unseen, unfelt. He liked to slip inside unlatched doors, too, when occupants were absent. He liked finding out about people.

Knowing funny little facts could pay off. Sometimes the payoff was slipping in the needle, the muttered comment that brought a flash of fear or fury to an unwary face.

Jesse Penrick liked *finding out* about people. But he didn't *like* people.

His watery, nearsighted eyes strained to see as much as possible. The wooden shutters were closed, but a broken slat afforded him a narrow field of vision, the portion of the living room that held a couple of wicker chairs and a wooden chest. As he watched, the occupant of the room came into view, carrying an awkward, lumpy bundle. The bearer dumped the load on the floor beside the wooden chest, then lifted the lid.

But Jesse's gaze was riveted on the floor and the red-and-

1

blue quilt—just like one his grandmother'd made—that gaped open to reveal its contents.

Jesse could have called the police.

It would have been exciting. Lights flashing. Sirens. Maybe even yellow tape like he saw sometimes in TV crime scenes. And Jesse could be a hero, interviewed on Channel 10. Hot stuff.

Instead, he waited, his gnarled hands gripping the window frame. In only a few minutes, the room was empty and dark, the bundle stuffed into the chest, the lights turned off, the car departed in a swirl of dust.

Jesse looked once over his shoulder, then trotted to the back of the cabin and the kitchen door he had learned to shake until the bolt slipped. He tiptoed inside. He had a little pocket flash which he aimed down at the opened chest. He tugged on the quilt. His impersonal blue eyes surveyed the interior thoughtfully, then he gave a satisfied nod. Without a qualm, he reached down and pulled. In a moment, he stared at the soft gleam of gold against his palm. That would prove he'd been here, all right.

He tucked the covering in place, closed the lid, then slid out of the house as silently as he'd come. Be interesting to see what happened next. And it would happen pretty quick, as hot as it was. He didn't have to be in any hurry. But, when the time was right, he'd make a little phone call. Be a hell of a shock. His thin mouth stretched in a wolfish grin.

TWO

Lucinda Burrows darted through the crowd, her brown alligator heels clicking excitedly against the concrete.

She'd done just as instructed, and the whole operation had gone without a hitch.

She was good at this.

Soon there would be more to do. Her green eyes glowed with excitement. She caught a glimpse of herself in plate glass and was pleased. She still looked young—and tonight she felt so young. To think this fabulous week had begun with a chance conversation at her favorite bookstore. After all the years of reading about adventure, adventure had come to her. She'd never thought it could happen!

She paused once, a little daunted now, because the crowds had thinned, and she was at the far end of the long drive that led to the highway. Then lights blinked twice in the darkness beneath a line of loblolly pines.

She took a tighter grip on her overnight bag and broke into an eager trot, stumbling a little in her eagerness, careening like a moth toward extinction.

THREE

The perfect crime.

Who said it couldn't be done?

The solitary drinker raised the champagne glass in silent toast.

To crime.

It was then—and did some dark gods in a shadowy corner of the universe clasp their sides and shake with mirth?—that the phone began to ring.

FOUR

Early Saturday morning,
September 19

Ingrid Jones had no idea she was being observed, she and
the whole expanse of Nightingale Courts. She was oblivious
to her surroundings this morning, although she was one of
the island's most fervent boosters. In the mornings, she
often took time to stroll out on one of the long narrow piers
to watch a passing sailboat or frolicking dolphins. At low
tide, she'd stand very still and enjoy the antics of solemn-
faced raccoons, the grace of small white-tailed deer, and the
industry of scavenging blue crabs. But today she marched
in the opposite direction, toward the row of silvery
mailboxes next to the honeysuckle-laden arbor at the
entrance to Nightingale Courts, her mind teeming with last
minute chores for the wedding. Thank heaven the blister-
ing heat had broken. Thursday and Friday had sizzled,
even for September in the semi-tropics. Today's breeze
held a hint of freshening. Not cool, certainly, but not
steamy. It would make the un-air-conditioned church
bearable. She needed to be sure the bridesmaids' dresses
were at the church in plenty of time. Max certainly did
have pretty sisters, all three of them. Though that one,
Deidre, was probably a real handful. Of course, anybody
with a mother like Laurel . . .

Thrusting her hand into Box No. 3, she pulled out
yesterday's mail. She hadn't had a minute to look Friday,
what with the tennis tournament for the bridesmaids and
the golfing scramble for the groomsmen. And last night had

certainly been spectacular—the rehearsal dinner aboard an island tour boat, complete with mariachis on one level, an Irish balladeer on the second, and a Mozart quartet on the third. And the food. You had to hand it to Laurel, she was really into round-the-world in eighty tastes. Ingrid herself considered American cooking plenty good enough and Low Country cuisine best of all, but the exotic foreign dishes certainly added spice. She just hoped Annie didn't have indigestion today, after that Indonesian curry and reindeer stew. Seemed a shame to kill a reindeer; but, as Laurel said, what was an ecological sacrifice if it was made in the name of love?

A tiny smile touched Ingrid's face. Dear me, if that woman couldn't talk about love. And in half a dozen languages, too. Well, it was going to be an original wedding, even though Annie had managed to tone down some of Laurel's notions. There was, Ingrid had to admit, certainly an aura about this union, though she wouldn't go so far as to call it, as Laurel did, a Cosmic Statement on Love.

It was only happenstance that she saw the splotch of red. She was turning away, her mind still teeming with items to be done, when the brilliantly red, uneven marking caught her eye.

Though it was intended to attract attention, of course, that vivid scarlet A emblazoned on Box 6. Attract attention and cause pain. Her hand unconsciously tightened on the sheaf of mail, crumpling it. She knew who was responsible. There was no doubt in her mind, though she felt an instant's surprise at his literary knowledge. But just an instant. As all old librarians know, you can't characterize readers. They come in all persuasions, from bricklayers to physicists, from the vicious to the angelic. So Jesse Penrick knew Hawthorne. It didn't raise her estimation of him. She had very strong feelings about Jesse Penrick.

She whirled to face his cabin and the inlet. Speak of the very devil, here he came, his boat gliding across the water, his blue-clad scrawny arms rising and falling with the oars. Returning from one of his cat-footed, voyeuristic nocturnal outings.

Ingrid hesitated for an instant. This wasn't the day to face down Jesse Penrick. This was a very special day, Annie and Max's wedding day, and nothing must detract from its beauty.

But she couldn't let the sleazeball get away with this latest dirty trick.

She was standing on the pier waiting, when he skinnied up the ladder, agile as a monkey.

"I want that mailbox cleaned up, Jesse. Today."

"Mailbox?" He had a slimy voice. Reminded her of old-fashioned hair oil. "Something wrong with a mailbox?" His watery blue eyes glistened with pleasure.

Take it easy, Ingrid warned herself. He was taunting her. He wanted her to lose her temper. That was part of the fun.

"Clean it up, or I'm going to throw you out of here. Your lease comes up next month. And don't think I won't do it."

He hunched his bony shoulders beneath the thick all-cotton navy blue turtleneck. He must have a closet full of them. It was all he ever wore, navy blue turtlenecks and tight dungarees. The better to move unseen through the night. The wind tugged at the strand of iron-grey hair that straggled across his forehead. His thin lips drew back in a snarl. "You just try it. You just try! I've been to see a lawyer at Legal Aid. You can't push me out on some trumped-up story. And I'll tell you why. It'd be discrimination. That's what the lawyer said: Dis-Crim-I-Na-Tion, and you can't do it, hear?"

She stared at him and knew she was close to exploding.

The snarl eased into a satisfied grin. "I'm going to get me the last laugh, you'd better believe it."

Ingrid was determined not to be drawn. This was a big day. An important day. The most important day for Annie and Max. She wasn't going to let a festering piece of sewage like Jesse Penrick ruin this day.

Without a word, she started to turn away.

"And if you don't take the check, maybe I'll speak out about some of the goings-on in these cabins."

Her head jerked around.

He grinned malevolently. "So maybe you won't be so high and mighty, huh?"

Ingrid's temper wasn't as easily triggered as that of her

employer at the famous mystery bookstore, Death on Demand, but even Ingrid had a flash point.

Her face flushing, she exploded, telling Jesse Penrick, in ringing tones and in full view of the Nightingale Courts, the sun-bright marsh, and the inlet, just how despicable she thought he was, in language both rude and Saxon-pungent, as might be expected of a very well educated ex-librarian.

FIVE

Annie Laurance slipped stealthily down the alley, crouching once behind a Dumpster to avoid an early morning encounter with Maisie Wellington, who owned the shop next to Death on Demand. It wasn't that she didn't like Maisie. She did, despite Maisie's disdain for mystery fiction. ("I mean, honey, it's so *gruesome*.") Annie objected mightily, however, to Maisie's determination to foist shell-pink lingerie on her. Annie preferred sleeping in a T-shirt and shorts in the summer and threadbare sweats on the occasional chilly days in January and February. (Oh, God, how could she reconcile seductiveness and comfort—although, actually, Max had always seemed quite enchanted with T-shirts and panties, and why should she have to change now?) And Annie found highly irritating Maisie's unshakable conviction that it was her God-given duty, as an older woman, to prepare poor little motherless Annie for Married Life.

Annie peered from behind the Dumpster and saw Maisie's plump rear disappearing into the service entrance of Lingerie for Loving Ladies.

With a leap as agile as a fawn evading a bobcat, Annie reached the back step of Death on Demand, fumbled with the key, and darted inside. As the storeroom door closed behind her, she let out her breath in an enormous whoosh.

For a moment, she didn't even move. She just leaned against the door and tried not to think.

9

However, it was beyond her capacity for thought control to ignore the monumental truth: today was her Wedding Day.

She was thrilled, terrified, excited, panicked, profoundly sentimental—and poised for flight. Until she thought of Max. Dear, wonderful Max. How did he feel right now? She glanced down at her watch. Almost eight. He would be showering. Her lips curved in a smile. She enjoyed thinking of Max in the shower, warm water pelting his broad shoulders and nicely muscled legs. In fact, Max was nicely muscled. . . .

Eight o'clock.

Annie swallowed. In half an hour she was due at the Wedding Day Breakfast. She wondered if, once past the ceremony, she would shed this proclivity to think in capital letters. It was the inevitable consequence of several weeks spent in close and continuing contact with Laurel, Max's mother.

Laurel . . .

She was unlike anyone Annie had ever met. Annie determinedly ignored the nervous, wiggly little thought deep in the recesses of her mind that Laurel was merely Max intensified. In fact, Annie refused consciously to entertain that treacherous supposition. Max, of course, was laid back. His unflappability, his poise, his imperviousness to worry, accounted for much of his charm. But he was *not* spacey. Max was wonderful, and late this afternoon he would become her husband.

Annie pushed off the door like a shot and catapulted into the coffee area and began to pace.

She was too young to get married.

She was too old to get married.

She struggled to breathe. Was she having a heart attack? She was too young to have a heart attack. Then why was she breathless and feeling as if her chest were an expanding cavity? She was too old to be acting like this.

Panting, she drew in gulps of the wonderful, soothing aroma of her bookstore, which was, of course, the finest mystery bookstore this side of Atlanta, with its glistening heart-pine floors and row after row of books, all the mysteries any reader could want and more, from Aarons to

Zangwill, and a coffee bar with Colombian, French, and Hawaiian blends, and a sleekly black, resident stuffed raven named Edgar, of course, in honor of Edgar Allan Poe, the dark genius who originated the mystery, and a resident (not stuffed) cat, also sleekly black.

"Agatha? Agatha?"

An ebony head lifted languidly from the coffee bar. In the light cascading luminously from the high south windows, the amber eyes glowed wickedly.

Annie flung herself toward the coffee bar and grabbed the sleek feline. "Agatha, love, I'm panicked."

Agatha hissed, wriggled like an eel, and wormed free, scratching Annie's right wrist as she dropped to the floor.

"Oh. You're on Max's side, I guess."

But Agatha had fled into the deeper shadows of the rattan-and-wicker reading area, no doubt seeking sanctuary beneath her favorite Whitmani fern.

Licking absently at her wound, Annie turned back toward the coffee area. She must get a grip on herself. She was committed. Three hundred eighty-seven guests were at various stages of dress this morning on the island of Broward's Rock in anticipation of a magnificent Wedding Day Breakfast, and Annie had to go. And to the Wedding at five P.M. Yes, dammit. Capital letters. Capital hysteria.

One chest-expanding breath.

Two.

Three.

She again drew deeply on the soothing scent of old bookbindings, leather, paper, and ink. Of course, mysteries. She would contemplate mysteries, immerse her mind in—

With a shock, she realized she'd scarcely been in the store since September began. She'd been too occupied with wedding plans—and with Laurel—but that was another story. Still, it startled her to realize she hadn't even looked at this month's display of mystery paintings. Obviously, Ingrid, her most patient and wonderful assistant, who would tonight serve as Matron of Honor (no, she *wouldn't* think about the wedding!), had ordered and hung the five—and weren't they excellent!

In the first watercolor, an imposing, broad-shouldered

figure sat in a high armchair behind a red brocade–covered bench. He held aloft a blackwood gavel, poised to bang against the bench. He wore a glossy black silk judge's cap, with gauze wings, and a long, official robe of heavy green brocade. Intelligence glowed in the dark eyes set off by almond-toned skin, a full black beard, and long sideburns. Dotting the painting like colorful butterflies were miniature renditions of a magnificent Buddhist temple, a tilted bronze bell, two golden hairpins, and the wooden hand gong often carried by mendicant monks.

A world sheathed in ice and snow glittered in the second painting. A monk, his habit covered by a thick traveling cloak, stood in snow-crusted boots by the edge of a frozen brook, staring grimly down at the body of a beautiful woman, held in the ice like a fly in amber.

Moonlight bathed a cliff face in the third painting, illuminating a grotesque figure, swathed in yards of crumbling bandages that covered both body and face. Against the rotting bandages of its breast, the creature pressed the unconscious form of a young woman. Two striking figures stared in astonishment and horror, a strong-featured, black-haired woman and a tall, well-built man with a bronzed face, bright blue eyes, and a dimpled chin. The man carried a limp, turbaned figure in his arms.

In the fourth painting, fantasy and reality warred. A brown-handled kitchen knife protruded from the chest of an actor dressed as a Munchkin, the knife obscenely visible against the yellow coat of his comic soldier's uniform. He lay dead on the Yellow Brick Road, staring sightlessly up toward the sound-stage lights. The middle-aged man kneeling beside the body had a tough face with a nose that had taken too many blows.

In the fifth painting, a traveler in bedouin dress but with a European face pitched a tent beside a dying camel. The desert wastes stretched endlessly, and a burning sun glittered in a cloudless sky. But there was neither despair nor fear on the face of the man, only utter and complete determination.

Henny Brawley, of course, was probably five furlongs ahead of the competition in discovering the titles and authors represented. She was always excited at the prospect of receiving a free book. Henny was by far the most avid mystery fan on the island. Her taste ran from Millar to Rice, Van Dine to Langton, Kienzle to Maron, and that wouldn't begin to cite them all. Moreover, she would immediately recognize this sub-genre (historical mysteries). She especially enjoyed Peter Lovesey and advised everyone who would listen to read *The Detective Wore Silk Drawers*. Henny also enjoyed dabbling in real mysteries, and had earned Annie's undying (perhaps quite literally) respect for her timely arrival at the bookstore in the recent affair involving murder below stage during an amateur theatrical rehearsal of *Arsenic and Old Lace*.

Recalling those difficult days, Annie groaned. Laurel had wrested control of the wedding plans while Annie was distracted by homicide. So, for the rest of the summer, Annie had engaged in guerrilla actions to try and regain mastery over the ceremony, one lightning foray at dawn to the seamstress, a clutch of impassioned midnight pleas to Max (these were usually very effective), several preemptive strikes on the telephone to various wholesalers and jobbers around the country.

As a result, the ceremony was not quite as Laurel had hoped. (A Cosmic Statement on Love.) But it also wasn't quite what Annie had envisioned (a dignified, simple exchange of vows) when she plighted her troth. Perhaps it would be fair to say it was a curious and original amalgam of the traditional—and the not-so-traditional.

And it would begin at five P.M.

The telephone rang.

Annie jerked around and regarded it warily. It was certainly too late for Laurel to call with new ideas. Surely she couldn't have any innovative suggestions, with the wedding only hours away.

The shrill ring sounded again.

Refusing to answer would be a cop-out. She hadn't reached that point. Yet. Besides, it was probably a book rep. Or one of those infuriating robots that opened the conversation with, "Please——don't——hang——up. This ——call——could——change——your——life." Or a friend. Or a wrong number.

She yanked the receiver up in mid-peal. "Death on Demand."

"Annie, my sweet." As always, Laurel's husky voice brimmed with good cheer, delight, and eagerness. Annie had a vision of blond beauty levitating by a phone. "I had a feeling you might be—well, just a little bit nervy. And when I couldn't find you *anywhere*, well, I knew you would have run to earth in your burrow." A pause. "The shop." In case Annie had by any chance missed her point. "And I thought, the very *best* thing I can do is help you take yourself *out* of yourself."

Annie pondered that interesting suggestion while the throaty discourse continued. It wasn't necessary to hear Laurel's every word. There were so many extraneous bits, asides about the glorious future of the world as a result of the recent Harmonic Convergence, the necessity of synchronizing with new vibrations, and the duty of each earthling to help cleanse the planet in preparation for the Momentous Events that would unfold in 2012, according to newly interpreted Mayan writings.

With the skill of much recent practice, Annie winnowed the bright phrases, always alert for any reference to the wedding.

But the kicker still caught her by total surprise.

"What?" she demanded. "What did you say?"

Simple, direct questions unnerved Laurel, eliciting verbiage festooned with qualifications, interpretations, explanations, and disclaimers, but the essential message remained the same.

"I'd better go see," Annie cut in hastily. She thumped down the receiver and raced for the back door.

Annie braked just long enough to wave at the entry-point guard, shot through the open gate, pulled the wheel hard left, and squealed off the blacktop onto a rutted dirt road that snaked around clumps of palmettos and dipped into sloughs. A plume of grey dust boiled in her wake. She flew past Jerry's Gas 'N Go.

Not far now.

The Volvo's chassis quivered at the jolts, but Annie kept her foot on the accelerator until she screeched to a stop just past the honeysuckle-covered wooden arch that marked the entrance to Nightingale Courts.

She turned off her motor, looked around, and wondered if Laurel had suddenly become a practical joker.

Because nothing disturbed the gentle, early morning quiet of this sun-burnished pocket of Broward's Rock. Nightingale Courts, a semicircle of seven cabins, faced the salt marsh. At high tide, only the tips of the spartina grass could be glimpsed. At low tide, the marsh drained to shining mud flats and shallow salt-pan pools. Just past eight o'clock on this lovely September morning, the tide was flowing in; a hungry dolphin out in the sound sliced through the water in search of a tasty breakfast of herring, mackerel, and whiting; a fisherman in a bright yellow tank top and cutoffs leaned against the railing at the end of one of the piers that poked through the marsh to deep water; a ringbilled gull zeroed in on an unwary mouse, and a well-hidden clapper rail cackled derisively. Three delicately plumed snowy egrets searched contentedly for crabs.

It could not have been more placid or cheerful, the balmy morning sunshine bathing the cabins, the weathered wooden piers, and, across the inlet, the thick clumps of yucca and sea myrtle that partially screened from view two ramshackle cabins. The sunlight glistened, too, on the shiny tin roof of Jerry's Gas 'N Go.

As far as Annie could see, she and yellow tank top were the only people up and about.

Feeling foolish, she stepped out of the Volvo and walked past the mailboxes toward the cabins. Built in the thirties as tourist courts, they'd fallen on hard times during the sixties, but had been bought and refurbished as rental units in the late seventies. Stuccoed a cheerful pink, they added a touch of California to the island. Annie had always enjoyed coming to Nightingale Courts to see Ingrid, who managed the property in exchange for her living quarters in Cabin 3.

Ingrid's door opened. She started down her steps, paused, then waved eagerly.

They met midway on the path.

"Ingrid, who's the man—"

"Annie, what are you doing—"

They stopped and looked at each other in surprise.

Annie spread her hands in puzzlement. "Laurel called

and said you were having a rip-roaring fight with somebody. Or, to be more accurate, she said, 'Ingrid is involved in a confrontational encounter with a somewhat sinister individual, and I do feel, Annie, that steps must be taken to assure her safety.'"

"Oh, for Pete's sake!" Ingrid laughed shamefacedly. "I always knew the island grapevine was unmatched for intelligence-gathering capabilities this side of the CIA, but still, I'm impressed."

Annie looked warily around, searching the grove of palmettos. "Where's Laurel?"

"I haven't seen her this morning, but I suppose— Oh, she must have been here when I had my run-in with Jesse Penrick. You know Jesse! As for Laurel, she was probably coming from an early morning session with Ophelia."

"Ophelia? Session?" Annie wasn't much given to the kind of psychic intuitions that regularly cast such dark shadows in the paths of Mary Roberts Rinehart heroines, but she felt an undeniable quiver in the nerve endings around her spine. "Sessions?"

"Oh, Annie, not to worry. It's all nonsense, of course, but no harm done. I'll tell you all about it later." Ingrid glanced at her watch and clapped her hands. "Good grief, we only have two minutes to make it across the island to the breakfast!"

That's how the rest of Annie's wedding day went, in a breathless, tearing, headlong rush, with no more time for worry, cold feet, or panic. If the day at certain moments reminded her strongly of the island's annual triathlon, with all its attendant noise, confusion, concurrent activities, and exhaustion of available volunteers, she didn't permit herself to dwell on the parallels.

The breakfast, outdoors at a beach pavillion on the ocean side of the island, featured grits, sausage, bacon, ham with redeye gravy, pancakes, scrambled eggs, and fresh pineapple flown in from Hawaii along with six hula girls, who softly crooned a Hawaiian love song and draped guests with orchid leis. Annie was delighted to see that Laurel had her hands full with Uncle Waldo, who had taken a fancy to a fat, fortyish wahine and wasn't to be fobbed off with only a lei.

Max, of course, was smashingly handsome (a grown-up Joe Hardy) in his yachting cap as he climbed into his speedboat to compete in the race that followed. It was the first time Annie had ever watched Max race, and she was appalled at the incredible speed the beautiful boats achieved. Laurel swooped up to join her. A finger lightly touched the trough between Annie's eyes. "It's never too early to think about lines, my dear. Now, you must just relax. Max *always* wins." Laurel, of course, was a vision of imperturbable Nordic beauty with her shimmering white-blond hair, ocean-blue eyes, and creamy gardenia-smooth complexion.

"Fast," Annie croaked.

But Laurel was right. Max won. Triumphant, wet with spume, he climbed onto the dock. Laurel shoved a box in Annie's arms. "You present the gift, my dear."

Max rooted happily in the tissue, then pulled out two peasants' costumes from Lithuania. *Let us rejoice*, the card read, *in brotherhood*.

"You and Annie can start a new fashion in sportswear that will bring together workers around the world," Laurel crooned.

Set up again, Annie realized.

Luncheon beneath the live oak trees near the harbor was another triumph—caviar from Russia, salmon from Scotland, lamb from England, rice cakes from China, and what Annie knew that Laurel would describe as a touching love dance from Burma, accompanied by a high, whining string instrument which reminded Annie sharply of cats stating differing objectives during an amatory encounter.

There was no opportunity to think—or to find out more from Ingrid about her morning argument or what she meant by Laurel's sessions—during the afternoon craft bazaar, when wedding guests were encouraged to browse among offerings by island artists and shop owners, wood carvings, paintings of the sea and antebellum mansions, shell jewelry, bird-life photographs, and antiques ranging from counterbalance candlesticks in heavy polished brass to eighteenth-century Charles Fraser watercolors of Carolina landmarks and more exotic creations from artisans around the world; inlaid Chinese boxes, Swedish crystal, Tibetan thanka paintings, Belgian lace, French gilt furniture, German cuckoo clocks, and primitive African art.

Annie wasn't sure of Laurel's intent with the bazaar (increase international commerce? cross-cultural germination? buy international; stamp out provincialism?). But an inkling came to her as they hurried into the church. Laurel beamed contentedly. "Now there, Annie, that wasn't so difficult, was it?"

Annie remembered the near panic she'd fought early that morning, and how it was swept away in the color and action of the day.

Her future mother-in-law nodded understandingly, though Annie hadn't said a word. Laurel's dark blue eyes filled with delight and anticipation. She stood on tiptoe and brushed her lips against Annie's cheek. "Oh, my dear, we've had a glorious day, and now for the crowning moment." Gently, she pushed Annie toward the door leading to the dressing area.

Ingrid was there already, of course, busy helping all the bridesmaids. Ingrid looked wonderful in the pale peach dress. She was calm and unhurried, even when Deidre stamped her foot and announced furiously, "This damn bodice is designed for a size forty cup, and I can't wear it!" The other crises were surmounted, a button popped off of one of Annie's gloves, the veil slipped sideways and hung like a broken sailboat mast, and the bridal bouquet disappeared. Ingrid had everyone at the proper spot, and just in time, as the processional sounded.

The wedding began, and if it wasn't traditional, it was perfect.

Annie watched with a smile as the ushers and the bridesmaids preceded her.

She walked alone down the aisle.

That decision had been hers.

And Max understood.

She came to him on her own. She was not a gift from another, not even symbolically.

But her wedding dress was not red, despite Laurel's plea

that red should be used in America as it was in China as the color of love and joy.

Laurel had been consoled at this defeat by Annie's agreement to carry a dozen cardinal-red roses. Red roses say, "I love you."

There was a red motif. Vivid red satin bows adorned the candle stands. The cushions where the bride and groom knelt were white with red embroidery. Roses blazed crimson behind the altar. (If onlookers detected a hint of rose in the creamy satin of the wedding gown, Annie would insist it was the spill of sunlight beaming through the vivid scarlet of the stained-glass windows at the back of the sanctuary.)

As the stately liturgy unfolded, Annie looked toward her groom. Her heart surged. He was almost too handsome— straight nose, firm jaw, serious mien. Then he gave her a sidelong glance from his rollicking blue eyes and winked.

The reception blazed with color and sound. Laurel had transformed the somewhat uninspired grand ballroom of the Island Hills Golf and Country Club into a paradise of blooms, including a frieze of bright red tulips flown from Holland. If there was not present a horticultural representative from every nation, it was no fault of Laurel's. She could point with pride—and did—to obscure botanical offerings from the heights of the Alps to the deepest recesses of the Amazon. The hours sped by with handshakes and kisses, laughter and toasts, a magnificent seated dinner (Annie wondered if T-bone steaks from Texas were yet another effort by Laurel to be international), the first dance with Max, the cutting of the cake.

The cake.

Well, Annie had to admit the gloriously, ebulliently, unmistakably carmine icing set it off.

Why not start new traditions?

Be open.

Be flexible.

Go with the flow.

Finally, amid happy shouts, a rain of confetti, and a blare of trumpets, they made their escape.

But not yet to the mainland and the forty-five-minute drive to the Savannah airport. Tomorrow, after attending the early service at St. Mary's, they'd arranged for ferry service. (Grumpy ferry owner Ben Parotti had tilted a beer, looked at Max blearily, and growled, "Well, this one time I'll do it.") Now, Max wheeled the crimson Maserati (a gift from Laurel) up the familiar coast road toward Annie's tree house. Laurel, of course, had wanted them to stay in the bridal suite at the island's finest hotel, The Palmetto House, but Annie wanted to spend one last night in her old home. By the time they returned from their honeymoon (and Max so far had refused to give even a hint of their destination), their new home on the golf course should be completed.

As the headlights dipped into the thick gloom of the lampless road, Max chuckled. "Remember the first night I ever brought you home?"

She smiled. "You said it was darker than the Black Hole of Calcutta. I never thought a city boy like you would go native."

The car coasted to a stop by the steps leading up to her house, and he took her hand. "A lot of things I didn't know then. The difference between hard-boiled and soft." (He didn't mean eggs.) "What B'con stands for. That Martha Grimes's titles are all names of pubs. Damn, I was an unlettered boor." He hurried around the side of the car to open her door. (Yes, it was sexist, but, after all, this was a special night.) "But," and he reached to help her out and then pulled her into his arms, "I always knew I loved you."

In a moment, she murmured, "Let's go inside." She had visions of the filmy silk nightgown hanging in her closet, waiting. Her bags were packed and sat in the living room next to Max's, ready for the morning's departure. Once inside the door, however, she turned to him and promptly forgot all about the waiting nightgown. (Maisie didn't know everything.)

And for an instant, perhaps longer, the shrill peal of the telephone didn't register.

"To hell with it," Max finally said urgently.

But Annie pulled away. She would not later claim that she had a premonition. That was the province of Victoria Holt heroines. But the persistent ring faintly stirred a chord of fear. Hardly anyone knew they were there—and wrong numbers rarely ring after midnight.

With an apologetic squeeze of his arm, Annie bolted across the room and scooped up the receiver.

"Hello?"

"Annie." The voice was high, frantic, frightened. "Oh, my God, please. Come quick. I need—" A scream, a moan, then the receiver was slammed into the cradle.

"Ingrid! Ingrid, what's happened?"

But Annie's voice echoed emptily on the dead line.

SIX

The night guard at the entry-exit gate, a college student from the mainland supplementing his income, stared at them in sleepy astonishment. There was little traffic into or out of the resort property after midnight. The ferry made its final run at ten, so residents and tourists alike found their pleasures on the island within the confines of the resort, enjoying the waterfront restaurants, the two night-clubs, the Island Hills Country Club (which, however, this Saturday night had been almost totally devoted to the continuing celebration of the Darling-Laurance nuptials), or pursued other indoor delights within the preserves of Halcyon Development, Inc. Little beckoned after dark in the island's original community near the ferry landing. The small-town main street offered one- and two-story build-ings, most of frame, a few brick: a furniture store, a five-and-dime, a doctor's office, a dentist's, the bank, the drugstore (old-fashioned, with marble-topped tables and wire-backed chairs), an insurance agency, a post office. The high school was two blocks from Main Street, as was the small Community Hospital. Most establishments closed at five on Saturday afternoons. Shades were pulled, lights switched off. Only Ben Parotti's Bar and Bait Shop offered a loud but noisome Saturday night, although chili dogs, soft cones, and gossip were available until eleven at the Dairy Queen.

So Annie and Max were out of the ordinary. Max leaned

on the Maserati's horn; Annie gestured frantically out the open window for the raising of the barrier.

The freckle-faced guard punched the button to lift the white wooden bar. "What's wrong? Somebody sick?"

As the sports car leapt forward, Annie called back: "Police. Call the police! To Nightingale Courts."

The guard's reply, if any, was lost in the high whine of the motor and the rush of wind through the open windows. Annie clung to a passenger strap above the door and remembered why it wouldn't do much good to call the police. Chief Saulter was in Germany, where his only daughter was scheduled to have her baby within a week. That left only Billy Cameron, a stalwart but youthful patrolman, who had the largest collection of Dick Tracy comics on the island. (And he never missed a mystery novel by the present author of the Tracy strips, Max Allan Collins.)

But something dreadful had happened to Ingrid, and Billy Cameron would be better than no one.

Annie struggled not to imagine what might have caused Ingrid's voice to rise in such fear and horror. "Faster," she urged.

But Max already had the sports coupe at eighty, and it took all his driving skill and a lot of luck to brake hard and avoid a collision with a bristly black boar that bared knife-sharp tusks before bolting back into the thick scrub. After dark, the island came alive with prowling, dangerous predators. But that was in the forests and swamps, Annie tried to reassure herself. It was still safe enough on Broward's Rock never to lock a door.

But Ingrid had screamed.

As they careened around the last curve and the head-lights threw the arch with its dark blanket of honeysuckle into bold relief, Annie felt an uncomfortable wash of déjà vu. Just as it had that morning, utter peace reigned at Nightingale Courts, although this was the somnolent and deceptive tranquillity of the darkest watch of the night. It is at night most often that three-foot cottonmouths rear their sleek heads above the water to glide in deadly pursuit of frogs and turtles, and sharp-teethed red foxes stalk marsh rabbits and nesting birds.

The headlights briefly illuminated a central expanse of gritty grey dirt with a sparse crop of grass and the cabins curving in a semicircle along the marsh. As the car jolted to a stop, Max switched off the lights.

All the cabins were dark. A lone lamppost to one side of the entrance arch cast a feeble golden glow that only emphasized the heavy pall of darkness. Out into the salt marsh and beyond into the sound, the presence of the water could be sensed rather than seen.

"I don't like this. Stay here, Annie."

As Max slid from his seat, Annie followed suit, not even bothering to reply.

A heavy fluttering noise caused her to grab his hand, then drop it immediately as she recognized the passage of a great horned owl.

She was right on Max's heels when they reached Ingrid's cabin.

"Ingrid?"

His call was soft, and Annie understood. It was so quiet. So *still*. Annie tried to batter down the horrid images that kept rising in her mind's eye. Ingrid would have rushed to them, if she were there. If she were able. *There's nothing wrong*, she reassured herself. *Some scare that Ingrid will explain. You've just read too many mysteries. That's why your heart is thudding.*

The screen door was closed, but beyond it, Ingrid's front door stood ajar.

This time Max didn't speak. He took Annie by the elbow and pushed her firmly to one side, then eased open the screen, kicked the door wide, and groped for the light switch.

Annie would never forget the scene that flashed into view: Max leaning forward in a crouch, his fists balled, ready to attack; the familiar shabby gentility of Ingrid's living room, petit point cushions on the cheerful chintz sofa, linen drapes in cobalt blue with a design of white shasta daisies, an eighteenth-century whatnot with her treasured collection of redware, and bookcases everywhere, reflecting Ingrid's many and varied interests— classic mysteries, Greek archeology, American history, Chaucerian England, Victorian antiques—and, in the center of the room, staring sightlessly up at the stippled plaster ceiling, the body spread-eagled on the blue-and-grey hooked rug. Even in that first shocked glance, Ingrid her prime concern, Annie recognized Jesse Penrick and wondered what in the hell he was doing there, clad as usual all in navy blue, except for his bare, white feet. A pair of sneakers and two socks lay beside him.

"Ingrid!" Annie pushed past Max, keeping to the left to avoid Jesse's body. It was too late to help Jesse now. Circling to the kitchen, she flicked on the light. No one. Nothing. But the back door stood open.

Max called from the living room. "No one in the bedroom or bath. Annie, she isn't here."

They searched again, avoiding looking at the body and most carefully avoiding sight of the sword protruding from his chest. They looked behind the couch, opened the front closet, checked the bedroom closet, peered beneath the canopied rice bed.

"I'll get a flashlight from the car." Max ran out into the darkness.

Annie followed and stood on the low steps of the cabin. Now she didn't give a damn about nighttime quiet. "Ingrid?" she shouted. "Ingrid?"

Up the road a siren sounded. Lights began to flicker on. A door opened and a man's slurred, deep voice demanded: "What the hell. What the hell?"

Shouts. Calls. Billy Cameron's dust-churning arrival. The slurred, deep voice rising again angrily, "Where's Ingrid? What the hell d'you mean, a body? Goddammit, where's Ingrid?"

Lights spilled from all the cabins now, except Cabin One. Car headlights crisscrossed the dusty central area.

Max took charge. "Everybody who has a flashlight, go get it and bring it back here," he ordered. "We'll start the search along the shore—"

"Wait a minute, Mr. Darling. Wait a minute!" Billy Cameron backed out of Ingrid's cabin and turned to face the milling crowd. His youthful face was pale. "Who's missing? Who're you hunting for?"

A bulky man in his sixties tried to shove past Max. "What the hell's going on here? Where's Ingrid?" He glared up the steps at Billy. "What're you doing in her cabin?" Despite crumpled khaki trousers, a faded cotton sports shirt that looked slept in, and the whisky-slurred voice, the man had an air of authority. He lifted his hand, quieting the chattering cabin residents pulled from their beds by the siren and the shouts. "What's all this about a body?" he demanded.

Annie answered. "Ingrid called. At my house. Just after midnight. She was frantic—she asked for help, then the connection was broken, so my husband and I raced over here." Annie gestured toward Max. *Husband.* "But when we arrived, Ingrid's house was dark. The door was partially open. We went inside and found the body—"

"Whose body, for Christ's sake?" Her inquisitor's nostrils flared. He was balding and bifocaled, with a large, moon-shaped face, powerful shoulders, and stocky legs. Not a man to trifle with.

"Jesse Penrick."

Max completed it. "He's lying in the center of the living room on his back. There's a sword stuck in his chest."

A low, shocked murmur rose from the watchers.

"Where's Ingrid?" The older man chopped off the words.

"We don't know," Annie cried. "Not in the house. Not anywhere we can find."

"Then we've got to search," he stormed. His blunt head swung toward Billy, and the lights from the patrol car glittered on his wire-frame glasses. "Goddammit, stop standing there! Let's organize. We've got to find Ingrid."

Billy flushed. "Who're you?"

"Duane Webb. Cabin Four. If it matters a goddam. C'mon. You've got a flash in your patrol car." Webb glanced toward Max. "You've got a flash. I'll grab one from my place. That gives us three. We'll split up."

"Women see quite as well as men in the dark," an acidulous voice announced.

"All right, Adele, you lead the women. Check down by the shore and the piers. You"—the commanding finger jabbed again at Max—"you go south. I'll—"

Billy yelled, "Wait a minute, mister! This is a murder investigation. You people are going to trample every-thing—"

"Cop, you go cuddle the goddam body. Jesse wasn't worth shit alive, and he's not worth that much dead. We're looking for a woman who's probably being held hostage right this minute by a killer. You worried about warm flesh or cold?"

Billy struggled to look as though he were in charge. Drawing himself up to his full six foot three, he said bullishly, "You people stay clear of this cabin. I'm going to radio to the mainland for help."

A motorboat roared to a stop at the far end of one of the piers. Everyone swung round to look toward a man in navy blue warmups who swarmed up a ladder, then jogged up to join them.

As he came into the light from the patrol car, Annie waved hello and saw total surprise in his eyes. Which was understandable. The last time they'd exchanged glances was at the reception, when he'd lifted a glass of champagne in toast to her and Max as they danced by. They knew him only casually, but they'd invited all the harbor merchants and their employees to the wedding. He worked for Betsy Raines at the Piping Plover Gallery, one of the shops that faced on the plaza side. Alan. That was it. Alan Nichols. The newcomer looked past Annie at the young patrolman. "What's going on? A boat out? I saw the lights from across the inlet. My cabin's over there. Can I help?"

Clearly, Billy Cameron wished the earth would swallow up at least a half dozen of these interfering bystanders. Before the policeman could explain what little he knew, Duane Webb accepted the offer. "Ingrid's missing, Alan. We're going to search. Be glad of your help."

"Sure thing. Do anything I can."

Billy said sharply, "Stay clear of this cabin," and started for the squad car.

He was intercepted by a plump little woman wearing a turban and a housecoat with cardinals fluttering among thumb-thick green vines. "Officer, Officer, is there a dangerous maniac running loose? Who's been killed? What's happened? I told Ingrid there was a black cloud. I could see it drooping above her head. It was so real I could almost reach out and touch it." Her voice rose into a keen. "Black. Black. The color of death."

"Ophelia, shut your goddam mouth," Webb snarled. "You're a bore and an idiot, and we don't need any of your witless maunderings. All right, let's get started, everybody." He wheeled around and headed for Ingrid's cabin.

"Mister. Hey, mister, you stay the hell out of that cabin!" Billy's face was red now with frustration.

Webb stumped toward Ingrid's carport, shouting over his shoulder. "Going to look in the damn car, then search the goddam premises. Which should have been done immediately."

The young policeman started after him, then whirled and ducked back into the squad car, leaning in to grab up his microphone.

Annie felt a quiver of dread. The microphone. Calling for help from the mainland. Oh, my God. Hurriedly, she poked her head in the squad car's open back window. "Billy, don't worry. I'll stand guard over the body."

He flashed her a grateful glance, then, as static crackled, turned back to his microphone.

Max was staring at her in surprise.

Annie gave a tiny jerk of her head, and Max followed her out of earshot.

She stood on tiptoe and whispered: "Help hunt for Ingrid. I'd better see what I can find out in her cabin. Because you know what will happen when Posey takes over."

Instant comprehension registered on his handsome face. "Oh, God," he muttered. "I hadn't thought about it. Of course. With Saulter out of the country, the world's premier ass, Circuit Solicitor Brice Willard Posey, will swoop across the sound. We'll never find Ingrid, he'll be so busy posturing. Right."

"Come on, come on," Webb shouted from the shadows near the cabin.

Max gnawed unhappily at his lip. "Annie, I hate to see you stuck in there with a corpse. But I don't want you out in the boondocks with a killer loose."

"I'm not worried about that. Only a very dumb killer would still be hanging around, after the massive amount of noise and confusion erupting here. I want to give that cabin a once-over, while I have the chance. Posey's such an idiot he wouldn't recognize a clue if it ran up and hugged him."

"True enough. Okay, honey. Have at it." He took time to give her a swift kiss on the cheek.

As he turned to go, she stared out through the darkness toward the inkier splotch that was the marsh. "Max, what's happened to Ingrid?"

He didn't answer. Instead, he reached out, gave her shoulder a hard squeeze, then pivoted to follow Webb.

Annie shot a quick glance at Billy, still talking rapidly on his radio, and moved swiftly toward Ingrid's cabin.

She wouldn't have much time.

She wasn't sure what she was going to do, but she had a deep-down, gut feeling that she'd better be prepared to figure out what had happened in Ingrid's cabin. Finding Ingrid was priority No. One, but Brice Posey had a genius for getting everything wrong. He was quite capable of deciding Ingrid's disappearance was immaterial to the murder investigation. She could hear him now, his piglike eyes bulging, his nose flared, "Irrelevant and immaterial, Miss Laurance."

Again, that funny little shock of surprise. She wasn't Miss Laurance any more. Mrs. Darling. Mrs. Maxwell Darling. Annie Darling. Annie Laurance-Darling?

Annie used the edge of her blue linen jacket to grasp the screen-door knob, trying not to smudge any prints. Of course, Max had touched it already and so had Billy Cameron. She used her shoulder to nudge the door wide enough to slip inside, then took a steadying breath.

It was time to stop ignoring the body.

Jesse's wasn't a prepossessing corpse. The face was a waxy yellowish color. Deeply grooved lines led from the sharply curved nose to thin lips, stretched now in a mockery of a smile. Locked in an upward glare, the lifeless eyes glittered, as if they'd once delighted in taunts and now enjoyed a final, malevolent triumph. But there was something oddly vulnerable about the pale white of his bare feet. Had he taken off his sneakers and socks? If so, why? Although Annie wasn't of a housekeeperish turn of mind, she observed that the thick bluish crew socks were once white cotton, tossed into too many washes with Jesse's perennial navy blue turtlenecks.

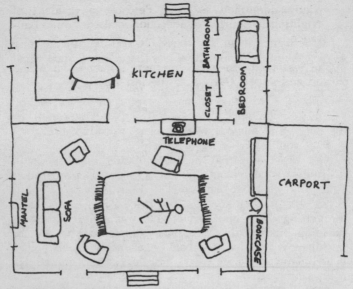

Annie shook her head impatiently. Time was fleeting. Posey might arrive at any moment and toss her out of the cabin. So, she'd better get busy. The first task of any detective was to describe the scene. What would Inspector Luke Thanet do?

She scrabbled in her purse, found a crumpled paper napkin (Annie & Max), smoothed it out, and drew a quick sketch, which she labeled SCENE OF THE CRIME.

She found a second napkin, headed it DESCRIPTION OF CRIME SCENE, and rapidly listed the following:

Murder victim found in living room in the residence of Ingrid Jones, manager of Nightingale Courts.

(Oh, Ingrid, dear Ingrid, where are you? Are you frightened? Hurt? Alive?)

Living room measures approximately—Annie stepped it off—*twelve by fourteen feet.*
Deceased found in center of room lying on back atop a hooked rug. Fully dressed except for bare feet. Sneakers and socks next to body.

Victim identified as Jesse Penrick, a resident of Nightingale Courts. Identification made by Annie Laurance.

She was ready to make her next notation when she paused and added *Darling* to the last line.

Front door open when discovery made.
Back door open.
Criminal not apprehended at scene.
Occupant of death residence missing. Search begun.

Annie stopped writing and lifted her head, listening to faraway shouts of "Ingrid? Ingrid?" It made it hard to maintain her impersonal tally, but she kept at it.

No indication of a struggle. Couch cushions in place, chairs in accustomed locations.
Drapes drawn for the night, hanging straight and unruffled.
Overlapping magazines on coffee table arranged with precision.
Telephone in place on table next to kitchen door, receiver resting snugly in cradle.
Hooked rug unscuffed on pine floor.

She chewed reflectively on her pencil. If someone had struggled with Jesse—and surely he hadn't stood there tamely, barefooted, and permitted his chest to be used for sword practice—why wasn't the rug rumpled and scuffed?

And a sword, for God's sake?

A sword.

Annie felt a tightening in her chest. Her head swung to the left, and her horrified gaze sought the mantel behind the couch. Ingrid kept mementos there, a blue brush pot of Canton ware from her trip to China, a knobby chunk of driftwood from Carmel, a ceramic sheepdog from Ireland.

Pride of place, however, was reserved for the highly polished oblong of mahogany above the mantel. Mounted upon it was the sword that Ingrid's great-grandfather carried at the Battle of Gettysburg.

The plaque was there.

The sword was not.

Annie looked back at the body.

And the door creaked behind her.

She spun around, then released her breath in relief as Billy Cameron hurried inside. He wiped his perspiring face. Billy had the wholesomeness of a rugby player, broad shoulders, strong, handsome features, and sandy hair with an appealing cowlick. "Posey's on his way. I got to get started." He whipped out a notebook, and it looked small in his hamster-sized hands. "Okay," he muttered, "okay. Call from Halcyon guard at 12:41 A.M. Proceeded to site." He looked up miserably at Annie. "God, I can't explain all these people and the mess going on outside. Here I am, Chief Saulter gone, everything up to me, and if I don't make a good report, Posey'll laugh at us, say we run a hick outfit." He shot a hostile glance at the corpse. "Trust Jesse Penrick to cause trouble, dead or alive."

"You're doing fine, Billy," she soothed. "Let's see. You arrived, took charge"—he nodded in quick agreement—"organized search while instructing participants not to infringe upon crime scene"—he scribbled furiously—"designated citizen to maintain security of murder cabin"— he looked blank, and Annie pointed at herself. Billy bent back to his notebook—"notified higher authorities, and returned to crime scene to initiate investigation."

Annie waited until he caught up, then proceeded. She helped him describe the crime scene, led him gently to the discovery of the apparent source of the murder weapon, then mused thoughtfully, "Why?"

Billy's eyes were blank.

"Why with a sword? Doesn't that seem"—she searched for the right word—"artificial?"

Billy's brows knotted. "Like in fake?" he asked. He looked down at the body. "Not very fake. He's damn dead."

It was Annie's turn to knit her brows in thought, wondering just how to explain.

"Ooohoooh! Oooohoooh!"

Annie and Billy both jerked around violently.

Standing in Ingrid's doorway was the turbaned little woman whose chatter of black clouds had infuriated the self-appointed leader of the search, Duane Webb. Ophelia, that's what he'd called her.

Ophelia's chubby face crumpled in distress. Vivid splotches of old-fashioned rouge made her cheeks look like red sails running before the wind. Mascara beaded her eyelashes and wisps of chartreuse hair peeked from beneath the edges of the turban. Chartreuse? Annie blinked, but the color remained true.

"That nasty old man. I told him wrack and ruin awaited his evil ways, and I was right." She clapped her pudgy hands together. "The spirits know." The frail voice dropped to a deep, almost masculine pitch. "And I am their vessel, serving at their will."

Billy stared as if an apparition from hell had alighted at his elbow, but Annie swiftly pounced on the kernel among the chaff.

"Ophelia," she demanded sharply, "what are you talking about? What evil ways? What's he done—"

"I've come to take charge," was the clarion call as Henny Brawley marched through the door, her dark eyes flashing, her fox-sharp nose quivering. She took in the scene at an eager glance and decisively pushed up the sleeves of her crimson warmup.

"Mrs. Brawley!" Billy's voice was an agonized bleat.

"Don't you worry, young man. I have come to devote myself to the investigation."

Annie had last seen Henny at the reception, not more than a few hours ago, though now it seemed like eons. She glanced at the grandfather clock next to the whatnot. It was just past two. In five hours the sun would be up. At the reception, Henny had worn a rose silk dress flecked with ivory swirls. The pleated skirt swung gracefully as she tangoed across the floor with Uncle Waldo. And Waldo had been only one of many partners. Once she raised a champagne glass to the newlyweds and mouthed, "*Totis viribus*, my dears." (Under duress, Max would translate the Latin: *With all one's might*.)

But neither the champagne, the vigorous rhumbas, chachas, and fox trots, nor the late hour seemed to have affected Henny. Not a line of fatigue marred her inquisitive, determined face.

Billy valiantly endeavored to stave off the inevitable. "How'd you know, Mrs. Brawley?"

"Police-band radio." Henny spoke absently. Her eyes were focused on the body. "Nasty piece of goods, Jesse Penrick. But why would anyone want to kill him?" She took a deep, satisfied breath. "Should be an amusing little show. Great sport."

Annie gave her a look of mingled exasperation and fondness. Henny really *was* a superb actress, as she had proved again in the fateful summer production of *Arsenic and Old Lace*. But her fascination and soul-deep identification with famous fictional sleuths was clearly reaching an absurd height. Henny's jaw jutted stalwartly; there was an unmistakable aura of command. Annie had a quick mental image of Walter Pidgeon portraying hard-playing, hard-fighting, clean-living Bulldog Drummond. And dammit, there wasn't time for theatrics. They needed to concentrate on Ingrid and what had happened in her cabin.

"Ingrid's missing!" Annie said sharply.

Henny's eyes narrowed. "The swine, they've got Ingrid! Well, they won't get away with it!" She paced the room, darting quick glances at the oval rug and its grisly burden. "Revealing," she barked. "Quite revealing. Clearly, Ingrid has been abducted. She is not a victim of foul play."

Billy's bewildered gaze followed her. "No foul play? How do you—"

The blare of a boat horn drowned out the remainder of Billy's question.

Billy gave a frantic glance at the door, then at Henny. "How do you know?" he repeated urgently.

"No disarray. No blood. No indication of violent altercation." Her accent was becoming progressively more British. "Further, why leave one body and remove another? No sense. Got to make sense. The swine have taken Ingrid for a purpose. Up to us to discover why." She pursed her lips thoughtfully. "And Jesse's shoes and socks off! Mark my words, that'll mean something."

Billy hastily began to scrawl in his notebook.

Henny crouched by Penrick and picked up one of the dead hands, let it fall. "No signs rigor mortis. Body still warm. Obviously, death occurred around midnight."

Annie tensed. She hadn't even thought about the time of death. Her attention had been focused on Ingrid. But midnight! For God's sake, that wasn't long before Ingrid called. What was Penrick doing in Ingrid's cabin at midnight? He was certainly not her friend. Why, they'd had a battle royal yesterday morning.

"Eyes haven't filmed over," Henny observed crisply. "'Course, that's only a rough guide."

Ophelia clapped her hands approvingly. "Oooh, you have a strong aura. A very strong aura."

The boat horn sounded again.

Billy hurriedly made a final notation, snapped shut his notebook, and waved his arms. "Hurry, ladies. Outside now. That'll be the circuit solicitor."

Posey bellowed. And kept on bellowing.

"Chaos. That's what this investigation is. *Chaos.*"

The searchers were straggling back into the central grassy area. Deep in conversation with Henny, Max stood by the honeysuckle-laden arbor. His blue blazer was snagged and his slacks looked like the aftermath of a mud wallow. Ophelia tugged absentmindedly on that sprig of chartreuse hair and oohed empathetically as Posey continued to shout and Billy Cameron's shoulders drooped lower and lower.

"Please."

A woman about Annie's own age, in faded jeans and a cream-colored cotton pullover, asked tentatively, "Have they found any trace of Mrs. Jones?"

Annie never thought of Ingrid as Mrs. Jones, and it seemed odd to hear the name from the lips of this young woman, who looked fearfully at the growing circle around Posey and Billy Cameron.

Annie spoke softly, too, in response. "No. Nothing yet."

"That's dreadful. Just dreadful. And so frightening." She wrapped her arms tight across her narrow chest and shivered. "I thought it was safe here. On Broward's Rock. I wouldn't have brought Kevin here if I hadn't thought so. And the noise and lights scare him. He won't stay in bed."

"Kevin?"

"My little boy." The young woman uneasily watched the moving shadows and lights. "Somebody said the one that got killed, it's the old man who lived there." She pointed toward Cabin One, the only one still dark.

"Is that where Jesse Penrick lived?" Annie asked.

"Oh, my God. So it is him."

Afterward Annie tried to remember her intonation. Was there a rush of relief? Or only shock? Or an emotion that Annie couldn't—didn't—quite identify? Or, more simply yet, was it very late on the morning after her wedding day, and had she been buffeted by too much strong emotion to be certain of any response?

Perhaps Annie's lack of reply alarmed the woman. She took a step backward. "I didn't know him. Not really." Her face was a pale blur in the moonlight. She twisted her head, looked behind her, then said hurriedly, "I'd better get back. I don't want to leave Kevin alone—not the way things are." She gripped her hands tightly together. "I've got to get back to Kevin." Then she darted through the shadows to the cabin near the other end of the semicircle.

Annie looked after her for a moment, disturbed. But this wasn't the time to worry about a stranger. Not until Ingrid was found. Annie glanced toward Posey. The circuit solicitor strode up and down, his chest poked out, gesturing vigorously at Billy. Shaking her head, she started for the arbor and Max, then paused as Duane Webb stumped into the bright beams of the police-car headlights.

Webb, too, showed the effects of a desperate search. His trousers and shoes were stained black from sloshing through tannin-dark pools, his muscular arms scarred with livid scratches. There was no slur to his voice now, though it was hoarse from shouting. He ignored Posey and honed in on Billy like a buzz saw.

"Get more men. Dogs. Lights." A muscle twitched in one cheek. "And divers."

The circuit solicitor's meaty face swelled with outrage. "Who are you?" Posey demanded.

"Duane Webb. Who the hell are you?"

"I am Circuit Solicitor Brice Willard Posey." His voice rang across the courtyard. Did he think a voter might be hiding in the cattails? Despite the late hour, he was wearing coat, tie, and vest. He was even more self-satisfied, overbearing, and obnoxious than when Annie had first met him. Her heart sank.

Posey took a deep breath, expanding his pouter-pigeon chest to its full extent, and proclaimed, "I am assuming control of this investigation—this incredibly botched and mishandled investigation—into the death of Mr. Jesse Penrick, who has been foully stabbed in the chest with a sword in the cabin of one Ingrid Jones, who has not come forward." Posey's pronunciation of her name clearly put Ingrid right on a level with Lizzie Borden.

"Ooooh," Ophelia crooned, pressing fingertips to each temple. "I should have *known*. Of course, I *did* know, but my earthly body interfered with the warnings. My psychic self, had I just permitted it full expression, might have saved them both. I saw the black nimbuses around—"

"Ophelia, stuff it," Webb rasped. "There's no time for your crap. My God, woman, Ingrid's out there somewhere"—he jabbed at the darkness—"and we've got to find her." He swung back toward Posey. "If you're the honcho, get a move on. Call the governor. Get some national guard troops. We need to cover this island like a—"

Ophelia's vine-decorated housecoat quivered like a wind-buffeted circus tent. "Now, you just listen to me! I *did* see black nimbuses. Right here this very morning when Ingrid and Jesse had that awful fight down by the mailboxes!"

The silence was sudden and absolute.

Everyone looked at Ophelia.

Henny's dark eyes rolled upward in irritation.

Webb's face spasmed. "Stupid bitch," he muttered.

But it was Posey's reaction that worried Annie. The idiot looked like a country-fair porker sighting a blue ribbon. He bounded toward Ophelia. "Now, ma'am, you're the kind of witness we need, the kind of witness who can help us solve this dastardly crime. You are important!"

A little stunned by this sudden attention, Ophelia tugged uncertainly on that vagrant lock of chartreuse hair, then bridled importantly. "You can just take it from me," she assured him, "the portents were *there!*"

Posey's overstuffed face curved into what he probably

thought of as an ingratiating smile. Annie was unpleasantly reminded of an alligator sighting a yapping Pomeranian.

"Now then, Miss—uh, Mrs. . . ?"

"Ophelia Baxter." She patted her turban coquettishly. "I live right over there." She pointed, then giggled. "Right between Jesses and Ingrid's cabins. Now, isn't that a coincidence!"

"You live right here," Posey repeated, with growing satisfaction. "And this very morning, the day of the homicide, you witnessed the missing woman and the murdered man"—his volume increased—"involved in a violent argument?"

The turban bobbed vigorously. "Yes, I did, and I wanted to march right down there and tell them that they were tempting Providence—because that's what it is, you know, when the tentacles of fate extend their—"

"Goddammit to hell!" Webb exploded, his voice reverberating like the crash of surf before a November wind. "This is bloody, goddam nonsense! This deluded woman has the intelligence of a sand crab. So Ingrid told Jesse off! So what? Who the hell hadn't? He was a disgusting, sniveling, hateful old bastard. I for one told him I'd bash his head in one of these days. And none of this matters—what matters is Ingrid! We've got to—"

"I know what matters," Posey rejoined irritably. "And I'm getting to the bottom of it." He swiveled back to Ophelia. "Mrs. Jones and Mr. Penrick quarreled violently Saturday morning?"

"Oh yes, yes, they did." She clucked regretfully. "Now, Duane, I'm sorry to say it, and no one knows better than I what a dear, sweet person Ingrid is, and I'm really very worried about her, wandering around out there"—the beringed fingers fluttered in the direction of the salt marsh—"but we all must tell the truth, or be shamed, mustn't we? And Mr. Posey just wants to know what happened, and I can say, because I was right here, and I saw every bit of it."

"Tell us—in your own words—just what you saw," Posey urged.

Despite Webb's frequent outbursts and Ophelia's difficulty in describing anything without copious references to spirits, portents, vibrations, and currents, her response left Posey delighted and Ingrid's friends distraught. The way Ophelia painted it, Annie thought furiously, Ingrid had done everything short of threatening Jesse's life in their unfortunate morning altercation.

"Now"—Posey all but smacked his lips—"you heard Mrs. Jones say, 'Jesse, you're nastier than the Marquis de Sade on a bad day. I'd like to slice you up for the alligators—and I'm warning you, I've had all I can take!'"

Annie'd heard enough. "Mr. Posey!"

His eyes slid toward her with all the enthusiasm of Hamilton Burger sighting Della Street. "Ah, Miss Laurance."

"Mrs. Darling," Max interjected immediately.

How dear, his bride thought, then she focused on her old and present enemy, and, with a good deal of effort, addressed him in a voice of sweet reason. There was no point in antagonizing him.

"Mr. Posey, I can assure you that Ingrid was not in a murderous frame of mind at all concerning Mr. Penrick. Actually, we talked about her little disagreement with him, and she dismissed it as one of those annoyances that crop up in the life of a property manager." Annie knew she was being rather creative over a very small exchange with Ingrid, but Posey didn't deserve any better.

Henny joined in. "As usual, Posey, you're going to miss the forest for the trees. Clearly, Ingrid Jones has been abducted. Any fool should be able to study the crime scene and deduce that."

Annie appreciated Henny's support, but devoutly wished for a smidgeon more tact.

"Ingrid's quite incapable of violence," Webb snorted. "Damn fool idea."

"Portents of death," Ophelia said huskily to the stars overhead. "I *told* them."

Max moved restively. "Posey, let it go for now. What matters is that Ingrid called for help—and we haven't found her!"

It was too little, too late.

Posey's face had the shine of the true believer. "As an accomplished and experienced investigator, I've learned to trust my instincts and to explore fully the contributions that can be made by witnesses, and, further, *I* avoid the temptation that besets *inexperienced* investigators to look beyond the obvious in a self-gratifying attempt to produce rabbits out of hats."

"*Not* attractive," Ophelia murmured. "Poor dear little rabbits squashed in boxes . . ."

An ugly red flush suffused Webb's face and neck. "Goddammit, she's missing!"

"Of course she is," Posey said complacently. "She has motive, opportunity—and she's missing." He flicked off each on three fat fingers. "What does that add up to?" He overrode the growing babble of dissent. "Guilt," he intoned happily. "Well, she won't get away from me. I'm going to issue an all-points bulletin for her arrest. That woman will never get off this island."

Webb lunged toward the circuit solicitor. "Do you mean you aren't going to put out search parties?"

"You've already searched," Posey pointed out silkily. "You didn't find a trace, did you?"

"That's right, for God's sake," Webb agreed. "We've looked everywhere within a radius of a couple of miles, and there's no trace of her, none at all—"

"So you would have found her body—if it was out there!" Posey thundered triumphantly. "No, you didn't find her because she's run away. She's hiding."

No, Annie thought. Ingrid can't be dead. She clung to one hope—Henny said there hadn't been another murder, and Henny, exasperating as she was, had a wonderful instinct for crime.

Webb lunged forward. "You goddam fool. She didn't run away. Somebody took her. As for a body . . ." He paused, swallowed, and said jerkily, "It's dark. We could have missed—" He faltered.

But Posey was oblivious to his distress. "Nobody dragged her out here and killed her. Why should they? And there was no struggle in her cabin. If she'd escaped from a killer and run out to hide, why, she'd have called for help when searchers came by." His heavy jaw jutted portentously. "No. This is all very clear to an *experienced* investigator. Jones is mad at this guy. She's threatened him. She takes down a sword—a sword that belonged to her—and shoves it into Penrick's heart—and then she hightails it out of here."

"Absurd!" Henny trumpeted. "No blood. No evidence of a struggle. And why is he barefoot? I'll tell you this, Posey, you're an amusing beggar, but incompetent. Now do you have the gall to tell me you don't intend to mount a full-scale search for Ingrid Jones?"

Posey ignored her and swiveled back to Ophelia. "Now, ma'am, we'll be taking your statement and—"

"Posey, old chap," Henny interrupted.

The circuit solicitor's bulky shoulders wriggled with irritation. "Mrs. Brawley, go peddle your papers somewhere else. This is a Murder Investigation, and I have my duties."

"One final query, my good man: Will you order a massive ground search for Ingrid Jones?"

"Of course not. But don't worry, we'll catch her. My men will be watching the coast. She won't escape the law."

Henny gave a judicious, all-for-the-Empire nod, swung about, and crossed to the latticed arch. She scanned it with a measuring eye, then began to climb, hand over hand. When she stood atop the quivering structure, she loudly announced:

"Calling all concerned citizens. I am hereby creating the Citizens Search for Ingrid Jones. We shall search in the woods, on the beaches, along the creek banks, and in the salt marshes. We shall not flag or fail. Citizens, unite!" And she lifted a clenched fist to the thin shouts of the astonished onlookers.

Annie was overwhelmed. Bulldog Drummond with overtones of the Former Naval Person.

SEVEN

Annie moved restlessly, clinging to the remnants of sleep. Hot. She was damned hot. She crinkled her nose and sniffed. Hmm. Coffee. Bacon. Her nose twitched. Marsh mud in the sun.

Her eyes popped open. She looked up blankly at a dingy swatch of canvas rippling in a breeze. A piece of wood was gouging her in the small of the back, she seemed to be lying in a trough, and this was too narrow to be her bed. A cot, an old-fashioned cot.

Max. The wedding. Their wedding night— Oh, Lordy. It was Sunday morning, the first day of her honeymoon, but Ingrid was missing and their honeymoon would have to wait.

She flung back an Army-issue blanket—no wonder she was hot—struggled to get up, and promptly got hopelessly tangled in a drape of mosquito netting.

Memory returned in a flood. As the night waned, Henny had taken time out from her Bulldog Drummond routine to contact her chief lieutenant on the Broward's Rock search and Rescue Squad, Madeleine Kurtz. Madeleine arrived with a cheery whoop of encouragement. She had glinty grey eyes, a foghorn voice, and stood a majestic six feet two. Henny and Madeleine set in motion the creation of a tent city. At their direction, Max and Duane unloaded a commandeered truck and laboriously erected on the dusty courtyard of Nightingale Courts what Henny proudly christened "Search Control Center." Annie phoned until her fingers ached, rousting out the members of the Cha Cha Bowling League, the Professional Women of Broward's Rock Island, the United Methodist Women, the Audubon Society, the Cultural League, the Triathlon Boosters, the League of Women Voters, the Women's Association of Broward's Rock, the Library Society, the Broward's Rock Municipal Hospital Volunteers, St. Francis of Assisi Altar Society, and half a dozen other organizations.

By the time the first mauve of sunrise streaked the eastern horizon, volunteers were arriving. In cars. On bicycles. Afoot. Many carried backpacks with survival gear, field binoculars, and compasses, wore no-nonsense swamp boots and could have passed for members of a Latin militia in their khakis and fatigue caps. Annie had blinked wearily in the daylight and stumbled past the arrivees toward a cot (Women's Side) in the tent city. As she fell into a deep sleep, she heard searchers receive their instructions as the search got under way.

Now, as she struggled to disengage from the mosquito netting (yes, Virginia, mosquitoes still thrive and multiply and attack in the Lowlands of the Carolinas, and no, they do not carry malaria, according to the Health Department), she realized she was ravenously hungry—and where was her husband of one night?

She looked down at her crumpled cream silk blouse and blue linen skirt and thought ruefully of the elegant grey dress she'd intended to wear today when they traveled. But despite the fact she looked about as attractive as the mangled hairpiece Edmund had carried to his mistress in Charlotte MacLeod's *Something the Cat Dragged In*, it was time to locate her new husband (on the Men's Side, of course) and see how he'd survived what little had remained of their wedding night.

The mosquito netting proved wilier than she. Finally, she dropped to the ground and rolled beneath it, thereby putting the finishing dusty touches to her costume.

She shaded her eyes against the brilliant morning sun. Ingrid would never have recognized Nightingale Courts. Yellow tape marked Cabin 3 as a Crime Scene (DO NOT ENTER). A television crew with minicams clustered around Madeleine, who stood statuesquely on an upended wheelbarrow and gestured vigorously toward the tent city. A long line of search volunteers inched by a field kitchen. So that was the source of those appetizing aromas.

Only the sternest sense of marital duty sent Annie in search of Max rather than directly to the end of the food line.

Wondering what sort of alarm might be raised if she strode boldly into the Men's Side, she temporized and sidled along the outside, squinting to see through the mosquito netting.

He was in the third cot from the end, sleeping on his back with his arms and legs outflung. Estimating his size, Annie wondered if a queen would be large enough and perhaps she should change the order to a king for their new house. She'd never before thought in terms of *permanently* sharing a bed.

Max's cot was the only one still occupied. With a wary look about, she dropped again to the ground, lifted the netting, and rolled under.

Using her hipbone to nudge him over, she perched on the edge of the cot and whispered, "Max. Hey, Max, wake up!"

One dark blue eye reluctantly opened and slowly focused on her. A flash of enthusiasm. An indistinguishable noise deep in his throat and two eager hands.

"Max! This is in public," she hissed, fending him off.

An expletive, beginning with a letter early in the alphabet, was *clearly* distinguishable.

"Max!"

They made a disreputable pair as they sat at the end of the pier, throwaway mess plates balanced on their laps. Her blue linen traveling suit was crumpled and dusty, and Max's trousers were snagged and stained. But their appearance was no more bizarre than that of Nightingale Courts.

From their vantage point, they could see the whole expanse of the inlet, the two cottages on the arm of land opposite, the glittering tin roof of Jerry's Gas 'N Go, the assorted boats docked at the long piers that thrust through the marshland toward deeper water, the semicircle of

cabins, and the huge, beige canvas tent. The tent domi-
nated the courtyard. A milling throng eddied from the
command post, a long table covered with maps and
telephones, to the mess line.

Max poked unhappily at an extremely limp slice of
bacon.

"Pretty good eggs," she observed.

"Hmmph." He gnawed disconsolately on toast coated
with government-surplus peanut butter.

"The lady dishing up the grits said there would be a
general meeting in about fifteen minutes."

Max stopped gnawing long enough to glance toward the
swarm of activity, then he glanced toward the sun. Abruptly, he put the crust on his plate and placed the plate on the
pier. "Annie—"

"No." She shook her head decisively. "No, she isn't dead.
Max, she *isn't*." She felt a surge of confidence, a certainty.
And she wasn't just whistling Dixie. She was betting her
chips on Henny and Henny's long immersion in every facet
of the mystery, from Dupin to Maigret. "No blood," Annie
said firmly. "No disarray. No *body*. Max, it wouldn't make a
bit of sense to kill Ingrid and take her body away. Why
leave one body and take another?"

He played devil's advocate. "The fact that she's missing
has convinced Posey she killed Jesse. Maybe that's what
was intended."

"That won't wash," she said firmly. "If she's never found,
who's going to believe she was guilty? This isn't the day of
Judge Crater. Why, the likelihood that she could escape to
the mainland and not be spotted by anybody is just zilch.
So, if she's never found, it will prove she's innocent, that
she was murdered, too. They think the reason Judge Crater
wasn't found was because somebody murdered him. No,
Ingrid has been kidnapped for a purpose, and it's up to
us—"

A tiny throat clearing, as delicate as the liquid call of a
tree swallow, indicated an end to the honeymooners'
privacy. Laurel smiled winningly down on them.

Max pushed aside his plate and stood. "Mother?"

Annie scrambled to her feet, too, tugging at her
wrinkled skirt with one hand and holding her plate with the

other. She wondered if his astonishment was at Laurel's presence (which would never astonish Annie, not here, not in Timbuctoo) or at her costume.

As always, Laurel was radiantly lovely. Her chiseled patrician features were aglow with good health and good cheer; her vividly blue eyes glistened with love for her fellow human beings. (And if those same blue eyes had a slightly spacey air to Annie, she put it down to uncharitableness on her part and quickly thrust the thought away.)

But Laurel's apparel *was* unusual, even for a woman who always matched her dress to her mood, with the infinite variety that implied.

A piece of dark brown cord cinched an absolutely plain, oatmeal-colored robe to Laurel's nineteen-inch waist. Simple leather sandals completed her attire.

No adornments. No jewelry. No scarfs. No hose. Not even a single button.

Annie knew that in a similar get-up, she would be about as alluring as Bertha Cool.

Laurel was stunning.

However, a tiny frown marred that smooth, aristocratic brow. "Maxwell, dear boy," his mother said hesitantly, "I wouldn't, of course, interfere in your honeymoon plans in *any* way. May I say, however—and I've enjoyed five honeymoons, my sweet—that I do believe this"—and her spread hand (no rings today) indicated the rackety wooden pier and the exposed mudflats of the salt marsh, steaming beneath the sun—"is carrying rustic simplicity to an *extreme.*"

"I couldn't agree with you more," her son said fervently.

"Oh, of course, of course. You and dear Annie have interrupted your plans to help search for Ingrid. I understand—and I applaud you both. . . . However, perhaps you dear children might take time this morning to—uh—freshen up."

If Annie had felt like Edmund's bedraggled trophy earlier, she now felt like a skunk-struck inhabitant of Joan Hess's *Malice in Maggody*.

"Sometime this morning, maybe. But we have to hang around now for the general meeting." At Laurel's look of inquiry, he explained Henny Brawley and Madeleine

Kurtz's formation of the Citizens Search for Ingrid Jones and the mobilization of Broward's Rock.

"That's very good." Her tone was the kind used by an indulgent adult admiring a child's mud pie.

Max quirked an eyebrow. "What else can we do?"

"I believe a physical search must, of course, be undertaken. But to combat evil requires *intense* mental concentration, and, of course, those of us who embrace an unlimited view of human achievement have recourse to other and more ethereal means." She beamed at them. "Ophelia and I have dedicated ourselves to this task—and I have no doubt but that we shall succeed." That winning smile. "I always succeed." It was said not with pride but with utter confidence.

It gave Annie the willies. God only knew what Laurel would take it in her head to attempt.

Max scented danger, too. His handsome face looked a little haggard.

"Mother, what are you up to? And how did you get mixed up with that dingbat?"

"My dear, Ophelia is not a dingbat. She is, indeed, a gateway to the beyond. But there's no time—" From the courtyard came a repeated clang. Annie peered around Max and saw Madeleine's substantial form now teetering atop the latticed arch, one arm industriously striking a pie tin with a metal spoon. ". . . for me to entrust you with the many and various avenues to enlightenment available to those who open their minds and hearts to the unseen but *vigorous* impulses which stream from the universe. In fact, I must *rush*." She turned to her daughter-in-law. "Annie, I need a key to the store."

The leap from the philosophical to the practical was too abrupt for Annie's earthbound mind. "Uh, what?"

"Death on Demand. Where may I find a key?"

Laurel excelled at non sequiturs. From the universe to the store in one mighty bound—what else was new?

The query reminded Annie that something else was askew. Because Ingrid, of course, had agreed to manage Death on Demand while Annie and Max honeymooned.

"The store!" Max exclaimed. "Annie, what will we do?"

"Keep it closed, I guess. I mean, we can't worry about that while we're looking for Ingrid."

Laurel clapped her hands. "Aha, the fates direct us when we are too blind to see."

Annie eyed her cautiously. Had it finally happened? Had Laurel's precarious mental balance tipped?

But her mother-in-law's smile was serene and blinding. "*I'll* take charge of the store. You needn't give it a thought. It's the perfect place for Ophelia and me to harness our energies and focus upon Ingrid. Now, Annie, I'm sure Ingrid has some personal effects at the shop. A favorite cup, perhaps? A compact? A sweater?"

Coffee at Death on Demand was served in white pottery mugs inscribed in bright red script with the names of landmark titles in the genre. Ingrid's favorite was *The Clue* (the first Fleming Stone book by Carolyn Wells) and she jealously guarded it from use by the G.P. (general public).

A little blankly, Annie offered, "You'll find Ingrid's cup in the bottom left-hand drawer behind the cash desk. And she keeps some other personal things in there."

"Good. Good. And the key to the store?"

Keys. Keys. "Vince Ellis at the *Island Gazette*'s keeping one. I don't know where Ingrid's are, and I think mine are in the drawer of the telephone table at the tree house."

"Vince will be fine. That's very convenient, since the *Gazette* offices are so close to the store." Laurel nodded complacently. "Everything works out for those who seek. That is the first byword of Harmonic Convergence, and the principle I always attempt to impart. Take care, my dears." The oatmeal-colored robe flared above her trim ankles as she turned.

From the courtyard, Madeleine's tattoo on the pie tin reached a crescendo.

Max looked at Annie, then after the departing form of his mother. "Laurel," he called, "where are you going? What are you going to do? And why are you wearing that funny outfit?"

"In the fullness of time," Laurel caroled reassuringly over her shoulder.

Annie sighed.

* * *

"Hey, Annie, Max, wait up a sec!" The pier quivered as Alan Nichols clambered up the ladder. He was still in navy blue warmups, and his looked slept in, too, but Annie noticed how admirably they molded to his muscular body. After all, she might be married, but she wasn't blind. Alan's curly chestnut hair was tangled, and he had shaved hurriedly, nicking his chin, but that didn't diminish his attractiveness, although he emitted a strong scent of evergreen. Annie had never been enchanted by men who used after-shave. His cheery blue eyes flashed an admiring message at Annie. He was that kind of guy. However, he greeted them dolefully. "Any word?"

Their faces told him.

He reached out and solicitously squeezed Annie's arm.

Max surveyed Alan with barracuda-like intensity. Just so might Selwyn Jepson's Billy Bull have eyed James Belsin when he made clear his interest in Eve Gill. Which was somewhat flattering. However, just because she was a married woman didn't mean every man she met had to treat her like a mother superior! She'd have to have a little talk with old green eyes.

Alan gave her another pat, then smothered a yawn. "I crashed a couple of hours ago, had to get some sleep. I thought maybe—" He looked past them toward the court-yard, then gaped in astonishment. "What the *hell* is going on?"

Annie explained. "Henny Brawley—you know her—she runs half the groups on the island, including the Broward's Rock Search and Rescue Squad. She's called out her forces and put Madeleine Kurtz in charge of a foot-by-foot search. Come on, I think Madeleine's going to make some announcements."

Annie discarded their breakfast plates in a trash bucket and the three of them joined the milling searchers. Madeleine, still balanced atop the arch, opened her address:

"Fellow citizens, greetings on behalf of Henrietta Brawley, director of Broward's Rock Search and Rescue Squad, and myself, Madeleine Kurtz—" She drew herself to her full height. Annie held her breath, but the arch continued to stand, I am honored to have been chosen by Henny to direct our all-citizen search for Ingrid Jones, who was ruthlessly abducted from her home last night. Promise to give the search my all. Henny regrets she can't be here in person. Busy investigating murder which occurred last night in Ingrid Jones's cabin. Henny requests assistance of all citizens. Anyone with *any* information as to the activities of the victim, Mr. Jesse Penrick, in days preceding his death, should convey that information to Mrs. Brawley post haste." Her foghorn voice gave a Gothic urgency to her message, investing each phrase with sense of mystery and intrigue. "Even *tiniest* facts may have untold import. Messages may be left at the command table."

Annie glanced at the listeners and saw several delving into knapsacks or pockets for writing material. She quirked an eyebrow at Max and whispered, "Henny is about to harvest a gigantic flood of irrelevant information. She's lost her marbles. This sounds more like Inspector Fox than Bulldog Drummond."

Max grinned. "Maybe she's found Bulldog's heartiness a bit of a strain."

"Shh," a nearby woman hissed, frowning darkly at them.

"We may safely leave the pursuit of the criminal to our inimitable Henny while we concentrate upon our task, finding Ingrid. Our situation: after midnight last night, Ingrid Jones telephoned her closest friend and long-time employer, Annie Laurance-Darling—"

"Mrs. Darling," Max growled.

"—and indicated she was in jeopardy. Before she could continue, she screamed and line went dead. Mr. and Mrs. Darling—"

"That's more like it," Max approved.

"Shh." Annie touched his lips with her finger.

"—arrived to find Ingrid's cabin unlocked." Madeleine pointed to Cabin 3. "Inside, they found the body of Jesse Penrick, who lived in Cabin One. Search of premises revealed no trace of Ingrid Jones. Another resident of the courts, Duane Webb, organized hasty search. This search yielded no clue to Ingrid's fate. During this time, the police arrived—"

As if on cue, a squad car rolled up to the arch. Since the way was blocked, literally, by a hundred massed bodies, Posey was forced to clamber out of the car by the arch. He looked about as happy as a cotton farmer with a boll weevil invasion.

Madeleine, obviously primed by Henny, gave a side-long, satisfied glance and continued in a husky bellow. "And that is why we have had to organize to search for one of our own—the authorities have *refused* to seek Ingrid."

Posey's face turned an interesting shade of puce, with perhaps a touch of orchid. Brusquely motioning onlookers out of his way, he picked up speed.

"Mr. Circuit Solicitor!" She might sound like a foghorn, but every syllable rolled majestically across the courtyard.

Annie began to have a good time. Her only regret was that Henny wasn't there to see the success of her minion's attack.

Posey stood on Ingrid's steps, his back to the crowd. But he knew there was a crowd. The politician warred with the prosecutor. It was no contest. He turned to face Madeleine, fury blazing in his eyes, but his mouth struggling for a smile. It was more revealing than he realized.

"Yes, Mrs., uh—"

"Madeleine Kurtz. Assistant director of the Broward's Rock Search and Rescue Squad, presently serving as ad hoc director of the Citizens' Search for Ingrid Jones. As leader of the volunteers, I demand to know what steps you are taking to investigate her disappearance." Madeleine clearly intended to give no quarter.

"As the prosecuting attorney whose duty it is to determine who shall be charged with the iniquitous homicide of your fellow island resident, Mr. Jesse Penrick, I am exploring the circumstances of his murder with all the facilities at—"

"What about Ingrid's abduction?" When Madeleine pursued a subject, she outdid a limpet.

The puce turned to magenta, and his geniality collapsed faster than The Old Man in the Corner (Baroness Orczy's famous detective) could untie complicated knots.

"There was no abduction," he thundered. "You people can search all you want to, but you're hunting for a

murderess who's vainly attempting to escape the conse-
quences of her crime. And I intend to swear out a warrant
for her arrest this afternoon!"

He turned, yanked open the door, and plunged into the
cabin.

Boos, hisses, and catcalls erupted from the crowd.

Madeleine gave a thunderous tattoo on the pie tin. Her
eyes blazed fanatically. "We shall not quail before our task!
We shall hunt in the swamps, through the woods, along
creek banks, in pastures. We shall remain faithful and
committed, and all of us, from myself to Ingrid's devoted
employers"—heads turned toward Annie and Max, waves
and smiles—"to our oldest living islander"—ninety-six-
year-old Matilda Kraft smiled smugly—"shall be in force
here, day and night, in this tent city, until Ingrid is restored
to us."

Hurrahs. Stamping feet. Huzzahs. An Amen or two. The
juiced-up recruits stormed to the command table and
eagerly lined up in groups of four to receive their assign-
ments.

"Night and day. Day and night," Max muttered.

Annie scarcely heard him. She stared at the closed door
to Cabin 3—and pulsed with fury.

"Calling Ingrid a murderess! I'd like to murder *him*!"

"Hush," Max urged.

"He can't get away with this! It's the most idiotic thing
he's ever done in a career that specializes in idiocy!" She
started for the cabin.

Max and Alan hurried behind her, Max warning, "Now,
Annie, cool it. We can't do Ingrid any good by making him
madder," and Alan asking, "What's going on? What's with
that guy? Annie, what are you going to do?"

Undeterred, Annie stamped up the cabin steps and
pounded on the door—then kicked it for good measure.

Posey yanked open the door. "Ms. Laurance—"

Max leaned over her shoulder. "*Mrs. Darling.*"

"Posey, don't be an ass!" Annie shouted tactfully.

Posey's cheeks puffed out.

She charged ahead. "You have no right to call Ingrid a
murderess. If somebody's killed her, it's going to be *your*
fault. You haven't even tried to find her, and we're citizens,

and I demand you help look for her. Get some helicopters; call out the national guard."

"Ah, Ms. Laurance."

"*Mrs. Darling*," Max said insistently.

Posey ignored him. "It is a felony to impede an officer of the law in the pursuit of his duties."

"Then you ought to be arrested," she fumed. "Who killed Penrick? Why? When? Get the answers, and we'll know who took Ingrid—and then we can find her."

"Oh, we'll find her, Ms. Laurance. Don't worry about that." And he slammed the door in their faces.

"*Mrs. Darling!*" Max yelled after him.

But Annie wasn't paying attention. She stood on the steps, her fists clenched, her face flushed, her eyes fiery.

"I'll find out," she snarled after Posey through gritted teeth. "Just you wait and see. I'll find out." She whirled toward Max.

Her husband, his face grave, looked at her and slowly nodded agreement.

"It's up to us, isn't it?" she demanded, stalking down the steps.

"Absolutely." Max's voice was crisp as he walked with her.

Annie stopped and looked toward the command post and the tent city. Search parties were beginning to disperse. "There are enough searchers."

Again, Max nodded. "Penrick's murderer knows what happened to Ingrid. And Posey won't look for him. So we will."

Alan's jaw dropped, and he stared at them in frank astonishment. He shoved a hand through his unruly chestnut hair. "How the hell can you do that?"

"Just like the police do," Annie said briskly. "Fact by fact. The first thing to do is hold a council of war on Jesse."

"He's dead," Alan observed blankly.

"Sure," Max agreed. "But why? That's the question."

Annie picked up the refrain. "Who hated him? Who was afraid of him? Who *was* he?"

"Oh, didn't you know him?" Alan asked. "He was a runty little guy, about five foot three, weighed maybe a hundred twenty pounds max, soaking wet. Had a mean face, rode a schlocky old green bike everywhere."

"I know *that.*" Annie was impatient. "I used to see him prowling around in the alley behind the shops. A scavenger. Always looking for anything thrown out that he could use or sell. You knew him, didn't you, Max?"

Max nodded. "I'd seen him around. Somebody told me he used to work at Hennessey's Marine."

"But we must find out more about him," Annie continued. "What was he really like? What kind of man was he?"

"A talky old bastard," Alan offered. "Used to hear him at Parotti's bar. 'People are no damn good, no *damn* good.'"

Annie looked at Alan in surprise. She'd only heard Jesse speak once or twice, but Alan had perfectly caught the oily high voice with its thick undercurrent of unpleasantness.

"Oh, that's wonderful," she said admiringly.

He gave a modest shrug, but followed up quickly with a gruff rendition of Humphrey Bogart and a mellifluous Ronald Reagan.

"Fantastic," she cried.

Max's eyes narrowed to slits. "But not really on point. How did *you* happen to know Jesse?"

"Just saw him around. I live over there." Resting one hand on Annie's shoulder, Alan pointed across the inlet at a cabin just visible through clumps of bayberry and sea myrtle.

The pressure of his hand was perhaps just a shade too friendly. Max's face congealed like Sgt. Buck's when he observed Col. Primrose with Mrs. Latham. The hand gave another squeeze. Annie gracefully slipped free and stepped a little closer to Max, who still looked like Agatha eyeing a field rat. Damn, married life was complicated. She would have to explain to Max that Alan couldn't help it. She'd seen him at work at Betsy's shop, and he was one of those kind of men who automatically come on to any women between thirteen and seventy. And he did have an undeniable charm. But this was no time for Max to get bogged down in hostility.

"Our job is to find out everything we can about Jesse," she said firmly, to recapture Max's attention. "Max, why

don't you get started rounding up information on Jesse and everyone living around here. And I'll sniff around here."
She glanced at the stuccoed cabins, glistening pinkly in the morning sunlight. They looked as serene as pop art. She wondered how Miss Seeton might have sketched them.

"Sniff around here?" Alan repeated.

Annie smiled encouragingly. After all, Alan didn't have their background.

"Sure," she said confidently. "This is just the case for a P.I."

Alan still looked lost.

"A private investigator," she explained kindly. "You know. Like V. I. Warshawski." (If she wasn't ignoring the snow on her morning five-mile run to Belmont Harbor and back.) "Or Mark Savage." (If he would take the time from his amorous pursuits.) "Or J. D. Mulroy." (She could always be counted upon to know what string to pull for helpful information.)

Their number was legend, and anything they could do, Annie could do better.

Maybe.

EIGHT

The onshore breeze didn't make a dent in Madeleine's tightly coiffed iron-grey hair. She saw off the last of the searchers, some armed with poles to prod the five-foot stalks of cordgrass near the shore, then swung smartly about and marched toward Annie and her companions. Madeleine wore a brown T-shirt that sported a golden halo over an upraised but obviously feminine fist. The legend read: SURE, GOD LOVES MEN. SHE GAVE THEM WOMEN.

"Ho there," she greeted them.

Annie smiled a welcome and noted looks of bland recalcitrance on the faces of Max and Alan. *Chauvinist pigs, without doubt. Maxwell Darling would hear about this.*

"Bully turnout," Madeleine bellowed happily. "Cracking good outfit." She pointed with pride at the command table, covered with ordnance maps and a full aerial view of the island. Three khaki-clad women talked intently over field telephones. Occasionally, they turned to give information to two workers standing before a blackboard, marking the location of search parties.

"Henny reorganized the Search and Rescue Squad when she took charge. This the first opportunity for all-out call to volunteers. She *is* pleased. Well, now, let's see." Madeleine rummaged in the front pockets of her baggy camouflage pants and triumphantly pulled out a list in crabbed printing, spiked with abbreviations. "Know you're on here. Oh, yes. Det. info." She jammed a hand into a hip pocket, pulled out a folded sheet of notepaper and handed it to Annie.

Annie recognized the handwriting at once. What was Henny up to?

"Good hunting," Madeleine bellowed. "Keep in contact with command center. Henny will send all messages through us." Giving a brisk salute, she swung away.

Annie opened the note and read aloud:

> "*On the trail. Jesse's boat (battered metal rowboat) missing!!! Fisherman (Jed Gates) noticed it in place at sundown Saturday. Know this will add to Posey's hare-brained conviction Ingrid fled. Nonsense, but will refute when all is known. Continuing to seek out Jesse's whereabouts Saturday. If I only had a bloodhound, who knows what I might discover! But fear not, we three sleuths shall triumph. H.*
> *P.S. More later.*"

Alan's blue eyes were bewildered. "What good would a bloodhound do with a boat?"

Annie wondered how to explain to Alan that Henny was, in her usual fashion, drawing upon a fictional sleuth's thoughts, in this case, Anna Katharine Green's Violet Strange in *The Golden Slipper*.

She decided the explanation was beyond Alan, said vaguely, "Oh, just a figure of speech," and moved on to the next postscript, with a worried glance at Max.

Clearing her throat, she read in a rush, "*P.P.S. Actually, we five sleuths. Laurel and Ophelia in psychic consultation. And who knows? Maybe ESP works.*"

"Oh, God," Max moaned. He looked accusingly at Annie. "I thought Mother was at Death on Demand."

Annie scarcely felt that Laurel's actions, wherever they might be taking place, were her responsibility. Since she couldn't quite think of a nice way to phrase that, however, she remained silent.

Max sighed. "I wish to God Mother wanted to save the whales. Or even chinchillas. I don't see why she has to be into this mind-expansion thing!"

Annie studiously looked down at Henny's note.

"I mean"—and his tone was aggrieved—"why can't she be like other people's mothers?"

Since there obviously was no good answer to this, Annie continued to stand mute.

Max shoved a hand through his thick blond hair. "Of course, she *means* well."

Annie thought about that well-paved road to hell. But she didn't need a marriage primer to remind her to continue to keep her mouth shut. As in tightly closed.

Alan saved the day. "Five sleuths? Hell, make that six. I'll help."

It did deflect Max's attention from the note. "That's all right. We can handle it."

But Alan wasn't to be dissuaded. "No kidding, I think Posey's a jerk. I'll do anything I can." He glanced at his watch. "I have to open the gallery this afternoon. Betsy's in San Francisco, so there's just me. But I'll come back tonight, so count me in."

Max was about as thrilled as Sam Spade with an invitation to a debutante ball.

Annie said warmly, "That's great, Alan. We'll look forward to seeing you."

Max waited until he was out of earshot, then said grumpily, "Like a hole in the head."

"Max, jealousy doesn't become you."

"I didn't get married to spend every waking moment with some hot-handed refugee from a perfume factory draping his paws all over you."

Annie grinned. "I didn't know you could wax so eloquent."

"I could do more than talk, if we could get out of here for a little while." His handsome face suddenly took on a look of cunning. "Listen, maybe we could slip away to your place. Just for a little while. I mean, I have to *shave*. And nobody'll miss us for—"

It must have been something on the order of great minds working as one, for Madeleine bore down on them, waving bath towels that looked like Army issue. "Annie! Max! Henny thinks of everything! She's delivered your luggage so you won't have to take a *minute* off from the hunt. And

Lavinia Melton's just finished rigging up the outdoor showers." She paused. "Men's Side and Women's Side, of course."

Annie didn't look at Max. Some sights are better left unseen.

Freshly showered and attired in a mint-green cotton top, white skirt, and white flats, Annie surveyed Nightingale Courts in the mid-morning sunlight and fought a wave of lassitude. She was so tired. Actually, she'd slept little for several days before the wedding, there was the high pitch of excitement of the wedding day, the trauma of Ingrid's disappearance, the restless and very short stint of sleep in the communal tent. She felt too tired to put one foot before the other. But Kinsey Millhone never surrendered to fatigue.

She looked toward Cabin One. Drawn window shades gave Jesse Penrick's home a dark, closed look, despite the pink stucco exterior. She remembered the last time she'd seen him. He'd worn his inevitable dark blue turtleneck pull-over and tight dungarees. His beaked nose, thin greyish lips, and squinty blue eyes with their malevolent cast created an unpleasant impression. He looked sullen, hostile, and angry, the kind of man people might well not like. But it took more than dislike to fuel murder.

She glanced toward Cabin 3. Ingrid's drapes were drawn, too, but that was only because she wasn't there to open them and let the sun shine in. Brilliant orange and yellow marigolds flourished in a front flower bed that glistened with pine needles, neatly herded there by a blower. Beside the carport, sweetgrass bloomed in pinkish masses like cotton candy. Beneath the carport sat Ingrid's car, a new blue Pontiac. The presence of the car brought a sudden ache to Annie's throat. Ingrid had been so proud of her car, the first one she'd ever bought brand new.

By golly, Ingrid was going to have the joy of that car for years to come! Determination burned within Annie. What was it about Jesse Penrick that had caused his life to end so violently? It was up to her to find out. She felt a surge of energy. Michael Gilbert's Henry Bohun rarely slept more than two hours a night, and look what he achieved as an investigator! Lifting her chin, Annie strode toward Cabin 2. Frilly white curtains hung in the windows, and green ceramic frogs perched on the front steps. Annie peered at the bright pink card taped beside the brass number. It read: OPHELIA BAXTER in black Gothic letters and *Psychic Consultant* in script. Oh, yes. Laurel's gateway to the beyond. A pudgy guru in a red and green housedress and black turban. With chartreuse hair.

The brass knocker was shaped like a pyramid.

Annie knocked, waited a moment, knocked again.

No answer.

A sudden movement drew her eyes to the left-front window. The curtain rippled, then a gorgeous, furry face peered at her.

"Anybody home?" Annie called.

The Persian cat rose on hind legs and began to shred the curtain.

Annie regretfully turned away. She wanted to talk to Ophelia Baxter, who had so artlessly revealed Ingrid's hot encounter with the soon-to-be-murdered Jesse Penrick. Time to find out whether that revelation had indeed been artless.

She passed Ingrid's cabin. Yellow police tape fluttered in the breeze. When had Jesse's body been removed? Was the autopsy done yet? When it was, how could they find out anything with Chief Saulter away? Maybe Henny would have some means of extracting information from the Southern Division Office of the Beaufort County Sheriff's Department.

Cabin 4 had a disheveled air. The drifting needles from the yellow pines lay as they had fallen, with no effort to marshal them. The morning paper had been flung midway between the circle drive and the front steps. Drawn shades closed out the sun here, too. She hurried up the steps and knocked, sharply.

The door opened slowly. Duane Webb stared out at her stonily, his bleary eyes magnified through his thick-lensed wire-frame glasses. He hadn't shaved yet, and the whitish stubble emphasized his receding hairline and sparse ring of greying hair. The scent of dust and old air rushed out at her, air that had been closed in for a long time. He was still dressed as he had been in those frantic hours of the night, in crumpled khakis and a faded sports shirt.

"Ingrid?" The slurred voice rose ever so little in inquiry.

Now she identified another scent, too, the sour reek of bourbon.

"Nothing yet. They haven't found her."

He turned away, shambled back into darkness.

Annie hesitated, then opened the screen door and entered.

Webb sank heavily into an armchair and picked up a tumbler half filled with whisky.

Although the room was dusty and cluttered with newspapers, it was well furnished. She stared in some surprise at the nubby linen-upholstered couch and matching chairs of Swedish design, with clean, plain lines. All the furniture coverings were variations of lemon. Against the south wall hung a huge modernist painting with splashes of black, orange, cobalt, and cherry. White bookcases, jammed with texts, books, and pamphlets, filled two walls. The chairs, the paintings, and the bookcases dwarfed the small living room. Annie felt certain they once had stood in cool, spatial elegance in another time and place.

It was a room that cried out for sunlight and laughter.

Without thinking, the words popped out. "Why are you sitting here in the dark?"

He slumped in the chair, staring at the tumbler that he held in both massive hands. His head looked like a candy skull for the Day of the Dead, pasty white with staring eyes. Deeply indented lines of pain were etched from nose to chin.

"Who the hell are you?" But the demand held little energy, as if the combative words erupted automatically. It was the roar of a toothless tiger.

"Annie Laurance." She spoke quietly, gently. "Ingrid's friend. We came last night, when Ingrid called. My husband and I." Which reminded her. "Actually, Annie Laurance-Darling."

"Oh, yeah. Yeah. I remember."

"I thought you were Ingrid's friend, too. You tried to help find her."

"I was. I was." The past tense weighted the words with

despair. "Ingrid. Kind of a harsh name. And she wore it like an armor. But she was gentle—and kind." He turned the glass of bourbon around, staring into the liquid. "Brought me soup last winter, when I was sick. She knew I wanted to die. But she didn't care, told me it was my duty to finish the course." A ghost of a smile tugged at his lips. "She loved mysteries, you know." He looked up at Annie. "Sure, you know that. She worked for you. She told me to think about Andrew MacWhirter in *Towards Zero*." A rumble that might have been laughter. "I told her to go to hell. She told me I was a spoiled kid. I asked her what the hell she knew about it. Turned out she knew a lot. She was alone, too. I'll bet you didn't know about Paul?"

He no longer looked at Annie. His mind was focused on knowledge beyond hers. She stepped nearer and sank into the chair opposite his. He stared into the whisky, and his words peopled the shadows with long ago places and dimly seen figures.

"Must've been a hell of a guy. For Ingrid to have cared so much. She showed me his picture." The glass in his hands moved around and around. "She doesn't have very many. They were young. Like you. Paul was going to be a professor. Chaucer. You ever read much Chaucer?"

"Not a lot." *The Canterbury Tales*, of course. She always recalled with sympathy Chaucer's plea at the end of *Troilus*, "Go, little book, and since there is so great diversity in English and in the writing of our tongue, I pray God no one will miswrite or mismeter you through ignorance of language, and wherever you may be read, I pray God you may be understood."

"Chaucer's full of laughter. And lust. And compassion. A man who loved Chaucer understood what life's about. A bloody struggle. A bloody damn struggle."

He fell silent.

"Ingrid and Paul?" Annie prodded gently.

Dark eyes focused on her abruptly. "Lou Gehrig's disease. That distances it, doesn't it? Name a goddam debilitating fatal disease after a big league baseball player. Makes it something that happens to other people. But it happened to Paul. They'd been married two years." He lifted the glass, drank deeply. "She got to watch him die."

Anger flashed now in those dark eyes. The whisky couldn't kill the pain. "So what the hell's the point? Why? A good-looking guy with a good mind, and he loves a good woman? So why the bloody hell does it have to happen?"

"I don't know." Her words drifted in the dim air, like autumn leaves in a November wind.

"Hell, no, you don't know." Anger still pumped his voice. "You're a bloody kid. You don't know anything."

She knew heartbreak when she met it. There might be the right words. Perhaps Father Dowling or Rabbi Small or the Reverend Randollph would have known them. She didn't.

He downed the rest of the bourbon in a gulp, reached for the bottle.

"But if you care about Ingrid, why aren't you helping in the search now?"

Those thick-lensed glasses turned toward the modernistic clock, green metal hands for the hour and minutes against a white background with yellow diamonds in place of figures. "If you don't find them in twelve hours, they're dead. After twelve hours, the chances go down faster than mercury in a blizzard." The hand tilting the bottle was steady. "Missing persons. Anything else is hokum. I was a city editor for almost twenty years. Story after story." He lifted the glass. "Body after body."

Ingrid didn't live in this room. She'd joined the shadows that moved in his mind.

"If she's dead, somebody's going to pay for it," Annie retorted angrily.

He laughed at that, and the sound was ugly. "Oh, you are so goddamned young. Pay for it? Oh, sure, sure. So you find the murderer. Big deal. Case solved. Four-column head in the *Gazette*. Wonderful. The State prosecutes and, lo and behold, gets a goddam conviction. That's great. And three years later, the bloody murderer'll be appealing the death sentence and appealing and appealing and still alive, while Ingrid's mouldered in a goddam grave. Kid, you'd better understand, nobody gives a goddam about the victim. All the rights are for the killer. But you'll find out." He raised his glass. "Here's to the education of Little Miss Do-Good."

Annie's head was beginning to throb. The room was suddenly suffocating. "You— you're disgusting. And no help to Ingrid."

"She's past being helped, you little fool."

Annie almost jumped to her feet, then she forced herself to remain. "Look," she entreated, "there's a chance for Ingrid. A good chance. It doesn't make any sense for a murderer to leave one body and take another one. Ingrid's been taken for a reason. Our best chance of finding her is to discover Jesse's murderer. You lived here. You can help me." She knew he could. No matter how much whisky he had drunk, his mind wasn't befuddled. "Who had a reason to kill Jesse Penrick?"

He gulped more bourbon, then his heavy shoulders began to shake. He was laughing.

"Who had a reason to kill Jesse? Oh Jesus, who didn't?"

"Why?" Annie demanded. "So he was hateful and quarrelsome. So what? What was there about him that could bring someone to kill him? What was he really like?"

"What was he really like?" His voice rose as he mimicked her. Slowly, the ugly laughter subsided. "He wasn't the kind of man you'd know anything about, kid. He was tighter with his nickels than a hophead with his last benny. He had a nasty tongue and a mind that crawled with venom like maggots on the underside of a rock. He liked sleaze, and he'd go all the way to Savannah to see dirty movies because he was too cheap to buy a VCR. Oh, Jesse was a sweetheart, all right." An ugly smile twisted Webb's face. "Who wanted to kill Jesse? Who didn't? If you knew him, you hated him. Oh, Jesus, I'd like to have taken his scrawny little neck in my hands and squeezed until his eyes popped out." A vein bulged in Webb's forehead and his eyes blazed. "God, I hated that sorry little bastard."

Annie wished desperately to be free of that room and its freight of misery and anger, but she persisted. "Why? Why did you hate him?"

"He liked to see people suffer. So I'm glad he's dead— and I hope it hurt like hell."

She stared at him for a long moment. Was he drunk? How well could he think? So she asked, "What time did you see him last night?"

At first, she thought he wasn't going to answer, then slowly the moon-face looked up at her. "Clever little bitch, aren't you?" He had no trouble articulating the words. "Go to hell."

The sense of enmity was so strong that Annie jumped up from the chair and began to back away.

"Actually, bitch, I saw him at Parotti's. That's where all the drunks gather on Saturday night. And I left just about the time he did. But I drove home, so I got here first. I could've waited for him. Somebody did. Glad they did. But it wasn't me." His tone was regretful. "Had a bottle to kill. Not Jesse."

"What did he *do* to you?"

Webb carefully placed the almost full tumbler on the table by his chair. He began to shake his head. "Oh"—and now his voice was weary—"he didn't do anything. I did it to myself." He buried his face in his hands.

He didn't look up as Annie closed the door behind her. On the cabin steps, she shaded her eyes. The September sunshine was blinding after the dimness of his living room—and the darkness of his soul.

Fear and anger warred in her. Duane Webb was angry and bitter. Was he also dangerous? Did he cease to look for Ingrid because he knew very well that she was dead? Had his urgent cry for an organized search been a killer's clever ploy? Was he drunk? Or was every word calculated to impress his devotion to Ingrid? Annie had never heard Ingrid mention his name. But Ingrid was a very private person. Annie had not known of Paul.

And she didn't yet know about Jesse Penrick and his neighbors. Certainly one neighbor wished him ill. What of the others?

A brusque voice rang through the air.

"Young lady! Young lady, come here!"

Annie looked up. A rangy, big-boned woman beckoned imperiously.

Noon Sunday

Confidential Commissions was not, of course, open on Sundays. As he unlocked the front door, Max admired anew his own cleverness in creating this most singular and original office. He had thought briefly of opening a private inquiry agency, but the Sovereign State of South Carolina has a most narrow view of the qualifications it exacted before awarding a private investigator's license (two years of work in an existing licensed agency or two years as a law enforcement officer). Of course, he could have opened a law office, had he been willing to take and pass the South Carolina Bar exam. (There is no reciprocity in South Carolina. Resident lawyers take a dim view of retirees flooding their state with part-time offices. No, the only route to law practice is to take the bar exam, and Max thought life much too short to be required to take and pass more than one of those, and he had done his duty in New York.)

In fact, Max was convinced that life was much too short to spend an inordinate amount of time doing any kind of work whatsoever. Since his more acquisitive forebears had amply provided him with successive inheritances, he was in the delightful position of being able to do precisely what he pleased.

Until he met Annie, with her apparently rock-hard conviction that all able adults must hold jobs.

He passed through the outer office and noted that the Whitmani ferns needed watering. Annie had chosen them. She seemed to have some kind of obsession with Whitmani ferns, something to do with Mary Roberts Rinehart's fondness for them in the sunroom of her Washington, D.C., home. (The house was also inhabited by the ghost of a previous occupant, Senator Primrose, as evidenced by furniture that went bump in the night and occasional blasts of frigid air. What interesting oddments had lodged in his mind through association with Annie.)

He opened the door to his office, switched on the light, and looked across the room at his enormous Italian Renaissance leather desk and Annie's framed photograph on one corner. Although Annie didn't know it, he spent more time enjoying her picture—and it captured her so well, her short blond hair streaked with gold, her serious grey eyes, and her eminently kissable mouth (damn, how long was he going to be sequestered on the Men's Side?)—than he ever did working.

Why did Annie have such an American view of life?

He eased into his well-padded, high-backed chair and switched on the vibrator. Well, of course, she was American and there was that strong vein of Puritanism. Fortunately, her Puritan ethic did not extend to sensual delights. He smiled contentedly at the picture—and the serious grey eyes regarded him with their usual intensity.

"All right, all right," he murmured. "I'm getting to work. Right now." That is, as soon as he ordered a nice lunch—perhaps mesquite-grilled sole—from the Island Hills Country Club. That call completed, he picked up a yellow legal pad and wrote:

JESSE PENRICK, LIFE AND TIMES.

Noon Sunday

Although she found the peremptory gesture off-putting, Annie responded because the unsmiling woman motioned from the steps of Cabin 5.

She was a very big woman. She wore a plaid shirt with rolled-up sleeves and brown slacks. Her black hair, streaked with grey, was pulled tightly back into a bun, emphasizing the strength of her features, a high-bridged nose, large brown eyes beneath heavy black brows, and a formidable chin. "Adele Prescott," she said gruffly, holding out a large, square hand, the nails cut short and unpainted. "You're Annie Laurance."

Annie nodded, then added hastily, "Annie Laurance-Darling."

Adele Prescott wasn't interested in her marital status. "Ingrid didn't stab Jesse. But nobody'll listen to me." Oddly, for so large a woman, her voice lacked resonance. "I can't get any satisfaction from that young man." An enormous sapphire in an intricate mounting of white gold flashed in the sunlight as she gestured across the courtyard.

Annie looked and saw Billy Cameron backed up against the steps of Jesse Penrick's cabin by Henny, who was leaning forward, her fox-sharp face alight with inquisitorial eagerness. Billy's normally pleasant countenance was set and stiff.

"If he's in charge, nothing will get done," Adele continued dourly.

Annie rushed to Billy's defense. "He can't help it. The circuit solicitor's taken charge since Chief Saulter's out of town. Billy doesn't have the experience to handle a murder case."

"I don't suppose he does have *that* kind of experience. But he's pretty good at sneaking in and out of back doors in the middle of the night."

Annie made a noise she desperately hoped sounded encouraging. What the devil was Adele Prescott talking about?

"I suppose it's his doing that no one's even talked to the residents of Nightingale Courts, *some* of whom are well pleased to see Jesse dead. Why, when I tried to tell him about the trouble between Jesse and that Webb man, he brushed me right off. Said the investigation was continuing and all important facts would be considered." She sniffed. "I just think he doesn't want anybody to know about him and Mavis."

"Who's Mavis?" Annie was bewildered. "Are you talking about Billy Cameron?"

"Of course I'm talking about him. I'd know that young man anywhere, coming and going at all hours of the night next door, when that baby's asleep. Pretty clear what those two are up to, and I wasn't the only one saw them. Jesse was talking to that girl the other day, and he had that sly look on his face. He was up to some devilment. He made her cry. I saw it. But I say, if you make your bed, you have to sleep in it."

Annie glanced involuntarily at Cabin 6. A child's pull toy, three baby ducks behind a mother duck, lay on its side by the front steps. A red rubber ball nestled behind a plastic dump truck. Last night, Annie recalled, a young woman had asked about Ingrid. And then she had hurried away to return to her little boy.

"Mavis?" Annie prompted.

"Mavis Beeson. Silly little empty-headed blonde," the woman said spitefully. "Bleached, of course. I've tried to talk to her, but she won't say a word about where she's from, or her husband, if she has one. She doesn't wear a wedding ring. But she sure doesn't lack for company—late at night. If you know what I mean."

The cabin door to number 6 opened and Mavis Beeson stepped out, holding a chunky toddler with curly brown hair. The little boy jiggled in her arms, repeating exuberantly, "Ding dong. Ding dong. Ding dong."

His mother stared apprehensively at the tent city and at Billy Cameron, glowering at Henny. Then her son reached up and tugged on her hair. "Ding dong, Mommy!" When she looked at him, her entire face changed, lightening, glowing, warming, the way a stark landscape brightens when sunlight emerges from a cloudbank. She held him up and nuzzled his tummy, then rained kisses lightly up his arm and behind his ear and on top of his head. He wriggled with delight.

"She looks like a good mother," Annie said.

"Spoils that kid rotten," Adele snapped, a lifetime of jealousy glistening in her dark eyes. "Minute she gets him home from the nursery, they're out in the back, digging, making mud pies, messy and noisy. I told her once no good comes of letting children think it's all right to be dirty. Children have to learn what's what." Outrage quivered in the thin voice. "Well, she knows all about dirt, I'd say."

Annie felt grateful for the hum of noise from the searchers, returning for lunch. An appetizing smell of vegetable soup rose from a steaming cauldron. She would have hated for Mavis to hear Adele's ugly comment.

But Adele wasn't finished. "Bet it was Jesse that painted that scarlet A on Miss Mavis's mailbox. Couldn't miss it when I got my mail yesterday. Maybe Miss Mavis saw it and decided to shut Jesse up."

Mavis felt their eyes upon her. Her head swung toward them. Unsmiling, she pulled Kevin tightly to her, whirled around, and darted back into the cabin.

"Scared to death. Serves her right." Adele gloated. "I told Ingrid she ought to boot our little Mavis out. Shouldn't put up with that kind of behavior. But Ingrid was just a fool about people. Why, it turned my stomach how nice she was to that nasty Duane Webb. The man drinks like a fish. And he butchered his wife and daughter. I told him that one day when he came outside, drunker than a lord." Her face turned an ugly saffron. "Do you know what he had the nerve to say? He said, 'What's it to you, you old bitch?' But Jesse got to him, all right. I don't know how Jesse found out." Mild curiosity lifted her voice, then sour surmise dropped it. "Probably at Ben Parotti's dirty old bar. He liked to drink there. Surprised he'd spend the money, but maybe he enjoyed the smell." She cackled perhaps in admiration of her own wit. "Ben sells beer and bait, and I don't know which stinks the most."

"Duane Webb killed his wife and daughter?" Horror buffeted Annie. Surely not even St. Mary Mead ever hid beneath its seemingly placid surface as much drama and despair and dark emotion as existed behind the pink-stuccoed exterior of Nightingale Courts. "How?"

"Driving drunk. After a Christmas party. People said they'd tried to talk him out of driving, but he wouldn't listen. Not the kind of man to listen. Well, he paid for it that time. Didn't see the stop sign and came out onto the highway and a semi smashed in the passenger's side. Wife killed instantly. Daughter died two days later. Christmas Day."

The self-righteous voice droned on, but Annie could hear only the crash of glass and the rending of metal and the high silver bells of Christmas carols and see a head bent in misery in a darkened room.

"Jesse Penrick told you this?"

"Oh, yes. He told all of us. Made him mad, I guess, that Duane wouldn't beg him to keep it quiet." She glared across the courtyard toward Webb's cabin. "Jesse liked to see people squirm. They had to dance to his tune. Duane wouldn't do it. Should have seen him the day Jesse put a toy car, one that was all crushed and dripping with whisky, on Duane's doorstep. Christmas gift."

"Oh, my God," Annie exclaimed.

Those unfeminine shoulders hunched impatiently beneath the plaid shirt. "You're just like Ingrid, feeling sorry for him. How about his wife and daughter?"

They weren't in pain, Annie thought. Not in the raw, scalding pain that seared Duane Webb's days and nights, until he drank himself into oblivion. Something of the sickness that must have swept Webb that Christmas morning swirled inside her.

"What a dreadful man," Annie cried.

"Drink leads men into—"

"Not Duane, Jesse! What a monstrous thing to do!"

The colorless lips twisted. "You, too. Just like Ingrid. Well, *I'm* not weak enough to be taken in by a man like Duane Webb. He couldn't turn my head!"

Annie didn't like the turn the conversation was taking. But Posey would probably come this way, too. Reluctantly, very reluctantly, she asked, "Was Ingrid interested in Duane?"

"Crazy as a sixteen-year-old girl with her first crush. Always carrying meals to him, and him mostly too drunk to care. I told Ingrid she was making a fool of herself."

Crazy in love. It was possible. Love doesn't count age or circumstance. Love springs to life like desert flowers, thriving on the thinnest sustenance, the rockiest ground.

Posey would claim that Ingrid hated Penrick for his treatment of Webb, that she'd quarreled with him in the early morning and that, facing him at the end of a day, she'd struck out violently when goaded too far.

Not Ingrid. Not gentle, almost frail Ingrid with her nononsense briskness that masked such a gentle, kindly nature.

Surprisingly, Adele was echoing her judgment. "Ingrid wouldn't have stabbed *anyone*. She may have been a lovesick fool, but she would never hurt anyone. Not even Jesse."

But Posey would listen to the last and discard the first.

Annie almost warned Adele Prescott to keep quiet, if Ingrid were her friend. But even as her heart urged her to do so, her head argued that she would be making a grave mistake. If Posey learned that Annie had interfered in any way with his witnesses, it would absolutely cinch his conviction of Ingrid's guilt. No. Annie's only hope was to find out more than Posey and do it fast.

"Did you see Jesse yesterday?"

Adele flashed her a sharp, suspicious look. "No. I always go to the flea market in Savannah on Saturdays. I set up and sell knickknacks I've picked up during the week. I didn't even get back to the island till after dark. The last time I saw Jesse"—her eyes widened—"why, that's funny. I stopped at Jerry's Gas 'N Go Thursday night to pick up a quart of milk, and I spotted Jesse in the phone booth!"

"What's funny about that?"

"Jesse using the phone. I never knew him to ever make a phone call. At least, I never saw him do it."

"Why wouldn't he make a phone call?"

"Oh, he didn't have a phone. Wouldn't spend the money for one. So far as I know, he didn't have a friend in the world. Who would he call?"

Annie tried to imagine living without a telephone and failed. "How did he make appointments or take care of business?"

"Business?" Adele snorted humorlessly. "Jesse Penrick didn't have any business. Except to snoop around. He was retired, lived on Social Security, just like me and Ingrid and Duane."

"Is everybody here"—Annie's hand swept the semicircle of cabins—"retired, except for Mavis?"

"Mavis and Tom Smith." The square hand pointed at the last cabin.

"What does he do?"

"Makes miniatures for doll houses. He's good at it." There was no warmth in her voice.

Annie looked at her curiously. Apparently there was no one Adele liked very much.

"What's he like?"

"Wears his hair in a ponytail." The thin voice dripped

disdain. Adele had all the right vibes to be a Gestapo inquisitor in an Alistair MacLean novel.

Annie suddenly had enough. She met Adele's sour eyes squarely and said, "So did Max, when I first met him. I thought it was the most damnably attractive thing I'd ever seen, so I walked up and introduced myself and asked him out." With the pleasure of seeing that formidable jaw drop, Annie wheeled around and marched down the steps and wondered what in the hell she was going to say to her short-haired—always—husband when the story made its rounds back to him, as it inevitably would. But Max had a wonderful sense of humor. Usually.

NINE

Unaware that the history of his hair length and its galvanizing effect upon Annie was about to become a topic of interested and occasionally ribald speculation in island watering holes, Max jammed an ink-stained hand through his short locks in complete frustration.

"Damn." He leaned back in his chair, which was still vibrating cheerfully but hadn't done a thing to ease the crick in his back from his extended—and fruitless—telephoning. He propped his tassel loafers on the desk—who cared if it had once been owned by a cardinal?—and flicked a second switch to add heat to the vibrations.

Easy does it, Maxwell, he told himself. Go with the flow. Remember? Surely he couldn't be catching Annie's intensity? He breathed deeply, thought briefly of his mantra (Laurel did mean well, and a woman's only son couldn't refuse a little thing like a mantra; it would be rudeness of the worst sort), and began to relax. He didn't bother to analyze what turned the trick—the heat, the added oxygen, or the chant.

But he was beginning to feel like himself, which was, of course, laid back, comfortable, unstressed, and mellow. It wouldn't add to his meager stock of information to attack the telephone like a Type A personality. He entertained himself for a moment, thinking of a number of interesting variations on possible expansions of the letter into descriptive summations, such as Airhead, Antbrain, and Asshole, all of which, in his view, aptly delineated people who threw

74

themselves through life without a passing glance at, much less a sniff of, the flowers.

Except for Annie, of course, his delightful, opinionated, high-strung, easily irritated, quickly angered, very sexy Annie. He beamed at her photograph. All the charm of a hedgehog, but much prettier.

Then he sighed. His dear little hedgehog was not going to be pleased at his unproductive afternoon. And Annie had such respect for his investigative abilities. (Of course she did.)

Besides, it was thwarting even to someone of his easygoing nature to throw out a net and come up with zero. Almost. Oh, he had a few facts, but not nearly enough. Always before, he'd found it easy to track down people's pasts. Thoughtfully placed calls to banks, insurance companies, police, credit bureaus, employers, local societies, and former neighbors (especially former neighbors), plus quick scans of newspaper files, reference books, and yearbooks could retrieve the damnedest information imaginable. Birth dates. Marriages. Divorces. Family. Schools. Organizations. Jobs. Gossip, both kindly and not so kindly.

Not this time.

Once again, he tugged in exasperation at his short, thick hair, and the phone rang.

He dived for it. Maybe something was going to pop.

"Max, my dear, what *are* you doing *there*?"

He blinked. "How did you know I was here, Mother?"

"I divined it, my dear." A sigh. "And I must say I'm disappointed." Laurel's husky voice fell away like a distantly heard train whistle in the night.

Max had been dealing with Laurel for almost thirty years. Now he tilted his chair almost to horizontal and tried to sound suitably serious. "I'm sorry to hear that, sweetie. What can I do that will fill you with parental pride?"

There was a thoughtful pause. For once, Laurel seemed to be at a loss for words. That *was* astounding.

Finally, delicately, she said, "Although I know you and Annie are most concerned about Ingrid's disappearance, and I respect that and understand it, I do believe—and I've had a good *deal* of experience—that a marriage must have a proper *beginning*." Pause. "Maxwell, one must *cleave* in marriage."

Now Max was at a loss for words. Could Laurel, could his mother— Yes. She could. And was. Although in his heart he agreed with her absolutely—and that was rare enough to be remarkable—he scarcely felt this was a suitable topic for discussion. But, obviously, some response was necessary.

"Uh," he began, and knew it lacked both resonance and pizzazz.

"Not that I would dream of interfering." The golden tone was a little hurried. "You know that I would *never* presume to impinge upon the lives of others."

This was so patently untrue that it distracted him for a moment.

"Oh. Do hold on, my sweet. Another line is ringing. I'll get right back to you."

Max cradled the receiver between his ear and shoulder, determinedly refused to think about his mother's well-meant (as always) but outrageous probing and stared pensively at the ceiling. What other avenue could he explore to find out something—anything—about the damn moles who lived at Nightingale Courts? Now, he had unearthed quite a bit on Ingrid. There'd been a nice story in the *Savannah News* when she retired after thirty-four years as a librarian there, and he'd found plenty on Duane Webb. Poor bastard. But astonishingly little had come to light about Jesse Penrick, Ophelia Baxter, Adele Prescott, and Mavis Beeson. As for Tom Smith—Max glared at the legal pad on his desk—the inhabitant of Cabin 7 was apparently invisible. No voter's registration, no bank account, no insurance policies, no

"My dear boy," Laurel resumed reassuringly, "I want you to understand that I am with you in spirit. Actually, I would be gravely concerned. But—you *are* my son."

That had never been disputed, so far as Max knew.

"Therefore"—and she trilled with relief—"I know that you will take care of first things *first*. And, of course, we shall all bend every effort to bring this to a rapid conclusion, both for Ingrid's sake and—"

Max interrupted firmly, though he would forever after wonder just how his mother might have intended to complete that sentence. "Mother, it is the most singular thing—I've had a sense of other spirits burning to aid us in our quest."

He almost felt a moment's shame, because Laurel was *thrilled*.

"Maxwell, how wonderful! I always knew that you, too, were one of us."

He had a vision of hundreds of oatmeal-robed figures and shuddered.

"My dear, have you received a little *hint* perhaps of where Ingrid is?" A breathless pause, intense anticipation.

"Uh." Max scratched at the back of his neck. "Uh, no. Can't say that I have."

Laurel sighed breathily. "I suppose you haven't yet reached that plane. And I'm afraid Ophelia and I have demanded too much of our contacts. Ophelia's faculties seem to be *blocked*."

Max wasn't persuaded that Ophelia, as he recalled the tubby, turbaned woman, possessed any notable faculties at all, so he wasn't terribly surprised. However, to keep the conversation away from himself and Annie, he would gladly have discussed the conjugation of Swahili or the impressive swimming abilities of the marsh rabbit (seven hundred yards when pressed), so he said in hearty sympathy, "Laurel, that's a damned shame."

"I *knew* you would understand," Laurel chirped. "So," she continued with brisk, satisfied assurance, "you'll get me a key to Ingrid's cabin."

Max shoved the lever and his chair snapped upright. Somnolence fled, replaced by intense concentration. "Mother, that's a Crime Scene. No admittance. You could get in a lot of trouble."

"If I had a key and said I was picking up something Ingrid had told me—"

"No. Absolutely and positively and definitively, no."

"Maxwell, sometimes you act just like your father—and that man was no fun at all!"

The connection broke with a bang.

Max glowered at the buzzing receiver. A confrontation between Laurel and Posey didn't bear thinking about it. Somehow he had to make it clear to Laurel that access to Ingrid's cabin was absolutely impossible.

Unfortunately, it wasn't easy to make any proposition clear to Laurel when her brain—that elusive, quicksilver, horrifyingly original organ—was focused on an objective.

The receiver buzzed like an angry wasp.

And dully, but with increasing volume, someone knocked on the locked front door of Confidential Commissions.

Annie stared helplessly at the blue eyes brimming with tears.

"Please, please don't tell anyone. If it gets into the papers, if Henry finds me—oh God, he'll take Kevin away."

Annie sat beside the crying woman on the tiny room's single sofa. The cushions were worn and lumpy, but neatly mended. A wicker chair with chipped white paint was the only other furniture. The room would have been depressingly dismal except for the scattering of brightly colored blocks, toy cars, and empty margarine containers, strung together with a bright red thread. Crayon drawings, random splotches of color, decorated the walls. The smell of modeling clay mingled with those of freshly ironed cotton, Clorox, and Jell-O.

Mavis Beeson leaned closer and grabbed Annie's arm. Long, cherry-red nails jabbed painfully into her wrist. "You got to *listen* to me. I promise I'll never see Billy again. I promise, oh God, I promise, but please don't let Henry find out!"

"Was Jesse going to tell Henry?"

The question, sharp as a stiletto, cut through Mavis's hysteria. Her hand fell away from Annie and slowly rose to clutch at her throat.

"Oh, no, no. We had it all worked out. He promised me—"

"Mavis, Jesus God, keep your mouth shut!"

Billy Cameron's shout exploded in the tiny living room. He stood in the kitchen doorway, filling it, and furious brown eyes blazed at Mavis. From the bedroom, Kevin's voice rose in a frightened wail.

Billy's usually pleasant face was almost unrecognizable, it was so distorted with fury—and fear. "She's worse than telling a cop," he stormed. "Don't say a word—or they will take Kevin away, for God's sake."

"Mommy, Mommy, Mommy!" Kevin's scream choked off into sobs.

Mavis looked at Annie with sick horror, then jumped up and ran to the bedroom. She reappeared, clutching the terrified little boy. "It's all right, honey, it's all right. Mommy's here." She stared at Annie, and said again, "Mommy's here," and her voice broke. Helpless tears streamed down her cheeks.

"Mommy, Mommy," the little boy wailed.

Billy reached them in two strides, pulling the girl and baby into his arms. He glared defiantly over their heads at Annie. "Last winter, I was on the road right outside Chastain. This girl with a baby ran out onto the highway, and in the headlights I could see her hair streaming in the wind. I knew she was scared, from the way she ran. Something bad had happened. I stopped and got them in the car. They were both crying, and she had blood running out of her ear where her husband had hit her, and the kid's arm hung funny. I brought them home here to Broward's Rock. Where they could be safe. I helped her get a job at the five-and-dime, and she's taking care of Kevin real good."

Annie stared at the bleached-blond head pressed so tightly against his chest and tried to understand. But Annie was free and independent and treated with respect. She lived in such a sane and well-ordered world that being beaten by a man was incomprehensible.

"Why didn't you go to the police?" she asked. For God's sake, Billy was a policeman. Hadn't they even talked about it?

Mavis half turned in Billy's arms. Tear-smeared eye shadow streaked her face. "Henry would kill me," she said jerkily. "Then what would happen to Kevin? I can't tell anybody! I got to get away. That's what I got to do. I got to get so far away, he'll never find us. That's what I should have done that night, but it was so cold and Kevin was hurt." She struggled in Billy's embrace. "I got to get away."

"Honey, honey, honey," Billy crooned, holding her gently and trying to break into that circle of fear. "I won't let him get you. I swear to God, honey, I won't let him get you." He looked over her head at Annie and nodded meaningfully at the door.

Annie hesitated, then rose and crossed the barren room. She opened the door and stepped out into the late afternoon sunshine.

Fragrance from an overgrown honeysuckle wafted on the breeze. The marsh stretched in glassy peace, gleaming a cheerful yellow from the wind- and tide-blown tussocks of cordgrass seeds. It was a lovely fall afternoon in the salt marsh, marred only by human misery.

Max built a steeple with his fingers. "On the face of it," he said judiciously, "I don't think there's anything to worry about." He managed a tight smile. He didn't really like his visitor, there was no getting around it. It wasn't that he was jealous, of course. But Alan Nichols was just a little too good-looking and a little too ready with his hands around somebody else's wife.

"So you think I can relax, huh?" Alan leaned back with a sigh of relief. "Well, to tell you the truth, I thought maybe Ruth was making too much of it. I mean, what the hell. So her mother hasn't called her yet! I guess Ruth has a goody-two-shoes picture of Betsy. And you know Betsy. She's probably having a grand old time out there." The lewd intent in Alan's good-old-boy tone was unmistakable.

That surprised Max. Not because he would have expected better of Alan Nichols. He'd expect damn little from Alan Nichols. But because it didn't fit Max's mental image of Betsy Raines. Of course, he and Annie didn't know Betsy well. However, the owner-manager of the Piping Plover Gallery was very active in the Broward's Rock Merchants Association, and they'd visited with her at several meetings and seasonal parties. In her mid-forties, Betsy was a successful businesswoman. She had a good figure, a nice manner, and remarkably pretty red hair. There was nothing about her to suggest a woman on the prowl. Max raised a quizzical eyebrow.

Alan flushed and tugged at his ear. "Hell, I don't mean to talk out of school. But I think Betsy likes to kick up her heels on business trips. You know, she's still a good-looking woman, and a widow. I mean, what the hell, Jack? I mean, she wouldn't be above picking up some guy in a bar. Maybe she's shacked up somewhere for a day or two and just forgot to call Ruth." Alan shrugged. "Hell, I don't know."

His tone implied he knew damn well, but was too much of a gentleman to say so.

Alan Nichols. Gentleman. His herringbone sports coat had a nifty red line in it which was picked up by the red silk tie knotted perfectly at the neck of an impeccable button-down, pinpoint Oxford cloth blue shirt. The effect was finished off with grey worsted slacks, sleek black tassel loafers, and a heavy silver ID bracelet. Probably stood in front of a three-way mirror and admired his ass after he dressed. Max was not impressed. What Annie saw in the curly-headed pretty boy was beyond his understanding.

Alan was beaming at Max now, in a perfectly good humor. "I'm damn glad I came over to talk to you. You've made me feel a lot better about it. It's silly to push the panic button just 'cause somebody missed a call. But I couldn't get through to the police here. That Cameron guy. And Ruth was so upset, I figured I better do something."

Max decided to overlook the unspoken implication that something—i.e., Max—was better than nothing. Perversely, he decided not to offer further reassurances. He glanced down at his legal pad. According to Alan, his boss, Betsy Raines, took a Delta flight out of Savannah on Wednesday morning en route to San Francisco on a buying trip for the gallery. "Did you see Betsy Wednesday morning?"

"Nope. She had an early flight, so I wished her a good trip when we closed up Tuesday."

"So far as you know, she made the flight?"

"Oh, sure." Alan looked surprised. "I mean, she must have. Otherwise, she'd have called or come back to the island."

Max wrote on his yellow pad. "Where's she staying in San Francisco?"

Alan frowned. "Oh, hell. I just looked at the copy of her itinerary. I'll have to check it at the shop and call you back. Some big-deal hotel in Frisco."

Although he wasn't a northern Californian, Max's hackles rose at the "Frisco." Laurel would stress that ignorance can't be helped and should never be condemned. Bully for Laurel.

"Okay," he said crisply. "You don't remember which hotel, but you can call me back on that. Let's see, she was going to stay five days. That means she should return Monday. Right?"

Alan slapped his knee in relief. "Sure. She'll be back tomorrow. Hell, I'm sorry I even came over here and bothered you." He started to rise.

He didn't sound especially sorry. Max gave him a short stare. Alan would always have the right words, but he came across like a used-car salesman touting a Jaguar with a Chevrolet engine. However, he had been alarmed enough about his employer to come to Confidential Commissions. Max could almost hear Annie saying, "You didn't check up on it? But Max, I really like Betsy." He waved Alan back to his seat.

"I didn't mean to imply we shouldn't do a little checking. It should be easy to locate her. For one thing, who was she going to meet? We can call some of her expected contacts and trace her movements."

"There I can't help you," Alan said regretfully. "I mean, it could have been anybody. An art dealer. A collector. All I know is, she took a bundle of cash with her and intended to come back with a Picasso. That's all she told me."

"Cash?"

Alan lounged in his chair. "Oh, that's no big deal in the art business. A lot of people want cash on the barrel head—and no close questions asked about where a painting came from. You'd be surprised how many collectors'll take a painting without provenance. Naw, that's no big deal."

Max knew contraband art was smuggled across borders every day. It might not be the ordinary course of business, as Alan implied, but there was a lot of cash dealing. In back rooms.

Alan was shaking his head. "Sorry I barged over here. But I didn't know what the hell to do when Ruth called. You know Ruth?"

Max shook his head.

"She's visited here a couple of times since I started to work for Betsy," Alan said. "A real uptight gal. Pretty cute, but no fire. You know the kind, keeps her legs crossed all the time. And my God, what grown woman asks her mother to check in every time she makes a plane trip? That's pretty neurotic, isn't it?"

With the frequent near hits enjoyed by America's airlines, which seemed a good deal more interested in being lean than safe, Max didn't think Ruth's anxiety was altogether unreasonable. If Alan didn't like Ruth, Max decided he did.

"Do you have her phone number?"

"Ruth's?" Alan looked like a lottery winner. "You mean you'll call her? Get her off my back? Jesus, that's swell of you, Max."

Max managed not to snarl as they said good-bye, although it goddam well did not make his day to bring a joyous smile to Alan's choirboy features.

He stared sourly at the telephone. But slowly his frown faded. The point was not Alan, but Betsy. Was she okay? Cheered, he rummaged in the bottom drawer for his Savannah directory and called Delta. It took two long waits on hold and three call transfers, but he finally had the information. Mrs. Raines's ticket had been used both from Savannah to Atlanta and Atlanta to San Francisco.

Immediately after he hung up, the phone rang and Alan was on the line with the hotel (the St. Francis) and Ruth Jenson's telephone number in Kansas City.

Max ended up on hold with the St. Francis, too, but was finally rung through to Mrs. Raines's room. He drew happy faces on his legal pad and wondered just how he should approach Betsy Raines when she answered. With a good-natured "Hey, we've got the distress flags out for you back here on the island"? He winced. Even to his uncritical ear that sounded asinine. How about, "Sorry to bother you, Betsy, but Ruth's been worried about you." Of course, he'd gloss over any possible reason for Betsy to have missed calling her daughter, such as a liaison forged in the hotel bar. He had a sudden clear memory of a Christmas party and Betsy Raines lifting her glass in a toast and the tree lights reflecting from her silver bracelets and red hair.

The hotel operator broke in. "No answer. Do you wish to leave a message?"

"Yes. Ask Mrs. Raines to call her daughter, please."

He'd done all he could do for now. His glance dropped to the bottom of the page and the telephone number of Betsy Raines's daughter, Ruth. Oh yeah, he'd better call her, tell her that Betsy had safely reached California. Then he would get back to work on the life and times of Jesse Penrick. Maybe he would yank the right string and it would lead directly to Ingrid.

He picked up the phone.

Annie welcomed the thick, heavy afternoon heat. She *liked* humidity, the sprinkle of sweat beading her face, the moist caress of the air. She passed the closed field kitchen, the odor of vegetable soup overborne by the scent of soap as Red Cross volunteers scoured their pots and pans. She'd missed lunch while talking to Adele Prescott and Mavis. Cabin 7 was next, but she had to have some sustenance and time to sift through what she'd learned. Dust rose in lazy spirals as she marched briskly along the grey dirt road. The sharp fragrance of the pines was as welcome as the shade from their silvery umbrella crowns. As the road curved, she left behind the muted activity of the search headquarters and glimpsed the shiny tin roof of Jerry's Gas 'N Go, the two old-fashioned gas pumps, and a plate-glass window.

A window that overlooked the road, the road that was the only access by land to Nightingale Courts.

Annie broke into a trot.

A bell jangled as she pushed open the door to the combination country store and gas station. An enormous woman in a pink gingham dress sat on a high stool behind the cash register. She faced the window. The small, wooden-floored store was crammed with well-stocked shelves. Refrigerator cabinets lined one wall.

"Found Ingrid yet?" She had a high, sweet voice.

The clerk, Shirley May Foley, knew all about the murder, the search, and Annie.

But she shook her head regretfully when Annie asked if any cars had passed around midnight.

"Can't help you there. Sure wish I could, but we close at eleven, and I was in kinda a hurry last night, so I can't speak to after, say, eleven-twenty. My boys, Beau and Bobby Joe, was coming to town to go huntin' today with their pa. So I hurried home to get started bakin'. I can say we only had one car after ten last night, and it was a reg'lar. You can't miss the lights—or the noise, either. That Webb man's car went by about eleven."

That confirmed Webb's story, that he'd driven home from Parotti's—Annie stiffened, like a dog on point. What was it Webb had said? Jesse had received a phone call and left about the same time. How long would it take for him to get to the Courts from the bar on his bike? Maybe five minutes. That meant Jesse'd arrived at his cabin around five or so minutes after eleven. Ingrid had called for help at midnight. Fifty-five minutes during which Jesse was murdered, then Ingrid was abducted. Ingrid had to have been removed in either a car or boat. It was unrealistic to think an abductor could carry her for any great distance. There had been so much noise and confusion last night that a resident abroad in a car *could* have returned unnoticed during the melee. As for a boat, Jesse's was missing. Annie's head whirled. The obvious inference, at least to Posey, was that Ingrid had escaped in it. But if the murderer had taken it, with Ingrid as a captor, didn't that mean the murderer *couldn't* be a resident of the Courts? If so, how had he returned? But he could have taken Ingrid in the boat to a hiding place and had either a car or bicycle waiting there. Annie wished she were better at chess or the kinds of thought problems that went: If one boat traverses two miles in three hours and a second boat, etc. She sighed.

Shirley May clucked sympathetically. "Sure sorry I can't be more help."

"You're the only one here at night?" Annie asked.

The big woman nodded cheerfully. "I work from three to eleven. 'Course, we have a garage boy, changes oil, things like that, but he got off at five."

"I don't suppose," Annie said with little hope, "that you saw anyone walking by around eleven?"

"Why, honey, anybody could slip among those pines, if they had a mind to."

"How about a boat? Did you hear any boats?"

"Don't hardly ever hear boats. You got to understand, the back storeroom's between me and the sound." Shirley

May leaned forward, her triple chin resting on an ample bosom, her china-blue eyes wide. "They got any idea who's behind all this?"

Annie wasn't going to dignify Posey's suspicions by repeating them, and Shirley May would hear all that soon enough. "Not really."

"Well, I think *I* know. You just come here and look at *this*."

She heaved her bulk off the high stool and presented a battleship-broad back to Annie as she moved heavily down the center aisle toward a door marked EMPLOYEES ONLY.

Annie followed into the storeroom and past cartons and crates to a back door and steps leading down to a patch of concrete.

The clerk pointed a fat finger at a small mess of ashes.

Annie looked at her in bewilderment.

"I think it's a *cult*, that's what I think. Now, nobody has no call to burn nothin' here. And this mess wasn't here Saturday night. But it was here this mornin'. I saw it first off, when I drove in. There's my car." She pointed just past the ashes to a rusted old Chevy.

Feeling it was expected, Annie crossed the oil-stained concrete and stared down at the remnants of a small blaze. Obviously, someone had set some brown paper afire. There was a curl or two that had survived and a dark stringy ash that might have been twine. She looked past the concrete. A dusty path led to a rickety pier that poked out through the marsh to deeper water.

It seemed to Annie quite an unlikely site for cult activities. "Well," she gently suggested, "I don't see why the, uh, cult would gather here—"

"If they didn't want to fire this whole shoreline, they sure had to!" Shirley May disagreed aggressively. "This here's the only patch of concrete till you get to town."

Which was true. If it mattered.

"And everything's dry as tinder right now, we had so little rain lately. Why, they didn't have no *other* place, if they were from around here."

Enthused, Shirley May found an empty box and upended it over the ash pile. "Maybe this'll turn out to be real important. Now, you tell the search folks."

They parted as firm friends, Annie purchasing a king-size (48 oz.) cherry-root-beer ripple delight and a Giant Baby Ruth, a prospective late lunch. As she strolled down the road, she decided a reasonable investigator couldn't expect to strike the kind of conversational gold that always seemed to befall P.I.'s like Lew Archer and Cheney Hazzard. Rounding the bend, Nightingale Courts came into view. Madeleine Kurtz looked her way and began to wave energetically.

Max scowled and tapped his pen on the legal pad. "No, I didn't get through to your mother. However, I left a message for her to call you, so I imagine you'll be hearing from her later today."

"You're sure she reached San Francisco?" Ruth Jenson's question was sharp.

"Yes, no doubt about it. Her plane ticket was used, and she checked into the St. Francis Wednesday morning."

"I don't understand it. . . ."

Max could think of no tactful way to inquire whether Ruth's mother had a penchant for picking up strange men for anonymous retreats. But her daughter would be the last to know, anyway.

"Perhaps she's gotten involved—uh—with a client. Too busy to phone you. Or maybe she forgot. All of us forget things sometimes."

"You don't know my mother very well, do you?" The question wasn't hostile, nor was the voice. In fact, Max rather liked Ruth Jenson's voice. It was level, brisk, pleasant. She continued, and there was no hysteria, only a quiet conviction, "Something's happened to her."

"Oh, now, Mrs. Jenson, surely that's leaping to conclusions unwarranted by—"

"No." The simple negative had the finality of a dirt clod dropped on a coffin. "You see, my dad was killed in a plane crash." A thin breath. "Ever afterward, Mother and I have always called each other whenever we had to fly. Oh, I know it's crazy, but we had to know, had to know at once that the flight was safely past. I was out of town Wednesday, but I left on my answering machine. When I got home

Thursday, I listened to my messages. Nothing from Mother. I called her house Friday, but there wasn't any answer. I called the gallery and all Alan knew was that she left town Wednesday."

"Maybe she thought she'd called," Max offered. "Or your machine didn't pick it up. Or she didn't leave a message for some reason."

"I appreciate your trying to find her, Mr. Darling." He was being dismissed. "At least, I now know she reached San Francisco. I'll call the police there. You see, I know something has happened—Mother is extremely responsible. She never breaks a promise. She wouldn't make me worry—not if she could call. So, I'm certain she can't call." For the first time, he heard the ragged edge of tears.

Her chances of being taken seriously by the San Francisco police ranked right around zero. Max didn't tell her that. Instead, he said, "You might get a private investigator there to look into it. It's a big city, and the police probably have to have more to go on than you can give them."

In a moment, her voice once again firm and controlled, she said, "I will. And thank you, Mr. Darling."

After he hung up, Max doodled restlessly on his legal pad. He'd thought this would be a quick call, marking an end to this distraction from his efforts to find out more about the residents of Nightingale Courts. Instead, he was growing increasingly anxious about Betsy Raines.

Ruth Jenson had had every reason to expect a telephone call that never came.

Was she wrong in a daughter's estimation of her mother's character? Had Betsy Raines looked for love in all the wrong places?

His legal pad looked like a war zone, slashes, cross marks, arrows, circled names (Jesse Penrick, Ingrid Jones, Ophelia Baxter, Duane Webb, Adele Prescott, Mavis Beeson, Tom Smith), and now heavily inked question marks boxing Betsy Raines.

He glanced down at his watch. Almost four. He wished Annie were here. Although her thought processes were often something on the order of Mexican jumping beans (erratic but interesting), he felt in desperate need of a

Watson to bounce his thoughts off of, then maybe the day's work wouldn't seem quite so fruitless.

Hell, he didn't even know where Annie was! He began to feel aggrieved. Why wasn't *somebody* (besides Laurel) evincing any interest in his efforts?

He didn't believe in sulking.

He believed in action. Once again, he lifted the telephone receiver.

Annie took another big bite of the candy bar—mmh, sheer delectable energy and to hell with blood-sugar levels—and stared at the note Madeleine Kurtz had given her.

Henny was busy, that was for sure. But what good she thought she was accomplishing—Annie shook her head and reread the message:

My dear chap! Oh, my dear chap! I am once again reaffirmed in my simple faith in facts. I abhor imagination; I just believe in evidence.

Reggie Fortune, of course, H. C. Bailey's plump, youthful-appearing, bighearted sleuth, who enjoyed all the good things of life, including his Rolls-Royce.

In a more humdrum mode, the note continued:

Traced Jesse's activities Saturday morning. Appeared at Shangrila Travel Services about 10 A.M. Requested information on round-the-world cruises, departed with handful of travel brochures. NEVER KNOWN TO TAKE ANY JOURNEYS. Such a departure from routine must be significant!

Annie drank deeply of her slushy from the Gas 'N Go. Henny was really reaching, although it did cast a different light on Jesse. It was the first fairly normal thing she'd learned about him. But, much more significant, in her mind, was Adele Prescott's interesting revelations about Jesse's propensity to play cruel jokes.

Annie finished the last bite of candy and began to walk toward Cabin 7. The more she discovered about the residents and their tangled relations, the more certain she felt that the answer to this murder lay near, very near.

Max was beginning to feel thwarted. Very thwarted. No word from anybody and no way to find anybody, meaning specifically Annie and Henny. Finally, he left messages at the command table for each to get in touch with him. What were they doing?

From the mailboxes, Annie learned that Tom Smith lived in Cabin 7. She realized, as she knocked, that no one had mentioned Smith, and so far as she knew, she hadn't met him. What was he doing when all the excitement erupted last night?

When the door opened, she smiled. "Mr. Smith. I'm Annie Laurance. Darling." She'd master it one of these days. "I'm a friend of Ingrid's. May I talk to you for a moment?"

His pale face stared at her with no change of expression. It wasn't deliberately unpleasant. It was simply devoid of reaction. When she had almost decided he wasn't going to let her in, he said dully, "All right."

He held the door for her. When she was inside, he turned and walked to a worktable and sat down. He picked up a miniature accordion and bent toward it. The room smelled of cloth, leather, paste, cigarette smoke, glue, metal, wood, paint, turpentine, and, faintly, underscoring them all, the unmistakable scent of marijuana. An entire wall was covered by shelving filled with every kind of assorted material. Another wall held shelf after shelf stacked with miniatures: tiny cracker barrels, ironing boards, washtubs, canned goods, minute telephones, 1870 typewriters, dairy products, furniture of all American eras from colonial to art deco, hats, musical instruments, figures from an America that existed now only in yellowed photographs (Oliver Wendell Holmes as a private in the Fourth Battalion Infantry, Tallulah Bankhead in a flapper's dress, Franklin Delano Roosevelt straining to stand with canes in the well of the House of Representatives), petite street cars, a wooden oil derrick, Model-T Fords, everything necessary to recreate a Lilliputian vision of the past.

It was as if she weren't there. Annie cleared her throat. "Do you fill orders, or just make what you want to?"

He was absorbed in pasting tiny white keys. He bent over his work, his fingers moving with delicate precision. He was a spare man with once-reddish hair, now greying and thinning, pulled back tightly into a ponytail. His worn blue work shirt opened at the throat to reveal a knobby neck. The shirt showed signs of neat darning. He put the last sliver of ivory in place, then looked up at her, not so much hostile as uninterested.

"Both. I fill orders and pick my own projects." He spoke in a lifeless tenor, each word receiving equal weight. He capped the cement tube, carefully cleaned a tool that looked a little like a dentist's pick, replaced it in a wooden case, then turned toward her.

"Do you want to order a scene?" He made no effort at salesmanship. He merely looked at her from empty pale grey eyes.

"You don't know who I am?"

"No. I'm sorry. Am I supposed to know you?"

"I'm a friend of Ingrid's. It was my husband and I who came last night and found Ingrid missing—and the body in her cabin."

"Oh." That was all he said. No questions. No comments. No exhibition of concern over Ingrid or expression of interest in the fact that a man's death had occurred not more than two hundred yards from where he lived.

"Didn't you hear all the noise last night?"

He nodded slowly.

"Did you come outside?"

He studied a spot several feet to her right. "I thought there might be a fire. But I looked, and decided nothing was burning."

"What did you do then?" She longed to grab his hunched shoulders and give them a vigorous shake.

"I went back to bed."

"You didn't come out to see what was happening? Or help in the search?"

"No one asked me to," he said simply. He dropped his

gaze to his hands, which lay limp and unmoving atop the worktable.

She was determined to break through his passivity. "Did Jesse Penrick threaten to turn you in for smoking pot?"

This time he looked directly at her, but his grey eyes were still blank and incurious. "No."

"Did you ever talk to him?"

He didn't respond immediately. One bony hand lifted and tugged at his lip. "He was at Parotti's sometimes."

"You talked to him?" Clarence Darrow couldn't have been more persistent.

"Sometimes." His hand reached out for a cigarette.

"What did you think of him?"

He lit the cigarette, watched a coil of smoke drift upward. "I didn't think about him."

"Did you like him?"

"Like him?" Those pale grey eyes revealed nothing. "I never thought about him."

"Did you know that he snooped around?"

There was just the merest flash in his eyes. And she could have sworn it was amusement. Then it was gone. "Did he?" Smith asked mildly.

Annie hated to admit defeat. Inspector Slack would never have given up. But she doubted that he would have done any better. Tom Smith was either just what he appeared to be, strange, remote, and passive, or he was as wily and devious as anyone she'd ever met. Helen McCloy would have had an instinct for the reality. Annie didn't.

She made a final effort. "What do you think happened? Who could have killed him?"

"I don't know." He yawned. "I think it's almost time for my dinner."

Annie's neck prickled.

He rose then, stiffly, as if he had been sitting at the worktable for many hours, and turned away from her. "I always fix my dinner at five." He shuffled toward the kitchen.

Annie didn't bother to say good-bye. She swung around and hurried toward the front door. As she opened it, she glanced over her shoulder. Tom Smith stood in the kitchen doorway. She felt a shock of surprise when she realized, as their gazes locked for an instant, that he no longer looked vacant. Instead, those pale grey eyes blazed with fear.

She plunged out the front door and down the steps, questions whirling in her mind.

"Mrs. Darling. Hey, Mrs. Darling!"

It took Annie a minute to realize she was being hailed. A smiling young woman in a khaki skirt and pink cotton knit top hurried toward her.

"Mrs. Darling, I'm Heather Frank. Freelance feature writer. You found the body, didn't you?" A slim, tanned hand poised over a notebook, and bright green eyes regarded her hungrily. "How did you feel? Was it horrifying? Exciting? Has it put your wedding night on hold? What can you tell me about Ingrid Jones? Do you think she's an escaped murderess? A victim? Could she be suffering from amnesia?"

Going over Reichenbach Falls would be a snap in comparison with fending off these pointed and dangerous queries. And Annie didn't have Holmes's arrogance as an armor. But if she didn't answer, she could see the lead: *Mrs. Darling refused to comment upon the possibility that her matron of honor went directly from the ultra-ritzy champagne reception to a rendezvous with death in the living room of her modest cabin. . . .*

"How long have you known Mrs. Jones? What is her relationship with the murdered man? Do you know who the secret love in his life was, the owner of the ring he wore on the chain around his neck?"

"The secret love of Jesse's life?" Annie demanded, startled. "What ring? What are you talking about?"

Heather looked like a cat guarding a bowl of cream. "Maybe we could exchange information. If you could tell me more about Mrs. Jones, how well she knew Penrick, I could tell you what I've learned from the autopsy report."

And if Annie declined to talk, she could project the continuing story: *Mrs. Darling was reluctant to discuss the relationship between Mrs. Jones and the stabbing victim. . . .*

Of course, she could deflect all attention from Ingrid and ignite a fire under Posey if she told this word-predator about Mavis Beeson and her lover, the young Broward's

Rock policeman. And suggested the reporter inquire why it
took Billy Cameron so long to reach the scene of the crime.

Too long. There was a definite lag in time from the call
made by the checkpoint guard to the arrival of Billy
Cameron. Where was Billy all that time on this very small
island? Had his beeper aroused him at Mavis's and he'd
hurried back across the island to get the police car? Or had
he not been at Mavis's cabin or at home? Could Billy have
decided to get rid of the threat to Mavis? Was he the killer?

Annie's mind churned. What, if anything, should she say
to this reporter? And how could she pump her for
information?

"Look"—Heather Frank radiated charm, while those
greedy emerald eyes remained alert—"let's just have a little
visit off the record. Don't you want Ingrid's side to get out?
Posey's down at your bookstore right now, talking to your
mother-in-law, getting a blow-by-blow account of Ingrid's
fight with Penrick."

Annie wished she could have seen Posey's first encounter
with Laurel. Somehow, though she knew it ultimately
would do little good, she had a feeling—Laurel might even
call it a presentiment—that Posey might have met his
match, and probably hadn't prized a helpful word out of
motor-mouth Ophelia, because Laurel liked Ingrid.

Of all times for Chief Saulter to be gone! And with Billy
Cameron suspect, they had no access to information about
the investigation. But, obviously, this ambitious young lady
had an inside track. Trust Posey to cozy up to the press.
Still, two could play that game. After all, Amelia Peabody
Emerson used the press to her own advantage. Why
couldn't Annie? She suppressed the niggling suspicion that
Max would not be delighted at a discussion of his honeymoon as a source of entertainment from coast to coast. If he
grumped like Amelia's husband, she knew the remedy to
that, too. (Reading mysteries did provide such moral
education. See selected passages, *The Curse of the
Pharaohs*.)

Annie smiled at her inquisitor and said warmly, "Do you
know, I hadn't thought about the power of the press to
present the viewpoint of the persecuted. Heather, it's
wonderful of you to give me a chance to tell you how

outstanding Ingrid is and how absurd it is for anyone to even consider her as a murder suspect." (She hoped she wasn't overdoing it, but true to Max's oft-expressed conviction, "You can't lay it on too thick," Heather was nodding in modest appreciation.) "Let's walk out on the pier, where we can have a really private talk."

It was quite cheerful on the end of the pier. Occasional sailboats passed in the sound, and the late afternoon sun was warm on their backs as they sat with their feet dangling. Actually, Annie enjoyed their talk. A Velda Johnston heroine could not have been more noble. With a bravely uplifted chin, she poignantly admitted to an eager Heather Frank that yes, indeed, she and her new husband were sacrificing their honeymoon to stay and seek their close friend, Ingrid Jones, whom she portrayed as a cross between Mother Teresa and Louisa May Alcott. She made a basic assumption that Heather's readers were quite unaware of Louisa's penchant for dashing off blood-and-thunder epics in between her children's books. Heather snatched at her offerings greedily, and would, of course, have hurried away without a quid pro quo, but Annie was too wily for that. In fact, she clamped her hand on Heather's arm.

"You said you'd tell me about the autopsy report."

Heather shook free of Annie's grip, scrabbled around in her shoulder bag, and pulled out a tattered copy.

Annie took it eagerly. She scanned it. Much she already knew. No surprises about cause of death—stab wound—but this was new! Penrick had suffered a contusion on the back of his head.

"Heather, do you suppose Penrick was unconscious when he was stabbed?"

"It doesn't say so. Maybe. What do you have in mind? That the murderer knocked him out, then stabbed him?"

"Why not?" Annie asked.

"Makes it premeditated," the reporter cautioned. "Murder in the first degree. There's always the chance of getting off with manslaughter, if a murder occurs in the heat of passion."

Annie understood the implication. "Ingrid didn't do it!" she said hotly.

"You know about her and Webb?" Heather's green eyes glistened with satisfaction.

Damn Adele Prescott. "There wasn't anything to know," Annie said staunchly. "I can assure you of that. I know Ingrid much better than anyone on this island, and her kindness to Mr. Webb was nothing more than that. Kindness."

But Heather was armed with Adele's tart-tongued interpretation and quite aware that a hint of romance and passion would sell copy faster than any description of altruism.

Once again, it occurred to Annie that she could direct the focus of the investigation away from Ingrid if she told the writer—or Posey—about Billy and Mavis. But she didn't want to do that. She knew Ingrid wouldn't want her to do that. Mavis's peril was real. All too often a wife's stories of beatings are discounted by both police and courts until it is forever too late for her. And what about the little boy who wriggled with happiness in his mother's arms? Annie wasn't prepared to risk their lives.

But maybe there was another way to deflect Heather. "Where's the stuff about a wedding ring? Nobody's mentioned that."

A beautifully manicured hand pointed to the box on the form entitled EFFECTS.

"Deceased wore no jewelry except for gold wedding ring found on neck chain also holding World War Two dog tags."

"Do you really think Jesse Penrick had a secret love?" From everything Annie had heard about the skinny, malevolent old miser, the notion seemed unlikely.

Heather brushed back a lock of gleaming dark hair. "What does it look like to you? Maybe it was *really* a long-ago love. See, he still wore his dog tags—those are metal squares with his name and unit and other information stamped on them. That's where the ring was, on the chain." She grew more excited. "It all fits. They could barely make out the initials on the inside of the band, they were so worn down. They think the initials are E. P. They're going to send the ring to a jeweler in Savannah to see if they can get a better reading." Heather stared off across the salt marsh, apparently oblivious to the crimson splash of the setting sun across the darkening water. "Yeah, yeah, yeah. How about this: A longtime acquaintance of Jesse Penrick surmised today that the reclusive and often belligerent island resident carried with him to his death a dramatic story of love and"—she paused—"love and desertion." She looked at Annie for encouragement.

Annie's eyes widened in astonishment.

Heather surged ahead. "Penrick's friend, who declined to be identified, indicated the World War Two veteran had never relinquished the identification tags that linked him to those long-ago days of danger and excitement. That the ring was found on this chain about the dead man's neck indicated its importance to Penrick, according to his friend, who wondered aloud whether the loss of a woman's love in those tumultuous days had twisted the Broward's Rock resident, causing his well-known hostility to women." The journalist asked eagerly, "What do you think?"

"Who said all that?" Annie asked, confused.

Heather waved her hand airily. "Oh, you know—that's like saying a source close to the investigation or an unnamed principal or a spokesman for the administration. I mean, you have to hang a story on *something*, or the city editor'll give you hell."

"Oh, I see. Well, I think you're really on to something. After all, as the French always say, '*Cherchez la femme.*'"

Heather, in turn, looked a trifle puzzled, but she nodded and snapped her notebook shut. "Well, I've got to get busy with all this." Salomé surveying the head of John the Baptist could not have been more satisfied.

As Annie waved good-bye, after warm protestations that yes, they would keep in touch, she hoped (a) that Heather wouldn't be able to sell her story, and (b) that if she did, Annie could manage to keep a copy from reaching Max. After all, Pam North did not tell Jerry *everything*.

But, as she gazed out across the water at the boats moving sluggishly at their slips, those were peripheral concerns. She gave herself furiously to think about Heather's revelations.

* * *

"Confidential Commissions."

"Hullo, Max, Henny here, returning your call. What's up, my dear chap."

"Not much." He hated to be reduced to this, but he was losing all pride. "Don't suppose you've seen Annie lately?"

"Haven't actually. Sure she's nosing about."

"How're you doing?" Max asked quickly.

"Making a good deal of progress. It's the facts that count. Full report will be made after dinner this evening at the Tent City. I trust you'll be there?"

He wasn't enthused at the prospect. But it might afford him a glimpse of his wandering wife.

"Food line opens at six-thirty. How's your investigation coming?"

"Lousy. Nobody knows anything about anybody."

Henny considered the problem. "And, of course, you can't ask the neighbors because that's who you're trying to find out about, the good people who live at Nightingale Courts. Max, of course! Get their rental applications."

"Their what?"

Henny laughed wryly. "Ah, the rich," she observed kindly enough. "The very rich. I don't suppose you've ever filled out a rental application?"

Actually, he had his business manager in New York handle that sort of thing. When he'd come to Broward's Rock, the mention of his line of credit and accounts in Morgan Guarantee Trust seemed satisfactory.

But Henny was plowing onward. "We of the lower classes, my dear, have to reveal everything but the name of our grandmother's shrink to rent property from the monied classes. Find out who owns Nightingale Courts."

It took Max only two more phone calls to make that discovery. When he was told, he didn't bother to write the name down. He managed a polite thank-you, then stared glumly at his legal pad. Of course, it came as no surprise that Nightingale Courts were part of the holdings of Harley Edward Jenkins III. After all, Harley was CEO of Halcyon Development, Inc., which had built the resort end of the island. Unfortunately, he and Harley were not exactly on friendly terms, not since Max had refused, on behalf of Confidential Commissions, to do a spot of photography for

Harley. Harley wanted a nice set of photos of a business opponent with a woman other than his wife. To sweeten a deal, as Harley had ingenuously put it. Max's refusal and his subsequent assessment of Harley's character had not made for cordial relations.

No. Harley wouldn't dream of letting Max see the rental applications for Nightingale Courts.

Max straightened the papers on his desk, turned off the light, and hurried outside. But he didn't go directly to his car for the drive across the island to Nightingale Courts and the Tent City. And dinner, so to speak.

Instead, he walked thoughtfully by the closed offices of Halcyon Development, Inc.

There was more than one way to skin a cat.

TEN

Later, Annie would wonder at her obtuseness, her lack of antenna. After all, as an ardent reader of Had-I-But-Known novels, from Mary Roberts Rinehart's first, *The Circular Staircase*, to Mignon G. Eberhart's fifty-ninth, *Three Days for Emeralds*, she should have been equipped to pick up on portents.

Apparently not.

Perhaps the root cause was her absorption in her own plans, for plans she had. Be that as it may, the ultimate outcome, she felt certain, probably shortened her lifespan by a good ten years because of the strain to her heart and nervous system.

As is common in the literature, it all began so innocently.

After dinner and a rousing pep talk by Madeleine, the search volunteers gathered around a campfire, well banked with a circle of earth, for a gospel sing and hot chocolate. Henny, with conspiratorial nods and beckonings, rounded up a motley group, which she briskly shepherded to the middle pier. She lifted a hurricane lamp to light the way as the last reddish streaks from the setting sun emphasized the swiftly falling darkness and the soulful strains of "Amazing Grace" floated across the water.

Laurel still wore her plain oatmeal robe and sandals. In the flickering beam of Henny's lamp, Max's mother looked about sixteen and fey. Annie wouldn't have been surprised to see her glide over the wooden planking of the pier without touching a board. Her hands were clasped in a sweet attitude of supplication, and her smooth, aristocratic features were uplifted.

Ophelia Baxter trotted along on Laurel's heels. She, too, wore a plain oatmeal robe, but there the resemblance ended. The tubby psychic looked like a blob of unformed ice-box cookie dough. The sprigs of chartreuse hair that escaped tonight's purple turban glistened almost as brightly as the bioluminescent zooplankton, Nocticula, glowing eerily at the water's edge.

Max, of course, was grousing about the food. "Fried chicken! Can you believe *fried* chicken! Don't they know about the American Heart Association's diet guidelines? And green beans swimming in grease from that ham hock. And what was that thing they called fatback?" He shuddered.

"I thought it was *especially* good," Annie rejoined.

"Real women eat real food," Alan said supportively, his arm brushing her shoulder.

In the intermittent light from the lamp swinging in Henny's hand, Annie couldn't see Max swelling like an irritated toad. But she could sense it.

Actually, she was surprised that Max had agreed to join this outing at all. Surprised and relieved, but, to tell the truth, just a tiny bit disappointed. After all, this *was* their honeymoon. So to speak. Why hadn't Max suggested they slip away to her treehouse to compare the results of their investigations? It would have been much more in character than trooping out onto a dark pier, chattering about *food*. Of course, she had intended to say no to any such suggestion, because she definitely didn't want to talk to Max tonight about what she'd learned and what she intended to do. Her thoughts on the subject were disjointed, but quite firm. She'd tell him tomorrow, after she'd accomplished her objective. If she did. She had a gut feeling that he would be opposed to her well-conceived program and would probably, in the inimitable fashion of all males, insist upon doing it himself. She didn't mind skirting the law, but was categorically opposed to Max doing anything that could result in his disbarment. Not that he practiced law. But he *could*.

So she'd leapt at Henny's call for a meeting, declaring

sotto voce to Max that they'd better not miss a chance to see what Laurel and Ophelia were up to. Still, it was a little disconcerting when he acquiesced without a murmur.

At the end of the pier, Annie sat with her back to a piling, Max and Alan on either side. Alan was a little too close, and his after-shave made her nose itch. She unobtrusively scooted nearer to Max, and he contentedly slipped an arm around her shoulders. Laurel stood at the pier's edge, the offshore evening breeze molding the shapeless robe to her slim and lovely figure. Ophelia flopped down beside them, murmuring plaintively about the splintery boards.

Henny put down the lamp and faced them, her arms akimbo, reminding Annie irresistibly of Letitia Carberry, Rinehart's irrepressible spinster adventuress who graced the pages of *The Saturday Evening Post* for so many years. There was the same aura of gallant determination and serious application which so characterized Tish Carberry from her wild ride in a runaway hot air balloon over Hollywood to her capture of a French village during World War One to her successful battle with rum runners during Prohibition.

"We shall triumph in our efforts to find Ingrid and to foil her kidnapper," Henny began forcefully. "I have called us together for a marshalling of forces."

Annie almost looked to see if Tish's geriatric sidekicks, Miss Lizzie and Miss Aggie, lurked in the shadows. But no, there was only their own group, Laurel, Ophelia, Max, herself, and Alan Nichols.

Alan cleared his throat, as if reluctant to begin. Then, after giving Annie a firm squeeze on her arm, he said diffidently, "Gee, I kind of hate to throw cold water, and I'd love to help if I thought there was any point to it, but I talked to some of the searchers, and, of course, you can't poke a stick in every foot of pond and swamp on the island, but if Ingrid was out there—I mean, if she tried to get away from the killer or something—it looks like they'd have found her by now. I mean, doesn't it look pretty much like if somebody took her, she's been bumped off?"

"Not at all," Henny trumpeted, with all of Tish's hardheadedness. "That's—"

Support came from an unexpected and, Annie thought, probably not especially welcome quarter.

Ophelia leaned across Annie and Max to blurt, "Mr. Nichols, you are *absolutely* in the dark." She waggled her fingers excitedly. "Without a glimmer of light!" Her high voice had a built-in whine that would have elicited an agonized "Pfui" from Nero Wolfe and immediate banishment from the office. "Ingrid lives!"

From across the water carried a resonant chorus of "May the Circle Be Unbroken."

Henny's fox-sharp nose twitched impatiently. She attempted to regain control. "Certainly Ingrid's alive. Obviously, if anyone went to the trouble to abduct her, it was for a purpose. I do presume we can agree upon that? If it were a mere matter of a double murder, why kill Jesse there and Ingrid elsewhere? Also, why hide one body and not another? And, as anyone with a thinking mind can deduce, the fact that no trace of her has been found only serves to reinforce the presumption that she has been kidnapped. In fact, every hour of search that passes without her discovery only convinces me more deeply that she is being held a prisoner at some isolated location. Let me put it briefly but, I trust, cogently" (Tish Carberry didn't suffer fools gladly):

"One. Ingrid Jones is not guilty of murder.

"Two. Therefore, she did not flee from the scene of the crime to escape the authorities.

"Three. Therefore, she was forcibly removed from the scene of the crime.

"Four. Therefore, since she has not been found, dead or alive, she is being held prisoner."

Alan moved restively, but Henny pressed onward.

"Five. Therefore, when it suits her captor, she will be released or her hiding place uncovered."

"Aw, now wait a minute," Alan interrupted. "That's bullshit, lady. I mean, I'm sorry, but that's a bunch of crap. Either she's hiding out, like that guy Posey says—"

At their chorus of dissent, he raised his voice.

"—okay, okay. You people say no way. You know her better than I do, so I give it to you. But if they haven't found her and they've looked everywhere, then she's been killed. I mean, what do you think's going on around here?

How could somebody kidnap her and hide her so that hundreds of searchers can't find her?"

Henny dismissed that with an impatient headshake. "Fiddle-faddle, that's easy enough to understand. The searchers have concentrated on areas near here and along the coastline. True, they've knocked on a lot of doors, but if a house is closed—the owners obviously out of town, everything locked and in place—all the searchers can do is call out, look in the shrubs, poke in the weeds. Ingrid, bound and gagged, no doubt, cannot reply or escape. The searchers can't break and enter, and as any fool knows, this island is full of out-of-the-way, hidden cabins and houses and closed-up boats. There're a hundred places she could be!"

There was an instant's pause. Annie didn't know whether Alan had been overwhelmed by logic or merely overwhelmed. He did, in fact, open and close his mouth several times, but Henny was hard to refute.

Annie had no desire to refute her. She wanted to believe, too, that Ingrid was still alive. And although Alan had trouble with Henny's logic, Annie had none. It all followed, once you were certain that Ingrid could not be the murderer, and of that Annie was absolutely, unshakably certain.

"Well, I think she's dead," Alan muttered.

"Oooh, oooh, no!" Ophelia wailed. "I *know* it isn't so!"

"Even a clear glass can distort perception," Laurel mused, still gazing up at the moon, now partially hidden by fast-slipping clouds.

"Pierload of fools. Young pup's the only one with any sense."

Duane Webb's raspy snarl drowned out Ophelia and Laurel's lighter voices.

"You behind that goddam notice?" he demanded of Henny, jamming his hands into his pockets. The lantern glow reflected off his thick glasses.

"What notice?" Alan asked, just beating Max to it.

"All the residents of Nightingale Courts are directed to report to the command tent at ten in the morning to have their fingerprints taken," Henny said shortly. "I had Madeleine put the sign up this afternoon."

"Fingerprints! Oooh, that's so *criminal!*" Ophelia cried.

"One must rise above the material," Laurel said placidly.

Duane snorted impatiently. "The last I heard, that corpulent dunce from the mainland had Ingrid ticketed as the mad slayer. How'd you change his mind?"

"Oh, I haven't gotten anywhere with Posey," Henny admitted irritably. "He's positively besotted with the idea of Ingrid as an escaping murderess. No, I got on the phone with Chief Saulter, in Nuremberg, and told him all the nonsense that's happened, and he's called Billy Cameron and instructed him to look both for Ingrid *and* the murderer—and the first place to start is by checking out the unidentified fingerprints on the murder weapon."

"What unidentified fingerprints?" Unconsciously, Max flexed his hands, and, worriedly, Annie tried to recall whether he'd touched the sword when they made their grisly discovery.

Henny barreled ahead. "Let's say I have access to information that hasn't been released. That's the main reason I called us together. We must pool what we've found out." She scanned their upturned faces. "I'll start.

"The cause of death, after you wade through pectoral and ventricle and all that, was a stab wound to the heart by the sword found sticking in his chest. Now, this is what captured my attention: The sword handle does carry fingerprints by Ingrid—and why shouldn't it, it belongs to her? but there are unidentified fingerprints on the handle, too, *overlapping* Ingrid's."

Annie opened her mouth, then shut it. Because, for God's sake, she knew whose prints those were. At a party Ingrid hosted in June, to celebrate the rousing success of the production of *Arsenic and Old Lace* by the Broward's Rock Players (and there had certainly been some impediments on the road to *that* triumph), Annie had impulsively entertained one circle with her description of Circuit Solicitor Brice Willard Posey. To emphasize a point, she'd lifted down the sword from its plaque over the mantel and brandished it, exclaiming: "Those who live by the sword shall die by the sword," and been the recipient of loud applause, although on sober recollection she doubted that particular sally was deserving of acclaim.

Her prints were on file, too. But if this apparent anomaly brought Chief Saulter into the case, even at long distance, and widened the search for Ingrid, let it go. Something might break before her prints were traced.

Max bent near. "Did you start to say something?"

"No. Oh, no. Just clearing my throat." And she did so.

"One odd point in the autopsy," Henny continued. "Jesse had received a blow to the back of the head. It occurred shortly before death."

"Was he knocked out?" Max asked quickly.

Annie made a conscious effort not to stiffen. Max could read body language faster than Agatha, and *she* was a marvel. As for Henny, she was a marvel, too. She'd zeroed right in on the most important clue Annie had managed to pry out of Heather.

"Impossible to say," Henny replied. "He could have been unconscious when stabbed. The autopsy is inconclusive there."

It was time for a distraction. "Well, obviously, the stab wound killed him," Annie said impatiently. "What I'm wondering about, who was the woman in his life?"

"Woman?" Ophelia squealed.

Henny was nonplussed. "Wherever did you hear that? No one I talked to mentioned a woman! They all agreed he didn't like women, had no use for them."

"He must have cared a lot for some woman," Annie insisted. "How else do you explain the gold wedding ring he wore on a chain around his neck?"

Henny put a hand to her mouth, and Annie knew she felt embarrassed that she'd skimmed over mention of the ring in the autopsy report.

Annie pressed her advantage. "It has to be important. He didn't wear any other jewelry."

"Maybe he was married once and got dumped," Alan suggested, "and he wore the wedding ring 'cause he never got over her."

Henny looked down at Max. "Did you find a record of a marriage?"

"No." His answer was unaccustomedly brusque. "Actually, it's been a little difficult to find out much about him at all."

"But you're the guy with the agency," Alan exclaimed in surprise. "Hell, I thought you could find out just about anything!"

Oh. snide, Annie thought.

Max, obviously, thought so, too. "Well, I didn't have any trouble finding out your boss made it to California."

That took some explanations. Max was describing his talk with Ruth Jenson when Duane barked impatiently, "Jesus Christ, Darling, we don't give a damn how you can pirouette on the phone. What the hell does this have to do with Ingrid? And what *have* you found out about Jesse? Anything to help find his murderer?"

"Who're you to criticize?" Annie snapped at Webb. "This afternoon you said it didn't matter a damn."

"Changed my mind," he said shortly. "Goddam, can't let some son of a bitch get away with hurting Ingrid."

"Mind over matter," Laurel said huskily. "That is all that is important," and she reached down to pat Ophelia's turban. "But it certainly can't do any harm for Maxwell to report on his efforts."

Max had yet to answer. They all fell silent, waiting, and the slap of the water mingled mournfully with the fading strains of "In the Garden."

"I have accumulated some information," Max said finally, very formally. "And I have further sources to draw upon. I hope to have a dossier on everyone who lives at Nightingale Courts by tomorrow morning."

"You don't want to share with us what you've learned so far?" Henny asked.

"No."

If Annie had been alert, it would have occurred to her that Max had had all day to phone and that he would, by this point, have tapped every *ordinary* source. She was, however, distracted.

"I know you will find out everything that matters," Henny said encouragingly. "I, myself, feel strongly that it is of paramount importance to find out everything we can about Jesse's actions in recent days. I am putting together a detailed reconstruction of his final day. It began, as most of you know, with an early morning confrontation with Ingrid.

But I have discovered other very interesting facts about Saturday:

"One. At approximately ten-fifteen A.M., Jesse Penrick entered Shangrila Travel Services on the harborfront and engaged the clerk, Karen Sommers, in conversation, inquiring about around-the-world cruises. He evinced interest in journeys departing Miami in October. He left the agency with brochures on the *Queen Elizabeth Two*."

"That's crazy!" Webb exclaimed.

Alan laughed. "Brochures don't cost anything."

"Had he ever been to the agency before?" Max asked.

Henny shook her head. "No record of it." She paused and waited until they stopped murmuring.

"Two. At approximately ten-forty, an acquaintance saw him looking through the window of the Piping Plover Gallery."

All eyes turned to Alan, who turned his hands palms up in a gesture of helplessness. "I didn't see him, and I'm sure he didn't come in. 'Course, Saturday's our best day, so maybe he poked his nose in, but I sure don't think so. And I *know* he's never been a customer. I mean, Betsy's stuff doesn't come cheap."

Henny continued briskly. "From there, I don't have any report on him until about one P.M., when he was spotted looking over the cars at the Oldsmobile dealership. I've tracked down all but two of the salesmen and nobody remembers talking to him."

"Nuttier and nuttier," Duane growled.

"But any out-of-the-ordinary action may be the key to his murder," Henny said portentously. "I shall continue to ferret out the facts. Now, can anyone else contribute?"

Annie hesitated, because she wasn't sure anything Henny'd discovered really mattered, but what harm could it do to pinpoint Jesse's activities? "For what it's worth, Adele Prescott said Jesse was using the pay phone outside the Gas 'N Go on Thursday night."

"So what?" Alan asked.

Annie shrugged. "It's odd, that's all. According to Adele."

Duane agreed. "Yeah, that could be important. Jesse was so goddamned tight, it must have been pretty major for him to spring for a quarter. He didn't have a phone, wouldn't spend the money for one. Said he liked to talk to people face to face. What he really liked to do was force himself on people when they didn't want to have anything to do with him. Like Tom Smith."

"Tom Smith! Oh hell, he doesn't exist," Max broke in.

"Oh yes, he does," Annie contradicted. "Cabin Seven."

"Of course, he does, my sweet," Laurel trilled. "Perfectly amazing miniatures. Even commode pieces in rose porcelain for antebellum mansions. Didn't you see his booth at the arts and crafts fair yesterday afternoon?"

Yesterday afternoon. The afternoon of their wedding day. Could it possibly, Annie wondered, have been just yesterday?

"Somehow I missed that," Max retorted. It was the nearest Annie'd ever seen him come to sarcasm with his mother. "I don't care if he's had a show at the Museum of Modern Art in New York, he's an invisible man. No bank account. No insurance. No voter's registration. No clubs, no slogans, no nothing."

"He's a little weird," Annie conceded. "It's kind of like he's not really there."

Ophelia pressed her fingers to either side of her turban. "A soul in limbo, estranged and forever alone."

Duane exploded. "Oh, shit, stuff it, Ophelia!"

"Reclusive," Henny said practically.

Ophelia scrambled awkwardly to her feet, trembling with indignation. "Duane Webb, you just shut your mouth! I do too know things that the rest of you can't see. You are all blindfolded by reality, that's what's wrong with you. Your minds are closed to manifestations of the spirit that span the past and the future." She paused, scrunched her eyes tightly closed and began to breathe deeply. "A black aura," she intoned heavily, "full of greed, a warped being focused on itself. Evil. It hangs here now; it clutches at us with spectral fingers; it envelops us in a miasma that stifles the soul."

"Jesus, what's with her?" Alan asked.

"Evil so close," Ophelia moaned. "Among us, the blackness of death." She knelled the final word in a trembling basso profundo.

Laurel made empathetic soothing noises.

"Oh, shit," Duane said wearily.

Ophelia's voice quivered. "You all say Ingrid's passed to the other side, and I *know* she hasn't! I *know* it. I held her scarf—and it smelled just like Elizabethan rose potpourri—and I pressed it to my eyes and I could feel her. She's frightened and her head hurts. Then it faded. If I just had—"

Laurel reached out and clapped a hand over Ophelia's mouth. "There, there, my dear. You've tried too hard today." Laurel's husky voice invited understanding. "Poor, dear Ophelia has *absolutely* given her all. Trance after trance, but just not quite enough to go on." She looked reproachfully at Annie. "I don't believe Ingrid had worn that scarf in weeks!"

"I don't know—" Annie began.

This was more than Duane could tolerate. "Stop all this bloody nonsense. It's obscene. Obviously, Ingrid's dead." He glared at Ophelia. "You and your stupid trances. They aren't real. You don't know shit."

"Oh yes I do!" Ophelia rejoined.

"If you know so goddam much, why couldn't you save your goddam cat you were so crazy about?"

Ophelia gaped at Duane. She gave a low moan, then lifted both hands to her face, turned, and stumbled away.

"Oh, my goodness," Laurel exclaimed. It was as near an expletive as she ever came. With a vexed shake of her golden head, she remonstrated gently. "My dear Mr. Webb, it is most unfortunate that you have distressed Ophelia. I'd best hurry after her. Really, *everyone's* quite exhausted. Perhaps we'll all feel better after a good night's sleep. Good night, Annie. Good night, dear Maxwell. Good night, everyone."

As she wafted, with surprising speed, in pursuit of Ophelia, Annie recalled, with a pang, that she had intended to find out from Laurel just how she and Ophelia had spent the day. And what, if anything, had transpired at Death on Demand. And, of course, Annie wanted to talk to Ophelia about her artless (?) revelation of Ingrid's quarrel with the victim, plus Ophelia's own relationship with Jesse. And what was all this about a cat?

In an uncanny echo of her thoughts, Henny asked sharply, "What happened to Ophelia's cat?" Henny had four Siamese, and she claimed each was as smart as—if not smarter than—Lillian Jackson Braun's Koko.

"Poisoned. And Jesse did it, sure as hell."

Annie lay tensely on her cot. It was almost midnight. She felt as if she'd been in this corner of the tent (Women's Side) for hours, but actually it had been shortly after eleven when their group returned to shore from the pier. The campfire had burned down to coals, and most of the volunteers had settled onto their cots, mute and exhausted after a long day of searching.

The good-nights among their group had been subdued and brief, though Annie had expected a little more from Max than a cheery "Nighto, sweetie. See you in the morning." Was the soul of romance absolutely dead? Not a single lingering glance, not even a fond pat. Had one day of marriage reduced their relationship to such a state? Furthermore—and she wriggled irritably—not even Alan had expressed any desire to spend further time with her, and that was so atypical of his kind as to be remarkable. For an instant, she felt a pang of concern. Had she suddenly become a frump? But, no. Both Max and Alan had edged close enough on the pier. Well, in due time, she thought, all would be revealed. She checked her watch again. Two minutes to the midnight hour. She would wait another fifteen, just to be sure everyone was asleep.

Max eased open the door to the Maserati, congratulating himself again on his forethought in parking on the far side of Jerry's Gas 'N Go. He turned the key, the engine sprang to life, and the car crept from beneath the shadows of a loblolly pine. He drove a mile without lights, feeling his way by guess and by God up the narrow sandy road. When he was almost to the intersection with the island's main blacktop, he flicked the lights on. The Maserati shot forward.

* * *

The stiff, uncooperative kickstand screeched. Annie hunkered down beside the bike in the darkest shadows of Ingrid's carport. The night was alive with surreptitious noise and ominous movement. Her heart raced uncomfortably at each crackle in the undergrowth. Was that a footstep in the blackness beneath the pines? She listened intently, but all she could distinguish was the wind in the pine branches, the slap of water against pilings, the scurry of nocturnal animals in search of prey. Easing onto the bike, she gave the stand a sharp kick and rode behind Ingrid's cabin across lumpy uneven ground to avoid the faint lights at the corners of the Tent City. She picked up the road as it curved away from Nightingale Courts. Pumping hard, she skirted to the far side of the Gas 'N Go, away from the single lamp that glowed above the phone booth.

With the lamplight left behind, the road was barely discernible between the darker lines of thickly massed pines, magnolias, sweet gums, and oaks, but Annie began to relax. Actually, it was fun to be wheeling through the night, though an occasional crash in nearby thickets made her devoutly hope she wasn't about to come face-to-snout with a feral hog.

She didn't turn onto the island blacktop. Instead, she crossed it to plunge onto an asphalt golf-cart path that would cut several miles from her journey. Did rats roam at night? And snakes? Her customary after-dark milieu didn't include swamps. She bent forward and pumped harder.

Max opened the pantry door in his condominium and smiled. After all, he'd had only the dimmest memory of this closet's contents, but there they were, his cleaning lady's rubber gloves. He picked them up, ignored the fact that they were somewhat sticky, stuffed them into a side pocket, then plunged back into the night. Not that he expected anyone ever to learn of his midnight foray, but an intelligent man doesn't leave absurdly obvious traces behind. Like fingerprints.

Not that he expected trouble.

In fact, he felt a kind of rollicking anticipation. He hadn't realized he had quite this aspect to his personality, this eager approach to the commission of a crime. Perhaps in another day and time (especially if he'd had financial pressures), he might have been quite successful as a Raffles. He would have to watch again his collection of old films about the gentleman crook. After all, he had a lot in common with some of those suave cinema thieves, especially John Barrymore, Ronald Colman, and David Niven. Suave, courageous, daring, devastatingly handsome, no doubt about it.

He paused beside a sweet-scented hibiscus in the almost empty parking lot to study the dark and silent environs of the harbor shops. The two waterfront restaurants shut their doors at eleven, and the Sans Souci and Lilly Mae's, on opposite sides of the island, were both discreet watering holes in secluded locations that closed at midnight. So only a late night stroller or perhaps young lovers might be expected to break the post-midnight stillness.

But a man can walk his dog at any hour.

Casually, Max strolled from the cover of the hibiscus and started toward the dark alley that ran between the shops, pausing occasionally to whistle for Fido, but keeping, however, as far as possible from the lampposts and their yellow pools of light. He was having a helluva time.

Annie jammed the bike behind the Dumpster and slunk through the deep shadows to the back door of Death on Demand. As she tried to insert the key into the bookstore's lock by feel (it was darker than Edgar's sleek black feathers in this damn alley; next meeting of the Broward's Rock Merchants Association, she was going to *insist* on better lighting), she heard the *whee-whee-whee-whee-whee-whee-whi* of someone whistling for a dog. Frantically, she probed and, finally, as the whistler neared her, made contact with the keyhole, turned it, pulled open the door and slipped inside.

She rested against the closed door, waiting for her heart to stop thumping. Of course, she had every right to be in her own store, but this was not the time for interruptions. And she needed to hurry.

She reached up and grabbed the flashlight hanging from a nail on the south wall. Flicking it on, she hurried through the storeroom, intent upon reaching the front cash desk.

An odd, most unexpected and, frankly, unpleasant odor assailed her. What in the world could it be? Her steps slowed. She turned toward the coffee bar, circled behind it, and aimed the light down.

No doubt about it. The smell rose from Agatha's dish.

A click of nails on the coffee bar announced the cat's approach. Agatha would, of course, be interested in this peculiarly timed arrival. Annie reached up and stroked her sleek cat, then bent to survey the bowl and its contents more closely.

Herrings.

Smoked herrings.

Or rather, the scraps of that meal, and not many of those.

Agatha dropped to the floor and began to twine against Annie's leg, purring loudly.

Agatha had not during the day learned how to open a tin of smoked herrings. No, the only answer had to be Laurel and Ophelia.

Annie turned the light on her pet.

Agatha's eyes narrowed.

"Are you all right?"

The purr was almost disgustingly vigorous.

Annie picked up the bowl and dumped the remains into the sink, then reached for a spoon to push the mess into the garbage disposal.

Agatha, moving with her customary agility, landed beside the sink, and before Annie could maneuver with her spoon, the black cat snagged a piece of redolent fish with one paw, clamped it in her mouth and fled.

"Agatha! Agatha, come back here!"

One of the least effective vocal exercises known to mankind is to yell an order at a cat.

Annie closed her eyes briefly. What if Agatha nestled her morsel next to one of the expensive collectibles, such as Hesketh Prichard's *November Joe, the Detective of the Woods* ($150) or S. S. Van Dine's *The Casino Murder Case*

($75) or E. Phillips Oppenheim's *Chronicles of Melhampton* ($125)? Agatha was very fond of nudging her way onto the shelf with the most treasured books. How she knew they were special, Annie didn't presume to understand.

Opening her eyes, Annie steeled herself, and, very slowly, swung the light toward the classic collection. No Agatha. So be it. She didn't have time now to look for her furry friend. Maybe the little glutton was crouched beneath a fern completing her odd feast. She made a mental note to stock up on collectibles. The shelf looked sparser than she recalled.

Smoked herrings for a cat. God, what else might Laurel and Ophelia have done?

Annie scanned the shelves. Private Investigator-Police Procedural, Horror-Science Fiction, Romantic Suspense, Psychological Suspense. So far, so good. She moved up the center aisle, past Caper-Comedy and Espionage-Thrillers, and finally to True Crime and the Agatha Christies.

A book lay open atop the True Crime section. Annie picked it up. Oh, yes, Allen Churchill's *They Never Came Back*, an accounting of famous disappearances. The book opened on the section about Judge Crater. She felt a prickle down her spine. Judge Crater walked up a New York street and was never seen again. Ingrid Jones telephoned from her cabin one September Saturday night . . .

Annie shook her head, snapped the book shut, and reshelved it.

It was at the front of the store, by the cash desk, that she found further evidence of Laurel and Ophelia's activities. On a square of posterboard, the public was invited:

TEST
your
E
S
P

Divine a title contained in the
velvet-swathed box, and it is
YOURS.

An arrow pointed toward the reading area, the cane chair and wicker table enclave along the south wall.

Annie didn't attribute her immediate visceral feeling of panic to ESP. It was merely the conditioned response of a mind familiar with the possibilities in a world inhabited by Laurel.

She found the velvet-swathed box on the first wicker table. (Where had they found the velvet?) Yanking the cloth loose, she opened the lid, turned the light onto the enclosed books and groaned.

Melville Davisson Post, *The Strange Schemes of Randolph Mason*, the author's first book of detective short stories, $250.

Mark Twain, *Tom Sawyer: Detective*, $95.

Arthur Upfield, *The Barakee Mystery*, review copy, $1500.

Robert H. Van Gulik, *The Chinese Maze Murders*, $310.

Edgar Wallace, *Four-Square Jane*, $150.

John Dickson Carr, *The Murder of Sir Edmund Godfrey*, $150.

Trust Laurel to show such exquisite taste. If she wanted to play mind games with Annie's customers, for God's sakes, couldn't she use reading copies?

Annie grabbed the books from the box, then stood, at a loss. Where should she put them? In the storeroom? Up in the attic? Behind the coffee counter?

A few minutes later, she surveyed an unbroken line of Sherlockiana on a shelf. All right. Let Laurel and Ophelia find them now! To make the retrieval of her treasures even less obvious, Annie darted from shelf to shelf, picking up books to put in the box.

These were perfectly good collectible mysteries that any reader would enjoy. The difference between these books and the others was price, and price, of course, was determined by a book's condition, rarity, and importance in the field. The six copies she was now placing in the box cost an average of $7.50. She nodded in satisfaction at the titles, *Academic Murder* by Donald Fiske, *As Empty as Hate* by Kyle Hunt (another of John Creasey's pen names), *Always a Body to Trade* by K. C. Constantine, *Not Exactly a*

Brahmin by Susan Dunlap, *The Dead Seed* by William C. Gault, and *A Death for Adonis* by E. X. Giroux.

She reswathed the velvet and was turning back toward the front of the store when she glimpsed an unexpected flash of red. Picking up the flashlight from the table, she directed the beam deeper into the reading area.

All of the cushions had been removed from the wicker chairs and placed on the floor in a kind of thronelike pile except for one red cushion. It was positioned directly in front of the pile.

Annie crossed the well-waxed wooden floor and studied this peculiar arrangement.

There were black cat hairs on the red cushion. The pile of cushions was deeply indented.

Agatha pressed gently against her leg.

Annie looked down at her cat, and was not reassured by the unblinking gaze. "Agatha, what in the *hell* has been going on here?"

Agatha flowed delicately to the red cushion and jumped onto it. She turned three times, then settled into a contented ball. One amber eye peered up at Annie.

Perhaps, Annie thought, it was as well Agatha couldn't talk.

"All right," she said briskly. "But I will find out. And that's your last smoked herring." It was time, past time, for Annie to retrieve Ingrid's extra set of keys from the bottom drawer of the cash desk and race back across the island.

Max studied the trapdoor in the light of his flash. It wasn't bolted. It was only a couple of weeks ago that the Halcyon Development, Inc., heating and air technician made his annual fall visit to check the unit on the roof atop Confidential Commissions. Similar units, accessed by similar trapdoors, existed atop each of the harborfront stores. Now, it would be clear sailing, if the trapdoor above Halcyon Development, Inc., was similarly unbolted.

Humming "Hail, Hail, the Gang's All Here," Max wriggled his broad shoulders through the square space, pulled himself up, and landed lightly on the gritty tarred roof.

* * *

Ingrid's keys jingled in the pocket of Annie's white skirt as she pumped past the Gas 'N Go. She slowed, keeping to the shadows. When the soft glow from the Tent City lights glistened through the trees, she swung off the bike. Almost there. She heaved a quiet sigh of relief and satisfaction as she shoved the bike back into its spot beneath Ingrid's carport. It should be clear sailing from here.

It was dark enough on the back side of Ingrid's cabin to satisfy Jack the Ripper. Annie slithered up the back steps, unlocked the kitchen door, and stepped inside, closing it behind her.

A faint aroma of rose potpourri hung in the still air. The blinds were closed. Not a vestige of light seeped into the oblong room. Annie frowned in concentration, remembering the layout of Ingrid's kitchen—sink on the back wall, overlooking the sound, stove and refrigerator against the wall to her right, small wooden kitchen table with two chairs directly in front of her, door to the living room centered in the opposite wall. She mustn't walk into the table. A clatter might arouse one of the sleepers in the Tent City.

Stretching one hand out in front, Annie began to tiptoe. She had reached the door, obviously open, as her hand patted only air, when a rustling, scrabbling noise—a sound unmistakably near—blocked the air in her throat and made her heart race with triphammer rapidity.

She wasn't alone in Ingrid's cabin.

The flashlight lying on the desk amply illuminated the filing cabinets. Max riffled through thick manila folders behind the divider tabbed NIGHTINGALE COURTS. Construction. Maintenance. Rental Applications. Repairs. He lifted out a slender green file, Rental Applications, and flipped it open. He began to smile. Oh, yeah. Hey, hey, hey. This was paydirt, all right. Annie would be—

"Max Darling," a voice drawled behind him. "Fancy meeting you here."

* * *

A footstep.

The click of a drawer closing.

Annie breathed shallowly and gripped the doorjamb.

Should she call the police? Oh God, the police consisted of just Billy Cameron. How long would it take Billy to come? Would he come? And if he did, wouldn't he arrest Annie for entering a proscribed crime scene? Wouldn't he do anything and everything to protect Mavis? Annie's mind raced. Maybe Billy Cameron was in the bedroom right now, a murderer returned to plant evidence to incriminate Ingrid. Or it could be anyone! Duane Webb, or that dreadful Prescott woman, or that pale-eyed Smith man.

Annie gripped her flashlight like a billy club. (They were made of rosewood around the turn of the century. Annie had one that had been carried by a captain in New York's Finest and was now mounted beside the mug collection in Death on Demand.) She crept forward.

She was acutely aware that almost any one of the suspects outweighed her. She didn't have the heft of either Penny Wanawake or Carlotta Carlyle. She would have to rely on speed and determination. And she'd never hit anyone over the head in her entire life. But the ready biff was certainly part of a good detective's arsenal. And she *had* to know who the intruder was. Perhaps it really was the murderer. She could solve the case and find Ingrid!

Adrenaline pumped through her. She lifted her flashlight-armed hand, turned the knob, flung open the door of the bedroom and charged.

It was in mid-flight, her weapon descending toward the crouched figure dimly illuminated by a pencil flash, that Annie breathed the unmistakable, distinctive scent of mountain-fresh lilac. In a flailing, desperate effort to avoid contact, Annie lurched sideways, tripped, and ended up flat on her back, breathless and aching. And furious.

"Annie, my dear," Laurel chided gently, "I know you are *always* in a hurry, but really, my sweet, is it wise to *launch* yourself so precipitously in the dark?"

ELEVEN

"Makes copies back and front, in five colors, and collates."
Henny closed the paper holder and punched three buttons.

Max studied the open liquor cabinet by the light of his
flash. He took no interest in mechanical details. The
information at hand, he was quite willing to let Henny take
charge of reproducing it. "Harley does himself proud." He
held up one bottle. "My God, does anybody actually drink
creme de menthe?"

"Sounds like Harley. Any scotch?" Serenely, she placed
the second rental application onto the machine to be
copied.

"Sure. Dewar's and Johnnie Walker Black."

"I'll take Dewar's."

Max's voice was muffled as he bent to open the refrigerator. "Ice maker, too. All the comforts of your home
bar." He found glasses, poured their drinks, handed one to
Henny.

She raised her glass in salute. "So you had 'further
sources to draw on' in compiling information on our
suspects?"

He smiled blandly. "How about a gentleman's agreement, Henny? You don't reveal my sources—and I won't
reveal yours."

The cheerful clink of glasses sealed their bargain.

Annie's hip throbbed from her fall, but she ignored the
nagging discomfort as she peered intently at the circular

120

loops in the braided rug. She ignored, also—or tried to—the husky humming that drifted from Ingrid's bedroom. All she needed now was to have to deal with Laurel! It was like trying to do brain surgery with a leprechaun tap-dancing beside the surgical instrument tray.

"Annie, love, could you come?" Laurel's throaty murmur rose confidently.

Taking a tight grip both on her flashlight and her temper, Annie bounced to her feet and hurried to the bedroom door. "Shh," she implored her mother-in-law. "If anyone hears us and calls the cops, we're in terrific trouble."

Laurel's hyacinth-blue eyes widened. "My dear, you sound so apprehensive! But there is a simple remedy—oxygen, that most life-giving of forces. Please, please, Annie, take a deep breath. One. Two. Three." The pencil flash waved in concert with the words.

Annie was infuriated to realize she was indeed breathing deeply. "Laurel, stop it! We don't have time to fool around. I need to—"

"Time is not our master, Annie dear. We can conquer time. As I have learned from dear Ophelia, the world can be ours through meditation." The ingenuous eyes brightened. "Just think about that, Annie, my sweet, and you will feel a sense of relaxation, even of exultation."

Maddened almost beyond endurance, Annie opened her mouth to explode, but Laurel deftly headed her off.

"Now, I called you in here because you, dear, of all people, can help the most to rescue our dear Ingrid. You see, I might make the wrong choice," and she pointed toward the clothing visible through the open door to Ingrid's closet.

Annie's mouth closed. She struggled for composure.

"Annie, I want you to think. Press your fingertips lightly to your temples, close your eyes, remember Ingrid in her favorite clothes."

Annie's mouth opened again, then closed. It might be quicker—and, God knew, simpler—if she did whatever damfool thing Laurel wanted. Then she could return to the living room.

Laurel stepped into the closet.

Annie squeezed her eyes shut. What was Ingrid's favorite outfit? Almost as she formed the question, a picture flashed into her mind: Ingrid cheerfully working at the cake booth during the hospital bazaar, clad in a white cotton sweater decorated with an imposing black cat among red geraniums and a cotton-and-linen skirt in a textured check of black and grey.

Her eyes snapped open and she hurriedly described the outfit to Laurel. "She gets so many compliments on that sweater. It's one of her favorites. She calls it her 'Agatha' sweater."

"So she *is* fond of Agatha," Laurel said brightly, nodding in satisfaction as she rummaged through the clothes. "That's what we thought—though the results were *so* disappointing."

Annie was aware of fleeting time—and the disaster that would occur should anyone notice will-o'-the-wisp lights moving about Ingrid's cabin—but one thing she had to know.

"Laurel?"

"Yes, dear?"

"Laurel, I can understand fish. But why smoked herring?"

"Oh, here it is, the *very* sweater. Oh, how marvelous." Laurel backed out of the closet and turned to face Annie, clutching the sweater tightly. "Oh, the herring. Yes, of course. I would like to make it clear, but reincarnation is so *complex.* I do fear that for once dear Ophelia was misguided. She had the most distinct impression that Agatha had once been a scullery maid in London in the 1890s—and that her young man had been seriously injured in an accident with a hansom cab."

Annie wondered if walking on quicksand might result in the same sense of disorientation she was experiencing.

Laurel took a quick step toward Annie. "My dear, don't you feel well?"

"Oh, I'm fine, fine. Of course, it all makes perfectly good sense. Smoked herring, of course. By all means." She began to back out of the bedroom.

Laurel gave a tiny shrug. "But Agatha was just—I hate to say it—just piggy—and when she'd finished her herring, she sank into the deepest sleep. Ophelia thought once it might be a trance, but her spirit was *inert* and no good at all to Ophelia."

Annie translated this to mean that Agatha experienced a blood-sugar lag and, having gorged herself, refused to be aroused.

"So," Laurel concluded, "our afternoon was wasted. But this"—and she held the sweater aloft—"should make *all* the difference. And it's all because of you. Now, dear, you can go back to your search." Her nod was magnanimous.

The clear implication was that Annie's endeavors, childish though they were, should be indulged. Annie stalked back to the living room. Oh, Lordy. Already one-thirty. She had barely begun.

Dropping to her knees, she returned to her inch-by-inch scrutiny of the rug. Her search was rewarded as she neared the blood-crusted area where Jesse Penrick's body had lain. She gave a whoop of triumph—pine needles embedded in the cotton.

Shiny brown, prickly, two-inch-long pine needles.

She was careful now, very careful, not to touch or disturb them.

But she could scarcely contain her excitement. This must be the same heady flush of cerebral delight enjoyed by Nero Wolfe when the answers clicked in place. She had taken that one tidbit of information from the feature writer, the revelation that Jesse Penrick had suffered a contusion on the back of his head, and built a theory.

The pine needles were the first tangible proof that she might be right.

Pine needles there, but no pine needles around the periphery. She jumped up and moved her flash slowly across the living room floor. No pine needles. She hurried to the kitchen, turned the beam down. No pine needles. Swinging around, she paced back to stare down at the braided rug. "They were stuck to his clothes!"

She said it aloud and looked up.

Unblinking blue eyes regarded her thoughtfully. Laurel was perched gracefully on the chintz sofa, Ingrid's white cotton "Agatha" sweater in her lap. She clapped her hands excitedly. "My dear, your search has been successful!"

"It didn't happen the way they think," Annie said eagerly. "He wasn't stabbed during an argument."

"Of course not," Laurel agreed approvingly. "He departed this life unknowingly."

Annie stared at her for a long moment. "That's right." Her voice sounded strange in her own ears. "How did you know?"

"Ophelia says it is a matter of emanations. When a spirit has been violently extinguished—and there would certainly be a flood of emotion when facing death—anguished reverberations come down through time. It is this power which often accounts for poltergeist events."

"So?"

A graceful hand indicated the living area. "No emanations." She tapped a finger to her cheek. "It is a *subtle* distinction, because he was done to death in this room. The autopsy report would have indicated movement of the body after death, had it occurred. Yet, there are no emanations. So, the solution is clear."

Annie wondered what kind of emanations would result if Laurel were violently removed from the premises. But, she reminded herself firmly, this was her mother-in-law. Until death did them part. Except, of course, Laurel would smilingly negate that last possibility. For a moment, the idea of an eternity spent with Laurel was almost more than Annie could envision without nervous collapse.

One day at a time, she reminded herself. Never had that sensible injunction seemed quite so imperative.

She even managed a smile. "Oh, of course, I understand. No emanations. Does Ophelia have any idea *where* Jesse was knocked unconscious?"

Laurel's headshake was pitying—and infuriating. "Annie, my sweet, it doesn't work like that." Pressing Ingrid's sweater to her oatmeal-colored robe, Laurel was earnest. "Ophelia is merely a receptacle. She receives emanations from her surroundings. Like this room. Or from objects." She held up the sweater. "Ophelia opens her mind and heart to vibrations from both past and present, the residue of which are retained in material objects. Because of her own purity of spirit, she can brush through that curtain which separates us from infinity and receive inspiration and guidance."

Heartily tempted to shout "Bullshit," as Texans are wont to do when provoked, Annie restrained the impulse and concentrated fiercely on what mattered.

Those pine needles didn't walk into Ingrid's living room and neatly dispose themselves where Jesse Penrick had been dumped.

And that was exactly what had happened.

He had been knocked unconscious elsewhere. Her eyes once again swept the room. There was nothing where he had fallen that could have caused a contusion on the back of his head.

This changed entirely the picture of Jesse facing his murderer at midnight in Ingrid's cabin.

Jesse had met his murderer somewhere else. He'd been knocked unconscious. He had lain on a carpet of pine needles until he was carried to this cabin.

Posey saw this crime all wrong. This was no murder of passion.

This was a carefully thought out, *premeditated* murder, and the cold-blooded plan had included killing Jesse with a weapon from Ingrid's home.

Posey's likely ridicule rang in her ears: *Isn't this a rather cumbersome theory, Ms. Laurance? Designed to fit circumstances you have merely imagined? Based on a scattering of pine needles?*

Annie's mouth firmed. But it fitted! It fitted with the contusion on the back of Jesse's head. It fitted with the pine needles where the corpse had been found.

If there were pine needles in his clothing— By God, that's all she needed.

"I'm getting there," she cried excitedly. She paced across the room, skirting the rug, of course. "Laurel, listen, it all makes sense. Somebody decided to kill Jesse and frame Ingrid for the murder. It was planned from the start. Don't you see? Because there was no reason for Jesse to come to Ingrid's house at midnight. That's crazy. No, it's a frame." She pointed dramatically at the rug. "Those pine needles prove it!"

Laurel nodded. "That's very well thought out." She

carefully folded Ingrid's sweater, then rose and glided across the room to brush her lips approvingly against Annie's cheek. "I'm afraid, however, dear, that there is one major obstacle."

"Obstacle?"

Poised in the kitchen doorway, Laurel sighed gently. "Mr. Posey is so *averse* to reason, isn't he?" She glanced down at the sweater. "There is so *much* to do," she murmured. "But surely I can find the time. I know, Annie, I'll talk to Mr. Posey." She nodded decisively, and her soft, golden hair rippled like sun-kissed water.

"Oh, my God, no." Annie heard the horror in her voice. She took a deep breath. "No. No, Laurel. I appreciate the offer. I do indeed. It is marvelous of you, but I believe it will be best if I talk to him. As you say, you, uh, have so *much* to do."

"That is true." The fine brow crinkled pensively. "Yes, that's true. Well, then, I will leave it to you, my dear." She smiled warmly. "I know you will do your best. And *not* lose your temper." She lifted a hand in farewell. "Until tomorrow, Annie dear." And she was gone, leaving only the haunting scent of lilac behind her.

The whispers were fairly low, but a faint undercurrent of bonhomie and scotch lifted them on the night air.

"Good night, Henny. Good hunting."

"Good night, Max. We'll have to do this again sometime. Most fun I've had in years. Maybe we both missed our calling. We'd make a swell pair of second-story men."

"Just like Raffles?" Annie inquired icily as she stepped out of the shadow of a palmetto to stand squarely in front of the two cat burglars on the dusty, moonlit road.

"Annie." Henny didn't sound the least chagrined. "You'll never guess what we were doing—"

"Oh, I don't know," Annie mused. "Picnicking? Canvassing voters? Trading chili recipes? Or perhaps something socially relevant. Planning a day-care center for working mothers?"

"Now, Annie," Max cajoled.

Henny patted Annie's shoulder. "Something tells me you

two have a lot to say to each other. See you in the morning. Reveille at six. Tallyho," and she trotted off into the night toward the Tent City.

She left behind a bottomless pool of silence.

"I thought I'd do a little more checking," Max said vaguely, after a while.

"It was somewhat disconcerting to find you missing from your cot," she replied crisply.

Max was quiet for a moment, then, his tone distinctly suspicious, he asked, "And what, my love, were *you* doing, roaming about at this ungodly hour?"

"A little checking," she retorted, trying hard not to sound defensive.

He began to laugh. After a moment, she did, too.

Each took a step toward the other, then a businesslike throat clearing arrested their movement.

"Heard rustle in the bushes over this way," Madeleine whispered hoarsely, obviously making a best effort to speak quietly. "Sorry to say, it's after hours, you know. Camp rules, you understand."

Which rather put a damper on further conversation.

The newlyweds gave each other a last fond farewell glance, then melted into the night. To the Men's Side and the Women's Side, of course.

Monday morning

Annie lifted her steaming mug of coffee in a cheerful breakfast salute to her mate. "At least the coffee's good." It smelled *wonderful*. But breakfast coffee always did, even if she hadn't brewed it from one of her favorite grinds.

"I will admit to quite pleasant breakfast interludes," Max said agreeably, "but I can't be quit of that communal tent soon enough."

Their paper plates, with the remnants of the Tent City breakfast (charred bacon this morning), rested on the pier beside them. Up at what Annie considered an obscenely early hour, they'd exchanged good morning nods from their respective spots in the shower lines (Men's and Women's, of course), then met at the chow line and carried their plates to the end of the middle pier.

Annie gulped down the rest of her coffee and wriggled impatiently. "I wish the search teams would get started. I can't wait to get into Jesse's cabin," and she rattled Ingrid's keys in the pocket of her skirt.

Max started to reiterate the protest he'd sounded throughout breakfast, but his bride cut him off.

"Nope. It has to be done. And I can do it. Don't you have any confidence in me? After all, nobody caught Laurel and me in Ingrid's cabin last night."

"Yeah. But that was the middle of the night, and this is broad daylight."

Actually, it was a murky morning, she thought, but refrained from saying so, heavily overcast, and the gun-metal-grey water had a sullen glitter.

"I'll be a lookout," Max said determinedly.

Just as determinedly, she said, "Waste of brainpower. You go on down to your office. With the info from the rental applications, you'll be able to put together dossiers on everybody. Then we'll really be in business."

He was finally persuaded, but gave her several rather endearingly worried looks over his shoulder as he walked down the pier. Annie waved encouragingly; then, as he disappeared from view, she drew her knees up to her chin and contemplated Nightingale Courts.

Despite the lowering sky and the telltale droop of most of the searchers, Annie felt a surge of energy and confidence. The searchers were discouraged, of course, because they'd found no trace of Ingrid, but Annie, banking on Henny's analysis, felt that every passing hour was further proof of a well-planned and brilliantly executed abduction.

From her vantage point at the end of the pier, she studied Nightingale Courts, all the cabins, the central area where the canvas tent snapped in the freshening wind, the honeysuckle-laden arch, the mailboxes—

Her glance riveted on the rank of silvery mailboxes, and she felt a prickle of excitement at the back of her neck.

The mailboxes—and premeditated murder.

Annie jumped to her feet. She looked across the inlet, at

Alan Nichols's cabin, at another weather-beaten cabin midway between Nichols's and Jerry's Gas 'N Go, then back to the semicircle of Nightingale Courts.

And knew that Jesse Penrick's murderer had been within this area on Saturday morning when Ingrid and Jesse quarreled. Because it had to have been that quarrel that prompted the murderer to carry the unconscious Jesse to Ingrid's cabin and kill him there.

She bent and yanked up her purse and pulled out the notebook in which she'd sketched down her impressions of the Crime Scene. Flipping to a clean page, she drew the Courts, the inlet, its piers, the gas station, and the cabins on the opposite bank.

Annie studied the results.

Her investigation was beginning to coalesce. Until now, her progress had been almost aimless, like the fictional P.I.'s of her acquaintance, from the Continental Op to Philo Vance. She'd wandered from cabin to cabin, trying to find out who hated Jesse Penrick, seeking to discover what his neighbors knew about him, searching for motives. But this map focused on a specific area and the persons who might reasonably have been within its boundaries early Saturday morning.

Her hand flew across the page:

SATURDAY MORNING

Possible observers of Ingrid's confrontation with Jesse:

1. Tom Smith
2. Mavis Beeson (And Billy Cameron?)
3. Adele Prescott
4. Duane Webb
5. Ophelia Baxter

She looked speculatively across the water. One cabin was obviously unlived in, and Jerry's Gas 'N Go wouldn't have been open yet, plus the clerk couldn't see the mailboxes from behind the cash register. The only vantage point would be from behind the store.

But Alan Nichols could see these piers from his place. So, she nodded and wrote:

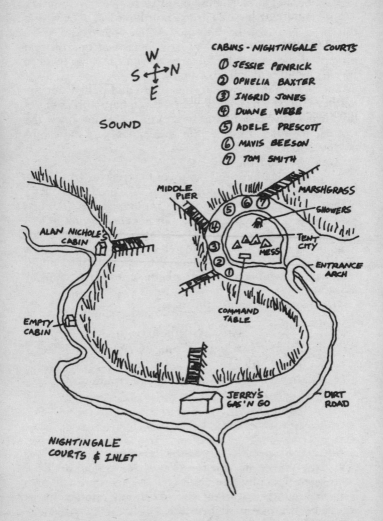

CABINS - NIGHTINGALE COURTS
1. JESSIE PENRICK
2. OPHELIA BAXTER
3. INGRID JONES
4. DUANE WEBB
5. ADELE PRESCOTT
6. MAVIS BEESON
7. TOM SMITH

SOUND

ALAN NICHOLE'S CABIN

MIDDLE PIER

MARSHGRASS

SHOWERS

TENT CITY

MESS

ENTRANCE ARCH

EMPTY CABIN

COMMAND TABLE

JERRY'S GAS 'N GO

DIRT ROAD

NIGHTINGALE COURTS & INLET

6. Alan Nichols.
7. Yellow tank top [whom she'd glimpsed when she'd arrived Saturday morning in response to Laurel's summons].

Oh, yes.

8. Laurel.

And to cover all possibilities, she'd ask Madeleine to announce that anyone who had been in the vicinity of the Courts that Saturday morning was requested to contact Annie.

But it was numbers 1 through 6 that held her attention. Maybe the murderer had been too clever, using Ingrid's fuss with Jesse, because it narrowed the possibilities from practically anyone on the island to a very few. Whether that idiot Posey would listen to this reconstruction or not, Annie felt confident she was on the right track. Now she had a starting point.

She gnawed on the pencil for a moment, then finished with a flourish:

CONCLUSIONS

1. The murderer put Jesse in Ingrid's cabin because of the Saturday morning quarrel.
2. The murderer could count on Ingrid being absent that evening because Annie and Max's wedding had received extensive coverage in the *Gazette*, right on a par with the hot pennant races. It was downright disgusting how Laurel had charmed Vince Ellis, the *Gazette* publisher. But as Norma Gold would have caustically observed, what else could you expect from a filthy little beast? Ergo, Ingrid's cabin was the perfect dumping ground for a corpse.
3. That meant the murder was already planned as of Saturday morning.
4. Which indicated that the motive for murder lay in some action of Jesse's prior to Saturday. So, dear Henny—as Bulldog Drummond, Tish Carberry, et al.—was wasting her time with her detailed investi-

gation of Jesse's actions on Saturday. Oh well, the
poor dear couldn't be expected to score every time.

5. Which further indicated that the murder was *not* the
   result of passion and didn't occur in the heat of anger.

Annie repressed the urge to turn a self-congratulatory
somersault. She was positive she had the murderer's name
on her list! Now, all she had to do was figure out which one
was the culprit.

Tom Smith was weird and frightened of something. He
claimed to have ignored Jesse, but if that were so, why was
he afraid? Time to dig deeper there.

Mavis Beeson was terrified her husband might discover
her whereabouts. But she insisted it "was all worked out"
with Jesse. What did that mean?

Billy Cameron could have seen Jesse and Ingrid quarrel,
or Mavis could have told him. How far was Billy willing to
go to protect Mavis and Kevin?

Adele Prescott was about as charming as a Borgia and
she apparently didn't like anyone—including Jesse—very
much. And she was awfully quick to ascribe motives to
others (Duane Webb and Mavis). Natural venom or a clever
smokescreen?

Duane Webb had reason enough to hate Jesse. But
would he implicate Ingrid, who had been so nice to him?

Ophelia Baxter couldn't wait to inform the authorities
about Ingrid's quarrel with Jesse. Was she eager to cooperate because she was hiding something? And she hadn't said
a word about Jesse killing her cat.

Alan Nichols was quick to respond in an emergency. Yet
he scarcely seemed the Galahad type. He claimed to have
only the most casual acquaintance with Jesse. Was that
true?

The sputtering cough of a gasoline engine drifted across
the water.

Annie looked up. Alan Nichols waved cheerfully from
the bow of his motorboat, which rode low in the water and
needed a new paint job.

She snapped her notebook shut. "Hi, Alan!" Was this
serendipity?

As the boat drew up to the ladder, he gave her an

admiring glance which would have made Max livid. There was something to be said for men like Alan. They certainly added a sparkle to life.

Tying up, he hurried up the ladder. "Saw you over here. I'm going out for a jog, but thought I'd check in. Anything happening?" As he came lightly over the side, he stood just a fraction too close. His chestnut hair tousled by the early morning breeze, his blue eyes bright and clear, he looked rested, good humored, and eager.

"Not a lot," she replied lightly. "The search parties are going to try one more time."

Alan forced a grave frown, but couldn't disguise the admiring gleam in his eyes. "Yeah. Well, I wish I could help. But I'm going to check in at the shop, then go into Savannah to meet Betsy."

"Oh, have you heard from her?" Annie asked.

Suddenly the frown was real. "No. No, I haven't. But I've got her itinerary, and to tell you the truth, this whole goddam thing about not being able to get her at the hotel has me nervous, and I just want to be there when the plane lands and have her tell me we're a bunch of damn fools for getting so worried and why don't I have the shop open?" He grinned, like a small boy with his hand in the cookie jar. "She'll give me hell, closing the store down to come in for her."

Annie had a sneaking suspicion Betsy would be pleased, even if she did complain. Obviously, there was more in Alan's feelings for Betsy than just the regard of an employee for a boss. For the first time, she wondered just how close they were. Alan *was* damned attractive.

"What are you doing today?" he asked.

Annie had quite an agenda ahead, but that didn't include sharing her thoughts with someone on her suspect list. She said casually, "Oh, nosing around. Asking questions. Which reminds me, Alan, did you happen to see Jesse and Ingrid Saturday morning?"

"You mean when they had their dust-up?"

"Yes."

"Oh, hell no. I was sacked out. Sorry. Why'd you ask?"

"I'm trying to find out who was out and about at that

hour. I'd like to know what Jesse was doing, where he'd been."

His eyes narrowed in thought. "Gee, hardly anybody'd be up that early on Saturday. But I'll ask around, see if I can find out anything. And listen, when I get back from the airport, if Betsy's game, I'll take the afternoon off and give you a hand. Okay?"

"Sure. Everybody's welcome," Annie responded.

"Great. I'll get back in touch." He scrambled down the ladder, stepped lightly into the boat and, in a moment, sputtered back across the inlet.

But Annie wasn't listening. Instead, her eyes bright with curiosity, she looked across the marsh at Nightingale Courts.

TWELVE

Mavis could not have been more obviously in flight had she been a cotton nightgowned, Gothic heroine sprinting down tower steps two at a time. Pushing Kevin in his stroller, she balanced one suitcase across the stroller bars and awkwardly clutched a crammed and overflowing shopping bag. A brown scarf hid her bleached hair. She wore a blue suit and high heels that sank down into the soft, grey dirt. She was skulking on the inlet side of the cabins, pausing as she reached each cabin to peer anxiously toward the central courtyard, then crossing the space to the next with a nervous burst of speed.

Annie recognized Mavis's strategy. It was precisely what she herself had done last night, slipping behind the cabins to cut through the pine trees to the road, out of sight of Nightingale Courts.

Annie waited until Mavis disappeared into the pines, then ran down the pier. On shore, she raced for the road. She was waiting when Mavis emerged from the woods near Jerry's Gas 'N Go. Eyes down, the young mother concentrated on maneuvering the stroller around a fallen live oak limb.

"Let me help you," Annie offered, stepping forward.

Mavis's head jerked up. Sheer panic flattened her face, making it almost unrecognizable. She gave a pitifully frightened noise, midway between a gasp and a squeal, and Annie thought sickly of the laboratory mice in *Murder Is Pathological* by P. M. Carlson.

135

"Don't be afraid. I didn't mean to frighten you. But you can't run away."

A pulse fluttered in the girl's throat. Hopeless tears brimmed in her eyes. "If I stay, Henry will find us. I know he will. Oh God, I have to get Kevin away."

"Nobody's going to hurt Kevin. I promise you."

"*You* promise. What can you promise? You're just like the social workers. Oh God, I hate all of you, you're so smug and so sure of yourselves and you make promises and you can't keep them. Tell me how you're going to keep a man from seeing his own son! And what if that awful woman next door goes to court and talks about—talks about me. And the judge, he hunts with Henry's daddy. Do you think he'll believe me if I say Henry hurt me, hurt Kevin? They'll say I'm lying, because of Billy. And what if Henry gets Kevin? Do you know what people do to babies sometimes, even their own babies? And I read about a lady, and she was important, educated, she was somebody, and she said her husband molested her little girl, but the judge said she couldn't prove it, and he wouldn't even believe the little girl. Oh, you tell me how it's going to be all right. I'll tell you something." Tears poured down her face now; she struggled to breathe. "I'll tell *you* something—Henry looks so nice and he can talk so nice. Oh God, *nobody'll* ever believe me about Henry."

"You can get a lawyer—"

"You aren't listening to me! What can a lawyer do? I talked to them at the county health department once. They said I could go to the police and ask them to get a restraining order against Henry. Do you know what that is? That's a little piece of paper. That's all it is, a little piece of paper—and Henry told me, if I ever left him, some day some way he'd get Kevin and Kevin would have years to pay for what I'd done. *Years!*"

"Mommy? Mommy!" Kevin's chubby arms reached up for her.

She knelt and put her arms around the little boy, her body wracked by sobs. He began to wail.

Annie dropped down beside them, her heart aching. "Don't cry, Mavis. I'll help you. I really will."

"You can't help. The only thing I can do is go far away and hide."

Annie searched in her purse for Kleenex. She needed Max with his ever-ready handkerchief. But thinking of Max helped. Max would back her up. She thrust a mass of crumpled tissues at Mavis and said briskly, "Look, nothing's hopeless. And I'm not going to tell you a bunch of lies. I know you're right, the law and the courts and the police can't keep a woman safe if a man is determined to hurt her. I know that."

God knew that was true. She'd seen too many headlines from every corner of the nation: MAN GUNS DOWN WIFE, CHILD DEAD IN ABUSE CASE, and the sad, too-late stories: "Coworkers reported today that the victim had sued for divorce and obtained a restraining order . . . ," or "The court awarded partial custody to the husband, because his former wife couldn't prove charges of cruelty . . ."

Mavis brushed ineffectually at her tears with the wad of tissues.

Annie patted her shoulder. "The reason most women can't help themselves in this kind of situation is because they have no way to protect themselves or their children. Right?"

Mavis nodded.

"All right. Here's what we'll do—we'll hire a security guard, two shifts. Somebody'll be watching you and Kevin twenty-four hours a day. We'll make it clear to Henry that there's no way he can get to you. You can sue him for divorce. We'll get Billy to testify about Kevin's condition and yours the night he picked you up."

Hope flamed, then died away. "But what about Billy? If that woman—"

"Somehow—I don't know how—I'll shut her up," Annie promised grimly. "Now that's just between you and me, but one way or another, I'll manage it."

Mavis shook her head hopelessly. "It isn't just Billy. How can I hire guards? I don't have any money. There's no way I can—"

"I said I'd help. I will."

Gradually, Mavis calmed and Kevin's sobs subsided. But she refused to return to the Courts.

"You have to be there at ten," Annie urged, "or Billy will have to start looking for you."

"At ten?" Mavis repeated blankly.

"They're going to fingerprint all the residents of the Courts. Look, you're safe enough for now. Just avoid the press and TV people. There's no reason for you to be mentioned in any of the stories, and, when this is all over, Max and I will help you. Truly we will."

Reluctantly, shoulders drooping, Mavis turned the stroller and walked with Annie down the dusty, grey road. Annie saw them safely to their cabin, then turned away. She was halfway across the compound, skirting the now deserted Tent City, when her brisk steps slowed.

It suddenly occurred to her that she may have been conned, or, if not led down the garden path, certainly diverted from the truth.

Not that she didn't believe Mavis's fear was genuine.

Yes, Mavis was surely terrified. But Annie wondered whether she'd interrupted the flight of a murderess fearing discovery rather than a battered woman seeking safety?

Annie glanced back toward Mavis's cabin. It could easily have been Mavis who moved stealthily through the night on Saturday, waylaying Jesse on his return from the bar, knocking him out, dragging him to Ingrid's, stabbing him, and awaiting Ingrid's return. But had she had time to subdue Ingrid and remove her to a hiding place and return in time to wander among the crowd?

Yes. Especially if aided by Billy.

Would that vulnerable, teary young mother kill?

She would do whatever she had to do to protect Kevin.

Annie felt a pang of chagrin. Miss Marple would not have been so easily deflected. She would have looked with a cold, clear eye at the attractive young mother, knowing that the following aren't necessarily true: lovers can't be guilty, children are good, mothers are loving, the narrator is the good guy, etc.

Annie should have directed some hard questions at Mavis: "Was Billy with you Saturday night?" "When did he leave?" "What did you mean when you said you 'had it all worked out' with Jesse?"

She was turning to march back to the cabin then and there, when she heard a stentorian bellow.

"Annie! Annie! Ho!" Her fatigue cap at a rakish angle, Madeleine Kurtz bore down on her, waving a folded square of paper. "Thought I spotted you on the pier, then when I looked up, you were dashing toward the road." Her tone implied that some people could afford the time for both relaxation and exercise, but others kept their noses to the grindstone. "Search teams reporting in regularly. No trace yet. Seems almost like black magic. Here's message for you. Got to get back to the phones." She thrust the folded-up square of yellow legal paper in Annie's hand, then wheeled around and strode back toward the command table.

Annie gave an exasperated sigh. Honestly, everything was contriving to keep her from her primary objective, a surreptitious survey of Jesse Penrick's cabin (were there vagrant pine needles there?), but she'd better see what Henny was up to.

The block-letter note was in a staccato style:

SUBJECT (JESSE PENRICK) OBSERVED ENTERING BIRD PRE-
SERVE (OPPOSITE JERRY'S GAS 'N GO) APPROX. 4 P.M. SAT. BY
J. D. HANRAHAN, GAS BOY. OBSERVED DEPARTING SAID
PRESERVE 4:20, CARRYING SMALL PARCEL WRAPPED IN
BROWN PAPER.

Annie peered closely at the bottom of the sheet. There was no signature, rather a small drawing of some kind. Then, a smile tugged at her lips. Dear Henny. Always irrepressible. Where had she come across a representation of the Green Hornet's Seal? Annie could almost hear the roar of his remarkable automobile, the Black Beauty, as the famed radio detective pursued wrongdoers.

But Henny was focusing on the wrong end. What mattered was what had happened to Jesse before Saturday. Who cared what kind of contraband stash he kept in the Bird Preserve?

Annie stuffed the note in her pocket. Now for Jesse's cabin. She started across the courtyard, then saw the bicycle parked at Ophelia's, a jaunty U.N. flag fluttering from its staff. Laurel's bicycle. Annie hesitated, then veered in that direction. After all, it would only take a minute.

As she banged the pyramid-shaped knocker, she prepared herself mentally. She wasn't going to be fobbed off. She was going to find out exactly what these two were up to and whether Ophelia was just a nut or perhaps a murderous nut.

The door opened—a few inches. Laurel squeezed through the aperture to join Annie on the front steps, then firmly shut the door behind her. She still wore the oatmeal-colored robe, no jewelry, and sandals. But she looked so fresh and soignée that Annie wondered if she had a half dozen of the robes, couturier designed. Surely no one could look as lovely as Laurel in just any old piece of dun-colored material.

A soft breath of lilac swept Annie as Laurel leaned close to whisper, "Silence is a jewel beyond price when a revealed spirit engages in astral projection."

Annie wished desperately for a cup of coffee or a personal astral projection to any other plane.

Laurel took Annie's elbow and gently tried to pivot her down the steps.

Annie remembered with crystal clarity how Laurel had resisted Annie's attempts to maneuver her out of Death on Demand last June, endangering Annie's trap for a clever murderer.

Two could play this game.

She planted herself firmly on the top step. "I have to talk to Ophelia."

"My dear," Laurel trilled, "Ophelia is just *too* popular this morning. A Scottish sea captain implored her to serve as his channel. Also the proprietor of a saloon in Tombstone, Arizona, in 1872, and an Aztec priest. *Fifteenth* century."

"How ecumenical," Annie observed.

"Ophelia," Laurel pronounced proudly, "is open to all influences."

"That must be rather tiring."

"My sweet, how perceptive of you!" Laurel patted Annie on the shoulder, not quite firmly enough to push her down the steps.

Annie reached out, grabbed the doorknob and turned it. "Laurel, channeling or no channeling, I do not intend to move one step away from here until I've talked to Ophelia."

Max hummed happily and poured another cup of coffee. Today was proving a sharp contrast to his luckless efforts yesterday. With the helpful information from the rental applications filled out by Ophelia, Jesse, Duane, Adele, and Mavis, he was pulling together quite detailed pictures of everyone's lives.

Everyone, that is, except Tom Smith.

He tapped his legal pad thoughtfully with his pen. Tom Smith. The man might never have existed. But surely something would turn up, if he kept looking.

His eye skipped down to his notes on Billy Cameron and Alan Nichols. Neither, of course, was a resident of Nightingale Courts. But Billy had a hell of a motive, because Mavis obviously had told him about Penrick's threat. As for Alan, Max included him on the general principle that he had a shifty look. Besides, he'd enjoy shoving a dossier under Alan's nose. It would certainly demonstrate to him that Max and Confidential Commissions could come up with the goods, despite Alan's crack on the pier last night. Not that Max harbored any resentment, of course.

Thunder crackled in the distance. The rain couldn't be far distant. Max thought wistfully of other indoor pleasures he would have preferred on a stormy afternoon. Surely someday his honeymoon would begin!

Ophelia sprawled limply in an overstuffed easy chair, her turban, cerise today, pressed against a yellowing lace doily. One chubby hand was daintily draped over her eyes, the other gently massaged the neck of the enormous Persian Annie had glimpsed in the window yesterday. As Annie plunged inside with Laurel at her heels, a deep voice (Ophelia must have a well-exercised diaphragm) intoned, "Water, water everywhere."

Resisting the temptation to make the obvious reply, Annie glanced around the cluttered room, then wished she hadn't. Ophelia's living quarters were apparently open to all influences, too, just like their mistress. An enormous poster of a many-headed Indian god hung on one wall, surrounded by Haitian voodoo masks. Bright red plastic tarot cards were scattered across the tabletop in front of her. A Ouija board leaned against a whatnot crammed with colored glass pyramids of every size and inscribed stones of various shapes. Almost every foot of space in the room was filled with tables—little ones, big ones, all topped by crystals of many kinds, including amethyst, rose and blue quartz, black onyx, and obsidian. A narrow path extended from the front door to the kitchen and another to the bedroom. Incense (reminiscent of mildewed socks) hung in such a thick cloud that Annie's eyes stung.

Ophelia's blue eyes were regarding her with alarm from beneath the spread fingers. Then they blinked tightly shut.

Annie began to wonder just how much of Ophelia was a deliberate sham and whether that mattered.

Laurel slipped gracefully across the room to hover over her psychic friend. "I'll get you some water, my dear. I know you must be terribly thirsty. Just rest *quietly* while I dash into the kitchen."

It didn't qualify as a dash, but, considering the impedimenta in Laurel's way, it was damned fast. And although her warning to Ophelia to keep her mouth shut was not the last word in subtlety, it proved that Laurel was as quick of tongue as of toe.

Ophelia dropped her hand to the chair arm, opened her eyes and stared at Annie with her lips pressed tightly together like Charles Darnay awaiting the executioner.

Annie itched to take a machete to the room and a bludgeon to Ophelia, but she reminded herself that she, too, could be subtle. If she tried *very* hard. She would be as smooth as V. C. Clinton-Baddeley's Dr. Davie and as patient as Georges Simenon's Inspector Jules Maigret.

"Ophelia," she said warmly, "I have so looked forward to having a really good visit with you."

Ophelia's shiny, black, self-applied eyebrows arched in surprise.

"Of all the residents of Nightingale Courts, I feel that you are the most sensitive to nuances, so I'm appealing to you for help." Annie smiled, with, she hoped, winning charm.

Laurel flew out of the kitchen, a glass in hand. "Here, Ophelia. Drink your *water*, and that's all we'll say about that."

"But I don't—" The sentence ended in a gurgle as Laurel thrust the glass at Ophelia's mouth and purposefully tilted it.

Over Ophelia's head, Laurel met Annie's eyes with a look of sublime innocence.

"Now, Ophelia," Annie purred, holding her steely smile, "if you've had quite enough water—"

"Enough," the channeler croaked. "Enough."

"Was there anything different about Jesse Penrick this last week? Anything at all out of the ordinary that you observed?"

"This last week?" Ophelia's interest was aroused. Her eyes narrowed and she tapped the fingers of one hand against the chair arm. The bluish-furred cat swiped viciously at them. "This last week . . ." she murmured thoughtfully.

Her demeanor was so straightforward that Annie looked at her with renewed attention. Perhaps there was a real woman behind the New Age facade.

"Let me see . . ." Ophelia's voice rose and fell as she sketched out her week, recalling places and events. Only twice had she seen Jesse. ". . . until Thursday afternoon late—and that was funny. He wasn't usually out of his house in the afternoons. He liked to come out late at night and roam. Sometimes he'd stay out till dawn. I'd see him coming in when I got up to let Princess out." And she petted the cat, who gave a warning snarl. "But Jesse was out in the heat—remember how hot it was Thursday?—all afternoon. He spent the whole afternoon at the end of the middle pier—and actually, he was still out there after dark, because I saw his pipe."

The end of the middle pier. That was where Annie and Max had breakfasted, two mornings in a row. It provided a panoramic view of Nightingale Courts, the inlet, and the shore. Could Jesse have been waiting for someone to come home?

And it was Thursday night that Adele had spotted Jesse Penrick using the pay phone at Jerry's Gas 'N Go.

Ophelia's voice took on a singsong quality. "Malevolent old man, but he got what he gave. That's what everyone comes to in the end, their just reward."

"Is that what you think he got?" Annie asked. "His just reward?"

But Ophelia refused to be drawn. "As you live, so shall you die. Today. Yesterday. Or tomorrow." Laurel nodded.

Annie's small store of patience was rapidly depleting. Was it a sense of constantly having to deal with utter idiots that made Holmes so irritable?

"Back to Jesse," Annie said crisply. "Did you see anything else that struck you as unusual?"

Slowly Ophelia shook her head, and the cerise turban quivered. The cat, irritated, jumped to the floor and ducked beneath a table draped in velvet. A small cloud of dust rose from the carpet.

"How about Saturday? When did you see him Saturday?"

Laurel interrupted. "We were out for a sunrise walk. To contemplate. I felt it *most* appropriate. I wanted all the forces of life to be in harmony for the wedding."

"They didn't cooperate, did they?" Annie asked dryly.

Laurel was too ladylike to do anything more than flash a glance of sad disappointment at her daughter-in-law. "We cannot," she said with great dignity, "harness earthbound spirits to our will. But, on the whole, the universe was in delightful alignment at the moment you and dear Maxwell exchanged your vows."

Annie was already sorry for lashing out. "Laurel, really, you did such a grand job. Everything was perfectly lovely."

"After all," Ophelia offered brightly, "he didn't pass on the other side until just past midnight."

That made it all right, of course.

Annie tried desperately to recapture the thread of her interrogation. "Saturday," she repeated sturdily. "When did you see him Saturday?"

"Oh, it was during our walk. He was coming across the inlet in his boat, and Ingrid was waiting for him on the pier. She was furious!"

This was the kind of witness that could do great damage to Ingrid in court. Annie thought how artfully Antony

Maitland could get a witness to rephrase his conclusion. "Now, Ophelia, actually, Ingrid was merely informing him that she was determined that he should move. Isn't that correct?"

"Of course, that's what she said. And that might have been the end of it," Laurel interjected, "until he threatened to reveal some things that were going on in some of the cabins." A delicate frown marred her face. "And Ingrid, I'm sorry to say, was swept by fury—and she lost her temper!"

With the very best will in the world, Laurel was sealing Ingrid's fate!

Annie sighed. Antony Maitland never had to deal with Laurel.

Then the import of the words registered.

"Laurel! He threatened to go *public* with something he knew about the other residents?"

Laurel and Ophelia nodded.

"Could this have been overheard?"

The blond head and turbaned head bobbed in unison.

Annie whooped.

Ophelia eyed her warily, but Laurel merely nodded imperturbably.

"Don't you see?" Annie demanded. "Now no one can claim Ingrid has the only motive! Oh, that's terrific." Jesse's final nasty barb opened a nice field of suspects for study, and Posey would hear all about it, as soon as Annie could get to him.

Annie pressed Ophelia for her knowledge of bad feelings among the residents of Nightingale Courts. Ophelia confirmed what Annie had learned about Penrick and Duane, and said she'd seen Penrick knock occasionally at Adele's back door, but she knew nothing about Penrick's relationship with either Mavis or Smith.

"And what did *you* think about Jesse Penrick?" Annie asked finally.

"He was a nasty little man," Ophelia snapped. "I hated everything about him." The heavily lipsticked mouth began to quiver. "He killed Barney, I know he did. He didn't like cats, ordered me to keep Barney away from his steps." Tears spilled down the pudgy cheeks. "He put out poisoned food, I know he did. And Barney came to the back door, he *dragged* himself to the door, and he was so sick, and then he died. I wish I could have poisoned Jesse. I'd have liked to watch Jesse Penrick die."

The wind kicked up swirls of dust as Annie stood between Ophelia's and Jesse's cabins. She gave a quick glance toward the command table, but no one was looking her way. Hurriedly, she darted past Ophelia's carport, then ran to Jesse's back steps. It only took a second to use Ingrid's master key and unlock the door.

As she slipped inside, she brooded over Ophelia's bitter words. How would she feel if someone poisoned Agatha? Agatha! She must remember to drop by the store and put down fresh food and water before she left for the mainland to see Posey.

Annie stood with her back to the door and surveyed Jesse's kitchen. It was the same size, of course, as Ingrid's, but there was nothing cheerful about this dim room. It smelled sour, and she spotted an overflowing garbage pail next to the refrigerator. There were no bright yellow curtains, as at Ingrid's, only plain off-white window shades. Annie switched on the overhead light, gave a little shrug, and opened the nearest cupboard. Might as well start there. Cans filled two shelves, boxed goods a third. She was turning away, when she paused.

How odd!

The canned goods were arranged according to contents, and they were in alphabetical order. Asparagus soup. Bean soup. Chowder. Minestrone. Onion soup. Beets. Carrots. Corn. Green beans. Spinach. Sweet potatoes. The same with the boxes. Bisquick. Oatmeal. Raisin bran.

Each can sat equidistant from its neighbor.

She poked into the broom closet. Everything in a particular spot, no higgledy-piggledy, let-things-land-where-they-might, as in Annie's kitchen. Jesse Penrick had fashioned for himself a geometric environment. A place for everything and everything in its place. He was not only hateful, he was, to slapdash Annie, really weird.

But there were no pine needles anywhere.

In the living room, Jesse's passion for exactitude was reflected in the precise arrangement of his pipes. Nine of them, all aligned a half inch apart along the back of a pine desk.

But the lid was ajar on the tobacco canister. On closer inspection, she spotted shreds of tobacco on the desktop.

The center desk drawer wasn't altogether closed.

The sofa cushions were askew.

Magazines were jammed haphazardly into a rack beside an easy chair.

A man doesn't alphabetize his canned goods, meticulously arrange his broom closet, align his pipes, then turn into a slob with the rest of his possessions.

Had the police searched these rooms?

Not in this manner. Chief Saulter demanded professionalism from his staff. Billy Cameron would never disarrange a desk, scatter pipe tobacco. Even Posey, with all his asinine traits, wouldn't leave a mess like this.

And, had the police searched, they would have neatly docketed papers, recorded information. They wouldn't have pawed about in the tobacco canister.

No. Not the police.

Annie felt the same unmistakable tingle she'd experienced earlier that morning on the pier when she realized the murderer had watched Ingrid and Jesse quarrel Saturday morning. Once again, she felt close, so close, to the killer, who had been here—looking for something.

She found further traces of a hurried search in the bedroom, clothes rumpled in their drawers, a lack of precision in the arrangement of the hangers in the closet.

Looking for something. Something small, obviously, if it could be hidden in a tobacco canister. And the search had to have been made by the murderer. A petty thief wouldn't have left behind the TV or the wooden tray on the bedroom dresser with its neat piles of pennies, nickels, dimes, and quarters.

Annie couldn't know what the murderer had sought—or whether it had been found—but she gave it a try. Twenty minutes later, she could have filled out an exhaustive report on everything from Jesse's choice in toothpaste (Gleem) to the depressing lack of personal mementoes. No photographs. No letters. Nothing to indicate he had not started and ended his life in this dingy cabin as an old man. And nothing whatsoever to indicate what someone else had sought here.

But she hit paydirt in the lower right-hand drawer of the pine desk, and suddenly Jesse Penrick came clear in her mind, dreadfully clear. She'd known him as a snoopy old man, poking into the trash barrels for anything of value, and she'd learned that he liked to hurt people, the crushed car on Duane's doorstep, the scarlet A on Mavis's mailbox. Now, she knew him for what he was, a scavenger of human frailty—for profit.

Perhaps the wonder was not that Jesse had been murdered, but that he'd lived so long.

He kept careful records, including the individual payment schedules.

The folder on Mavis made her the angriest. There were several photographs of Mavis and Billy, and the final neat notation, *Sept. 15, $5.*

The sorry, sorry bastard. So that's what Mavis meant when she started to explain that "it was all worked out" with Jesse. No, he wouldn't inform Mavis's husband of her whereabouts, not so long as she paid him five dollars a week.

Tom Smith's folder contained a single clipping headlined, WHERE ARE THEY NOW? It was yellowed and the dateline was in August several years ago. The story sketched the backgrounds of nine anti-war activists of the late sixties, who had disappeared after bombings or draftboard break-ins. Six were still wanted for various crimes. There were several smudgy photographs. The sums listed on this payment schedule were irregular but began about a week after the article was published and ranged from ten to forty dollars weekly.

Obviously, Jesse kept a close eye on his neighbor's success with his miniatures and adjusted his rate accordingly.

She puzzled over Adele's folder. It contained a list of payments, averaging a hundred dollars a month, but it was harder to discern what Jesse had found in Adele's background to provide a basis for blackmail. There were only two other items in the folder, a newspaper clipping and a map. The clipping was a three-column photograph of an attractive woman in her mid-thirties standing before a classic antebellum mansion. The cutline read: *Lovely Susan Prescott welcomes guests to Hounds Hill for the April house-and-garden tours*. The hand-drawn map of the island contained a half-dozen or so residential streets. Each street was marked with two addresses, one circled. And that was all. Quickly, Annie copied the map in her notebook.

There was no payment schedule in Duane's folder, only a slender stack of news stories on the deaths of Mary and Sheila Webb, Duane's arrest for drunk driving and his conviction (two-year sentence, eight months served, remainder suspended).

Jesse had underlined in red several dates in the obituaries, Sheila's birthday, Mary and Duane's wedding anniversary. That last date was September 19, the day Annie and Max wed, the day Jesse Penrick was murdered.

The wind rattled a loose shutter on the roof of Duane's cabin. Annie knocked for the third time on the kitchen door.

He might easily be in there, sitting and drinking in that dark, overcrowded room.

Annie fingered Ingrid's master key. She was a little bit afraid of Duane. There was an aura of unsatisfied violence and anger around him. She shook her head impatiently. Aura, indeed. Had she spent too much time around Ophelia and Laurel? Still, it took a little internal prompting to decide to open the door. (Think what Cordelia Gray would do. Or Norah Mulcahaney, if she had a search warrant.) Inspired by such stalwart examples, Annie inserted the key, unlocked the door, and poked her head inside, calling out, "Mr. Webb?" She *could* pretend she'd found the door unlocked.

She edged inside when there was no answer, her heart hammering. It took only minutes to be certain Duane was absent. His cereal bowl and coffee mug were still on the kitchen table along with a crumpled morning newspaper. A

brown cotton sweater was tossed carelessly on the telephone table in the living room, the bed unmade in the
bedroom. But there was no telltale trail of pine needles.

The printer clattered, vibrating on its plastic stand. The
printout dangled to the floor and began to curl.

Max relaxed in his chair, now almost horizontal, and
studied the ceiling. The dossiers were done, and they
contained a wealth of information, birth and death dates,
job histories, gossip, personality profiles. Somewhere in all
that jumble of fact and fancy, there had to be a lead to
Penrick's murderer.

Penrick himself turned out to be damned peculiar, as
well as consistently unpleasant. One of those "Step on a
crack, break my back" mentalities, shrilly insistent that his
personal belongings be arranged with meticulous order,
refusing to permit odd or irregular-shaped furniture or
decorations in his house, always wearing a navy blue cotton
turtleneck and tight dungarees.

Max decided to read it all from scratch, give it a fresh
eye. He was just the fellow to find a revealing bit of
information. Pouring himself a fresh cup of coffee, he
settled down with his papers, with only an occasional pause
to admire the outstanding job he'd done.

Adele Prescott's antique-filled living room astounded
Annie. Despite the room's small size, a Bristol glass
chandelier hung from the ceiling, casting a bright glow on a
collection of Meissen china plates, nineteenth-century
papier-mâché trays with gold leaf and mother-of-pearl,
three American rococo pier-glass mirrors, two Chinese
porcelain vases, and two gilt torcheres. Each piece was the
finest of its kind. Annie knew these were not reproductions.

Her cheeks flushed with pleasure, Adele pointed out
several pieces to Annie, taking special pride in a pair of
elaborately dressed Japanese dolls of the late Edo period
and a green stone mask from Teotihuacan. "You like my
things," she observed with satisfaction, and she smiled. It

was the first warmth she'd ever exhibited, and Annie felt chilled.

"You certainly have an eclectic taste," she said, straining to reconcile her initial assessment of Adele, while simultaneously making a surreptitious survey for pine needles.

"I've *always* liked only the best. All my life."

Then how did you end up in Nightingale Courts? Annie wondered.

The big woman caressed a Russian straw work box. "Once I had a lovely setting for my treasures." She scowled. "A man will always go after a younger woman, especially a wealthy man. You'd better remember that." She picked up a jade letter opener.

Annie's face froze, then she contained her irritation. People see life through their own experiences. Obviously Adele's past was full of betrayal. Had she always been strident and overbearing? And how to reconcile Adele's appearance with her obsession for beautiful objects? Had her collector's regard for precious things made Jesse Penrick even more odious in her eyes? Why had Jesse clipped the article on Hounds Hill? Had Hounds Hill been Adele's "lovely setting"? Who was the Susan Prescott who stood on the steps of the antebellum mansion?

"Did you once live at Hounds Hill?"

Adele's nostrils flared. A vein began to pulse in her throat. "Who've you been talking to? That hateful Duane Webb? Yes, I lived there. It was *my* home. *Mine*. And someday I'll have a beautiful home again—then I'll have room for my things. Is that why you've come? To throw Hounds Hill in my face?" Her thin voice rose shrilly.

"Oh no, not at all. I just heard someone say something once about Hounds Hill, but no, that's not why I came." For an instant, Annie was tempted to tell her about Jesse's folder. But not yet. No need to put her on guard. Annie flashed her a conciliatory smile. "I'm trying to find out more about Jesse's activities. You told me you saw him at the Gas 'N Go pay phone Thursday night. Did you see him on Friday or Saturday?"

Adele shook her head impatiently. "I certainly didn't spend my time keeping track of him!"

Time to try flattery. "Mrs. Prescott, you are obviously a

woman of intelligence and cultivation. I know you would never have invaded your neighbor's privacy, but I'm just asking you to take a moment to look back. Anything at all you might have noticed about Jesse Penrick this past week might be helpful."

"Why should you care about that disgusting creature?"

"I don't care about him at all. But his murderer abducted Ingrid. Finding the killer is the best way to find Ingrid."

Adele replaced the letter opener on a small Hepplewhite mahogany console table and picked up a silver music box inset with a delicate rose-quartz filigree. She lifted the lid. As a Strauss waltz tinkled, sounding like a melody distantly heard in the night, she stroked the quartz, her blunt fingers gentle. Either the music, the soothing touch of her possession, or Annie's mention of Ingrid touched her, because she finally answered grudgingly, "I saw him Wednesday night. Couldn't sleep, so I went out on the pier. It was late, I think, around midnight. He'd been out in his rowboat. He tied up at the pier, right under one of the lights. When he climbed up the steps, I got a glimpse of his face. He had a nasty, pleased look on his face."

"What did you think he'd been doing?"

"Peeking. Like he always did. I told him once he was a voyeur. He had nasty eyes."

Annie gave a final hasty glance for pine needles, knowing as she did so that they would be impossible to spot against the dark patterns in the Oriental rug. She felt she'd managed all she was going to learn through subtlety and indirection. So—

"Tell me, Mrs. Prescott, why did you pay Jesse Penrick a hundred dollars a month?"

A broadside to the head couldn't have startled the woman more. Her face was suddenly as white and ridged as bone. "What did you say?"

"What did he have on you?" Annie pressed.

But that was the wrong question. With a sinking heart, Annie knew it when she saw relief flame in those dark eyes. Relief followed by fury, quickly controlled.

"I don't have any idea what you're talking about," Adele Prescott announced. "You're confused." But the hand reaching out for the doorknob trembled.

* * *

Barbie's voice on the intercom was cheerful, as usual, and informal, as always. Max suppressed a sigh. How could he expect clients to be awed, as Annie assured him they were when approaching Nero Wolfe, if Barbie always called her boss by his first name and played country music on her radio? As Waylon Jennings bemoaned the loss of another love, Barbie said, "You awake and everything? Some guy named Alan Nichols is here to see you, and he's in a swivet."

Max could care less about impressing Alan Nichols. Or about Alan's state of mind. But his not to reason, his merely to serve mankind. "Sure. Send him in."

Max rose, held out his hand, and forced a welcoming smile. He didn't know what irritated him the most, Alan's haberdashery-perfect appearance (white silk blazer—*white*, mind you!—pink shirt, blue silk tie with white polka dots, and navy gabardine slacks), or his billboard-perfect looks. What could Annie see in the curly-haired creep?

But, Max realized abruptly, Alan wasn't his usual ebullient self. In fact, the scared, sick look in his eyes was unmistakable. "Max, listen, I'm really worried! I met Betsy's plane—she was due back from Frisco at nine-fifteen—and she wasn't on it!"

Ominous clouds pressed closer from the west. An occasional flash of lightning indicated the storm was near. In its second day, the Tent City had acquired a down-at-heels, ragged appearance. The plastic trash cans overflowed, the mosquito netting billowed in the wind, and an occasional yellow plastic cup rattled across the dusty ground.

Across the courtyard, most of the residents of Nightingale Courts stood sullenly near the command table. Annie glanced at her watch. Almost ten. Time for the fingerprinting. Madeleine Kurtz appeared to be checking the residents off a list. She swung about and looked impatiently toward Adele's cabin. Spotting Annie, she made energetic hailing motions.

Quickly, Annie nodded affirmatively, then made elaborate just-a-minute motions and turned away to trot toward the last cabin. She hadn't spotted Tom Smith among Madeleine's group, and she wanted to ask him a few questions in private. When she knocked on his front door, it swung open.

"Mr. Smith?" She pushed the door wider. Her nose wrinkled at the room's heavy odor, that not very pleasant mixture of paints, smoke, leather, and wood. "Mr. Smith?"

Light spilled from the kitchen. The living room was dusky. The door to the bedroom was closed.

Annie raised her hand and rapped firmly against the door panel. The sound was loud enough to wake the dead.

No answer. She stepped inside, leaving the door open behind her. But, abruptly, she felt certain he wasn't there. The cabin had an empty air. There was no sense of another human's presence. Still, she opened the bedroom door cautiously, again calling out his name. She preferred not to come face to face unexpectedly with the cabin's odd occupant.

The bedroom was as bare as a monk's cell. A single narrow bed, with a woolen army blanket pulled up neatly over the pillow. One maple chest. One straight chair. Not a mirror, not a book, not a picture. It was in odd contrast to the living room, with its innumerable shelves and boxes containing his workstuff. The door to the bathroom was ajar. She crossed the room cautiously until she could see within. It, too, was empty.

So was the kitchen. Empty and clean, with no dishes out to indicate when he'd last eaten there. The back door stood open.

Annie shivered. Where was Tom Smith? Why did this cabin have the feel of a place long emptied of life?

Laurel smiled benignly, apparently quite willing to assume a hostess's duties even in the most unlikely of circumstances.

"Annie, my sweet, so nice of you to join us. I've been reassuring Ophelia. It isn't at *all* difficult to have one's fingerprints taken. A bit messy, but not *difficult*. I was last fingerprinted in Budapest, and the *dearest* little inspector told me I had the most divine hand. Quite sweet, and very *helpful* to international relations."

Duane Webb ignored Annie's arrival and stared broodingly out at the whitecapped waves in the sound. Adele Prescott shot her an icy glare, then resumed her angry pacing by the tent entrance. Mavis jounced Kevin on her hip. She smiled shyly.

Madeleine bounded up to her. "Got everybody corralled but that miniature man. Searchers report *no* trace. Storm coming. May call everybody in."

Annie nodded and opened the note Madeleine thrust at her. She raised an eyebrow at the lengthy missive. Goodbye Green Hornet, hello—?

I know if I just had a moment to take my *shoes* off, I'd feel much better, but duty calls. Continuing to trace Jesse's actions Saturday. He arrived Parotti's Bar and Bait Shop approx. 7 p.m. and was in, for him, a jovial mood. Jesse described with relish to Sam Hinchley (shrimp fisherman) the movie he'd seen last week in Savannah (*Locker Room Lovers*). Talked about big plans, going to go to London, looking at a new car. Approx. 11 p.m. telephone rang, a call for Jesse. First time Ben Parotti ever remembered anyone calling him. A hoarse voice. Parotti not sure whether man or woman. Jesse to phone, apparently message made him angry. He swore, "Goddammit, better not be," and hurried out into the night. Feel Jesse's actions on Saturday now well documented. Expanding scope of probe. On Friday afternoon, Jesse stopped in Island Five-and-Dime, bought a wedding anniversary card. Next stopped at Hennessey's Marine, where he priced a new motorboat. Progress of investigation gratifying. As you know (proven by the Second Law of Thermodynamics): "Everything wears out. Everything breaks down. Something's got to give." And *I'll* be there when the truth outs.

The signature came as no surprise. George Bagby's Inspector Schmidt, he of the aching feet and patient pursuit of evildoers.

Annie dismissed Henny's charades from her mind and

focused on her information. She knew much of it, of course, and a good deal of it seemed extraneous. But the wedding anniversary card—

She came up beside Webb. "I stopped by your cabin earlier, but you weren't there."

"Nobody asked you to drop by," he said sourly.

"I just had a question, something you didn't mention yesterday. Surprised me. Maybe it'll surprise the police."

He pulled his gaze away from the sound, focused on her. She wished the thick bifocals didn't magnify his eyes so, giving them an almost daunting power.

"Yeah?"

"The anniversary card—how angry did it make you?"

She had her answer. Not in words, but in the burning fury of those blue eyes, fury quickly controlled. Duane Webb, for all his bristly speech and manner, had himself well in hand. The flame subsided, and he turned back to his survey of the sullen waters. "Don't know what the hell you're talking about."

Adele Prescott stopped pacing and strode to the command table to glower down at Madeleine. "Is this your doing?" she demanded. "Arranging for all of us to be fingerprinted?"

"Why should you object?" Madeleine retorted, equally aggressively.

"I'm not a criminal, and I don't appreciate being treated like one."

"Honest as the day is long. Right, Adele?" Webb said in mock admiration. "And you can't help telling everybody so, can you?"

"I've established a reputation for trustworthiness. It's essential in my business."

Webb gave her a contemptuous glance. "Hell, I'd rather have a house robbed blind than have you stay in it for even a day. Ophelia's a fool, but she's right about one thing. Ugly spirits contaminate their surroundings."

Adele's face purpled. She jammed her hands deep into her windbreaker pockets. "You don't even have a house anymore. If you're so smart, why do you have to live in a rented cabin? You drank yourself out of house and home and murdered your wife and daughter, to boot."

An ugly grin made him look like a malevolent moon. "Touché, you old bitch. But you don't have a fine home anymore, either, do you? How much do you enjoy being a caretaker of other people's houses? Adele Prescott, house sitter. That's a far cry from the days you used to lord it over everybody as the mistress of Hounds Hill."

A muscle twitched in Adele Prescott's jaw.

"Ugliness begets ugliness," Ophelia murmured sadly. "Hatred sows hatred." She pressed her fingers lightly against her temples. "Somewhere out there, Ingrid's spirit seeks us, but we cannot hear her if our ears are filled with a discordant jangle."

"Screws up the messages, huh?" Duane asked sarcastically.

Sudden tears brimmed in Ophelia's eyes. "None are so blind as those who *think* they can see."

Laurel fluttered near her. "My dear, you must *conserve* your emotion. You know that we are near a *critical* juncture."

Ophelia sniffed raggedly. "Oh, I know. I must not become upset. I must not. I must not."

"You're all crazy. That's what you are, nutty as a Christmas fruitcake." Mavis Beeson's eyes swung from face to face. "I don't know why I ever came to live in this horrible place." At her tone, Kevin's small arms tightened around his mother's neck. Her lips trembled, but she lifted a reassuring hand to smooth back a curl from his face. "I wish I didn't have to see any of you ever again."

Webb looked at her pityingly. "If wishes were horses, the sun would still shine on many a golden kingdom." His voice was weary.

Mavis stared at him uncomprehendingly, then her face changed. Eagerness warred with uncertainty in her eyes as Broward Rock's sole police car pulled up to the honeysuckle-covered arch.

Annie darted up to meet Billy Cameron. She didn't want to be overheard. "Billy, can I visit with you for a minute?"

He loomed over her. Although he had to be around her own age, he'd always seemed younger, younger and unsophisticated, like an awkward St. Bernard puppy. But today his normally open, friendly face had a new hardness.

He didn't look young, friendly, or bumptious. He looked like a very large and very wary man.

Very wary.

"What do you want?"

Annie hesitated, then said irritably. "Look, I haven't told anybody about you and Mavis." She kept her voice low.

But he darted a hunted glance at the waiting group. "There isn't anything to tell," he said roughly. "I don't know what you're talking about. Mavis and I hardly know each other. If you say anything else, it's a lie, 'cause you're trying to protect Mrs. Jones."

So he was going to brazen it out. Couldn't he see that lying would only make it worse?

"Billy, listen to me. You want to find Penrick's murderer, don't you?"

"The real murderer, yeah."

"Then tell me this: Did the laboratory find pine needles sticking *to* Jesse Penrick's clothing?"

THIRTEEN

Mid-morning Monday

Agatha was not happy. In fact, Agatha was furious. Her amber eyes glistened balefully and her tail whipped with increasing velocity.

There were those who would scoff at imputing such emotion to a cat, deeming it anthropomorphic.

Annie knew better. And even though she was going to have to race to reach the ferry on time, she scooped up the sleek, taut-muscled feline and murmured, "I'm sorry, love. I know you've been ignored. I know just how you feel—and I'll understand if you make a report to the SPCA. Come on, now"—and she nuzzled her cheek against her pet's neck— "lighten up."

Agatha was, gradually, calmed and appeased, and grudgingly appreciative of a tasteful serving of salmon.

As a result of that essential interlude, however, Ben Parotti's ferry was giving its final whistle, indicating impending departure, when Annie roared aboard, the last car to make it. Simultaneously, the storm struck, the first large drops pelting the Volvo's windshield. Annie gave a whoosh of relief and switched off the ignition. Ben, sensibly clad in a bright yellow slicker, leaned out of his high cabin to yell, "Annie. Hey, Annie!"

Annie grabbed her umbrella (no Broward's Rock inhabitant ever traveled without one), slipped out of the car, and struggled against the wind and rain to the ladder at the base of the tower. She peered up anxiously. Ben was a fanatic

159

about his schedule. What could possibly impel him to delay the ferry's departure to talk to her?

He bent over the railing, his grizzled, leprechaun face both irritated and impatient, his eyes narrowed against the force of the wind. "Listen here, why're those damfool women out in Max's speedboat in this kind of weather?"

It would not be wrong to say that Annie felt a distinct sinking sensation, though the ferry rocked sturdily beneath her.

Ben's finger stabbed the air. "You'd think any man would know better than to let damfool women out in a boat like that, even in good weather. But how could we tell his mother she couldn't take it?" Ben was grumpy, anti-establishment, always wore tobacco-juice-stained coveralls, but he had a corner on some of the most thriving markets in town, his combination beer hall and bait shop, the ferry, and the only covered boat slips on the island.

"Laurel's out in this?" Annie cried, and she gestured at the driving rain and at the white caps glittering atop the choppy waves of the sound. Laurel and Ophelia must have driven across the island like demons, too.

"She and that damfool woman in a turban. Took the boat out about five minutes ago. You tell Max I think he's a damfool, too." Parotti punctuated his disgust with a piercing shrill of the whistle, and the ferry lurched away from the dock.

Annie was drenched by the time she reached her car. She'd planned to marshal her thoughts for her upcoming attack on Posey. Instead, she gripped the steering wheel and stared grimly out at the rough water. Where the *hell* were Laurel and Ophelia, and what did they think they were doing?

Barbie sounded regretful. "You'll just have to hang on, Annie. He's on long distance."

Static crackled. "Tell him I'm on a short fuse—and I'm about to drown."

"About to town?" Barbie yelled. "It's hard to hear you." Why do people always yell when they can't hear you?

The first phone Annie had found was outdoors, of course,

and her umbrella was more a sop to convention than a protection. Her cold, wet skirt clung to her legs like plastic wrap; she began to shiver.

Five moisture-laden minutes crawled soddenly by before Max came on the line.

"Hey, Annie, I can't talk long. It looks like Betsy Raines is missing for sure. She wasn't on the flight to Atlanta this morning, and I just talked to a maid at the hotel. Said the last time she saw the woman in 1113 was about noon Thursday. Nobody's seen her since. The bed was just used the first night, but all her luggage is there, except the maid remembered she was carrying an overnight case."

Annie tried to assimilate this unexpected news and keep her teeth from chattering. What a hell of a time for Laurel to cause trouble!

"Max, I—"

"So I've got to—"

"Max, wait! Your mother. Laurel. She's out in the speedboat. Now. Out on the sound somewhere. She and Ophelia."

A moment's pause. "Isn't it raining?"

"Raining! My God, it's a deluge. I'm standing at an outdoor phone, and I'm wetter than a damn duck. Yes, it's raining."

"Well, I guess they'll get wet. Listen, I've got another call—"

"Max, Max, aren't you going to do anything? Send out help? Look for them?" A sudden gust pulled the umbrella ribs straight up. Annie felt like a bucket of cold water had been dumped over her head.

Max, who, of course, was sitting snugly in the warm and dry environs of Confidential Commissions, chuckled. Annie thought it quite the most odious sound she'd ever heard. "Annie, honey, relax. Laurel can take care of herself. She's regatta class. She doesn't mind a little rain."

On that, Annie hung up.

She was still fuming as she tried to do something about her appearance in the basement women's room of the county courthouse. Part of her distress sprang from a welling uneasiness. How could Max not be worried? Didn't that indicate that her husband of—she drummed her fingers—her husband of not quite two days was not really in touch with reality? She tried not to think how spacey his mother was. It wasn't profitable to think along those lines. Moreover, at the moment, she could only cope with so much stress. She sighed and looked without pleasure in the discolored mirror. Not that she was vain. But it was hard enough to deal with Brice Posey without looking like a leftover extra from *Les Miserables*.

Still shivering, she gave her lank hair one final swipe. God, she looked like a cross between Celia Montfort in *The First Deadly Sin* and Claudia, that charming baby blood-sucker in *Interview with a Vampire*. Maybe she'd scare Posey to death.

Cheered at the thought, she fished in her purse, found her small notebook and flipped it open.

Five minutes later, she surveyed her list with satis-faction.

EVIDENCE:

1. Penrick suffered a contusion on the back of his head.
2. There was nothing upon which he could have struck his head if he were standing in the center of the living room when stabbed, and there is no indication the body was moved after death.
3. Pine needles are present on the rug where his body was found.
4. There are NO pine needles elsewhere on the rug or, indeed, anywhere in the living room.
5. The police laboratory reports pine needles adhering to Penrick's clothing. (Posey might not be happy at Billy Cameron having revealed this information, but he couldn't dispute it.)

CONCLUSIONS:

1. Penrick was rendered unconscious prior to his death. Otherwise (if stabbed where found, and lividity indicates this is so), he wouldn't have suffered a contusion on the back of his head.
2. Penrick's unconscious body must have lain on a carpet of pine needles.

3. Penrick was transported to Mrs. Jones's cabin and then stabbed with the sword which occupies a prominent place in her living room.
4. This method of murder indicates prior planning, so the selection of Mrs. Jones's living room as the murder site is obviously part of a plan to implicate Mrs. Jones.
5. This information indicates indisputably (surely an attractive word to Brice Posey) that Penrick's murderer must have observed the disagreement between Mrs. Jones and Penrick on Saturday morning.
6. Therefore, the conclusion is inescapable that the following must be seriously considered as suspects in his demise: All residents of Nightingale Courts and any others in its vicinity about 8 A.M. Saturday.

Annie paced the small anteroom of the women's lounge. This next part was tricky. She didn't want to end up in the county jail for housebreaking, but how, without indicating her own forage through Jesse's cabin, could she successfully sic Posey on to those very interesting folders in Jesse's pine desk?

"Oh, oh, oh," she said aloud, and practically broke into a tap dance. Of course, of course. Quickly she scrawled the final lines.

OBVIOUS LINES OF INVESTIGATION:

1. An immediate search of Penrick's papers should be instituted by authorities to garner more information about the dead man's activities and to look for possible motives for murder.

Even though Posey didn't like her, how would he be able to resist that pompous passage?

2. Penrick's relationships with all the residents of Nightingale Courts must be explored.
3. A door-to-door canvass should be instituted along the inlet to see if residents have any information about Penrick or his activities. (He was observed on Wednesday night returning to the Courts in his boat while looking very pleased in an unpleasant way.)

Annie gripped the notebook like a lance and hurried out the door. Annie Laurance-Darling off to war! But she did wish her shoes would stop squishing as she walked.

"God, was it that much?" Max whistled.

"That's what Hagerty said. And it was damned hard to get it out of him—until I explained why I was calling." Buddy shoved a hand through tousled brown curls. "You know how bankers are."

Max did indeed. Hardly any banker would enjoy divulging that he'd loaded a customer's attaché case with $220,000 in unmarked twenty-dollar bills.

"He said he'd told her it was a big risk, taking cash. He wanted her at least to put the money in a cashier's check." Alan looked miserable. "I told her, too, 'cause I knew it was a lot. She just laughed. Jesus, do you think she got hijacked?"

"I don't know. But we better get somebody to check and see if her attaché case is in that hotel room."

"Not here?" Annie never thought the news that Brice Willard Posey was unavailable would strike such dismay in her heart.

"The circuit solicitor is at present actively engaged in an ongoing murder investigation on behalf of all residents of the county." The hatchet-faced secretary was leathery skinned and adenoidal, but she spoke in a ringing tone that sounded suspiciously like the intro at a campaign contributors' dinner.

"That's why I need to talk to him," Annie said insistently.

The secretary pushed rimless glasses higher on a beaked nose. "Are you a member of the press?"

Annie got the point. She pulled her notebook out of her purse, leaned against the desk with one hip, and said breezily, "Right. *Island Gazette*. Beverly Gray, at your service."

As she figured, old horseface had never thrilled to Clair Blank's stirring stories about Beverly Gray, who met mystery everywhere from the college campus to the Orient. Horseface had probably arrived full-blown, rimless glasses intact, as a forty-year-old virgin.

"Of course, Miss Gray." She picked up a mimeographed sheet from a stack on the corner of her desk. "The circuit solicitor, as always, attempts to keep the people's representatives *fully* informed of his efforts on behalf of the citizens of this county. The telephone number at the bottom of the page will provide hourly updates as further information is received." She concluded with a toothy smile that rivaled the shark of *Jaws* for awesome display of dentures.

Annie smiled in kind. "Thanks so much. But I do love to talk to Mr. Posey in person. He adds so *much* to a story. Do you have any idea when he'll return?"

"Oh, I just can't say. I believe he's gone to the scene of the crime and may be out there for hours. Despite the inclement weather."

"That's very brave of him," Annie murmured.

There was an instant of suspicion in the reptilian eyes, but Annie bore it with choirboy innocence. (Anyone reading Joseph Wambaugh would know just what a multitude of sins that description could cover.)

"If you want to leave the name of your paper, I will give him the message when he gets in."

Annie decided not to push her luck, though she was tempted to provide the number of Death on Demand.

"That's all right. I'm going to the scene of the crime myself. I'll find him there."

Out in the hall, she glanced down at the mimeographed sheet. Though why Posey would be back in Ingrid's cabin—

Stark words leapt from the page:

. . . *nude body of a middle-aged, unidentified woman discovered early Monday floating in a lagoon in the Savannah National Wildlife Refuge* . . .

Oh, my God! The Savannah National Wildlife Refuge— but that was on the mainland, halfway between the island and Savannah—how could it be?—Henny had been so sure that Ingrid had been kidnapped—and now a body—the Refuge—

Annie plunged down the hall for the stairs.

* * *

The whirling red light atop a sheriff's car cast a warning glow despite the thick grey curtain of rain. Annie turned the Volvo off Highway 17 at the entrance to the Refuge, which was blocked by two sheriff's cars. A slicker-clad deputy waving a lantern struggled toward her. Beyond the barrier of cars, a single-lane dirt road snaked into the river-bottom hardwood swampland. By now, it would be a wallow of mud, navigable only by four-wheel-drive vehicles.

The full force of the storm struck Annie as she climbed out of the Volvo. Before she had been wet; now she was pummeled by wind and rain. Her shoes fell immediate casualties to the sucking mud.

"Crime Scene!" the deputy yelled. "Refuge closed."

She hadn't come this far to leave Ingrid alone in this hell of water and wind. "I've come to identify the body." An enormous rumble of thunder drowned out her words. "The body," she screamed. "Identify it!"

It seemed forever that she struggled behind the deputy through foot-dragging mud. She realized, with a thinking part of her mind, that it wasn't really far. Six hundred yards, perhaps. Barely into the Refuge. They bent against the wind and the pelting rain, exposed on the high road bounded on both sides by rush and cattail-rimmed bayous. They came around a curve. A second blur of light, white lights this time, marked a cluster of men, all slicker-clad, at a spot midway down the bank to the water.

Struggling down the bank, bristly cordgrass plucking at her bare legs, Annie glimpsed a puffy, greyish hand—or what was left of it. A deputy moved, and she saw the body.

No nightmare ever compared with this hideous reality, this swollen, bare, deteriorating flesh.

Annie gave a low moan and struggled not to faint. The deputy turned back and reached out to give her support.

The bloated face was beyond knowing, nibbled upon by swamp creatures, scraped against the rooted bottom, but Annie's gaze fastened on an earlobe and the large silver hoop earring.

"Oh, God, it isn't Ingrid. It *isn't.*" Ingrid didn't have pierced ears.

Then Annie covered her face with hands and cried. Life should never end like this.

Never, never, never.

FOURTEEN

A hot shower and clean clothes, a cheerful cotton dress in peach with periwinkle-blue seashells, helped some. But not enough. Not nearly enough. Max took one look at her face as she walked into his office and he dropped his legal pad, said quickly into the telephone, "Call you right back, Henny," hung up, and hurried around the massive desk to take her into his arms.

Despite the best of intentions, she began to cry. "Oh, Max, Max, it was so awful. Like refuse thrown away. Just thrown away. And they don't even know who she is!"

He sorted it out finally. "A body—but not Ingrid."

She scrubbed at her face with his handkerchief, gulped for air, and said gratefully, "No. They don't know who she is—but Max, it was—"

"Don't think about it," he ordered.

She wished her mind would obey. She didn't want to think about it, but would she ever forget it? She squeezed her eyes shut and nestled into his arms.

Max gently massaged the taut muscles at the back of her neck. "Annie, you can't do anything about the woman in the Refuge. I'm awfully sorry you thought it might be Ingrid and saw her, but it won't help you or her to keep thinking about it. And we have plenty to worry about here on the island. Ingrid's still missing and now it looks like something's happened to Betsy Raines in San Francisco."

She opened her eyes and heard the latest news on Betsy with a feeling of growing horror. What was happening to residents of this lovely pocket of the Low Country? An unknown woman dead, Ingrid missing, Jesse murdered, and now Betsy unaccounted for in distant San Francisco.

Max's phone rang. He shot it a worried glance, but stayed close to Annie.

In a moment, Barbie poked her head in his office. "San Francisco P.D. on the line, Max."

"Go ahead, Max," Annie urged, "I'll be all right." She knew her smile was wan, but she nodded decisively.

Max squeezed her shoulder. "Sure?"

"You work on Betsy. I'll concentrate on Ingrid."

"All right." He turned for the phone, but took time to scoop up a sheaf of printouts. "Here's all the stuff on the Courts residents. Maybe you'll find something in there."

She took them gratefully. The printed words would be a barrier of sorts between her thoughts and the memory of the rain-riven bayou and that bloated heap of flesh that had once been a woman.

Carrying the papers into the front office, Annie paused by Barbie's desk.

The secretary looked up, her eyes wide. "Did Max tell you—Mrs. Raines is missing and she had $220,000 with her. Her daughter's called five times and Alan's going crazy. He thinks maybe he should fly out to California and help look for her."

"He can't do more than the police," Annie said. But she felt sorry for Alan. She knew just how he felt. She wanted so desperately to find Ingrid. Well, she'd better keep after it, now that Max was diverted into the long distance inquiry on Betsy. She clutched the printouts tightly. Maybe there would be something in them, some fact that would catch her eye and lead them to Ingrid.

She settled in a comfortable wingback chair and welcomed a cup of coffee from Barbie.

She began to read, and arched an eyebrow in surprise.

Jesse Penrick had a solid work record. Somehow, Annie hadn't expected this. He'd logged in sixteen years at Harbester Marine Salvage in New Orleans and nine years at a local marine store on Broward's Rock. (Owned by Ben Parotti, of course. Annie was beginning to have an appreciation that Harley Jenkins III wasn't the only successful entrepreneur on the island.) According to Oscar Harbester, Jesse was damn bright with machinery ("The old sourpuss could fix anything!"), but ill-natured, hostile, and vindictive. "Don't ever get crossways with Jesse," a coworker on the island declared. "He was a nutty son of a bitch. Every damn tool had to be exactly in its place, not a quarter inch out of alignment."

Annie underlined that comment. Here was corroboration of Jesse's passion for order, and she intended to make sure it didn't escape the attention of the circuit solicitor, along with the list of evidence and conclusions she'd composed in the basement women's room of the county courthouse. But when would she ever have a chance to present her list to Posey?

The front door to Confidential Commissions burst open and Henny shot inside. She shook a huge black umbrella, then furled it and stalked toward Annie.

"What's all this about Betsy?" She stood with her hands on the umbrella crook and with her head cocked to one side. Beneath her rain cap, only a fringe of fluffy hair was exposed. As Annie told what she knew, Henny paced, like an aging bird, tapping the floor with the umbrella point and frowning acerbically.

Despite her rapid-fire report, Annie was mentally skimming her file of fictional detectives. Something about Henny reminded her of a small, dusty-brown sparrow. Oh, of course!

She paused in her description of the hotel maid's actions and asked, "Inspector Cockrill?"

Henny flashed a brief smile of commendation, but motioned for Annie to continue. As she concluded, "Cockie" fastened bright, birdlike eyes on Annie and exclaimed, "There's more to this than meets the eye—and I am *not* persuaded that there is no connection between Betsy's disappearance and this flood of criminal activity which the island has suffered since Saturday."

Annie sorted out the negatives. "You mean you think Jesse's murder and Ingrid's disappearance and the problem with Betsy are related?"

"I certainly do."

"Oh, Henny, that's absurd. Why, Ingrid barely knew

Betsy, and Betsy disappeared in San Francisco." She suddenly felt a sharp disappointment in Henny. Usually, Henny's mind worked as well as those of some of her fictional favorites, say, John Appleby or Inspector Ghote. But she obviously was way off base with this preposterous linkage.

Henny drew herself up. "I have only one idea—to preserve truth." Wheeling, she charged back into the rain.

Annie sighed and picked up the printouts.

She scanned the rest of the information on Jesse. Sixty-four. No record of marriage. Dropped out of high school at sixteen. Shipped out of New Orleans as a wiper on a freighter. Joined the Navy in 1939. Honorable discharge as Seaman First Class in 1946. Effects found on body: wristwatch but no other jewelry, except for wedding ring on chain around neck. Billfold containing Social Security card, driver's license, membership in Adult Film Club of Savannah, one ten, two fives, three ones. Clothing: navy blue turtleneck cotton sweater, blue denim pants, tank-top white cotton undershirt, white cotton boxer shorts. Sneakers and worn white socks found beside body. (Why, for God's sake?) Shirt and undershirt bloodstained with knife rents. Billfold in hip pocket. Front pant pockets empty and only partially elongated, indicating a possibility they had been searched.

Once again that elusive hint of something small, something missing, something the murderer desperately sought.

Annie thoughtfully smoothed the sheet. So many unanswered questions. She sighed and looked at the next printout.

Tom Smith. Resident of Broward's Rock since 1978. Miniaturist. Sells from his house and at flea markets. No advertising, word of mouth. Drinks two beers every Saturday night at Ben Parotti's Bar and Bait Shop. Responds when greeted. Never initiates conversations. Never voices opinions. Will talk about football. No known friends.

Max had marked a vigorous check by a series of sentences:

No bank account.

No insurance.

No driver's license. (No car. Travels by bicycle or bus.)

Pays bills by money order.

In rental application listed Los Angeles address. No record of a Tom Smith ever having lived at the address.

Max had circled his final comment in bright red:

The invisible man.

What else, Annie thought, could be expected of a man with a past that had to stay hidden? It shouldn't take even Posey long to trace the persons listed in that article on missing activists. Then they would know the truth about Tom Smith.

But would that truth lead them to Ingrid?

Barbie opened Max's door. His irritated voice boomed out: "*Why* can't you open the attaché case?"

In a moment, he strode into the anteroom, shoving a hand through his thick blond hair. He dropped into the chair beside her, his usually good-natured face twisted in a scowl. "Red tape. For God's sake, here we've got a woman missing, and the idiot hotel won't even open a piece of luggage without a damn court order. I wonder if they'd insist on an order from the fire marshal before they'd use a hose on a flame!"

The phone rang, and he popped up again. Annie wasn't sorry to see him go. Determinedly, she concentrated on her own quest.

OPHELIA BAXTER. A Gemini. Forty-six. Born in Cucamonga, California. Two years of college in Long Beach. Worked as flight attendant on local airline until fired for overweight. Married three times, to a fireman, a Zen motorcyclist, and a wood carver. A waitress at a health food store. As a result of a mystic experience in 1978 (a choir of angels humming Om in ragtime), she set out to find an untrammeled center for occult visitation.

Annie grinned. Both the staid, moneyed residents of the Broward's Rock resort area and the down-to-earth natives would be astounded at that assessment of their island. They would agree Broward's Rock was lovely, idyllic, and unspoiled. But an "untrammeled center for occult visitation"?

As she continued to read the printout, however, Annie decided there might be more to Ophelia's choice than geographic and spiritual location.

"All I know is," explained James Madison, who had served as chauffeur to a wealthy reclusive widow, "Mrs. Simpson got this idea voices were talking to her—and they made her real nervous. Then she met this lady out in Colorado at some kind of mystic place, and she convinced Mrs. Simpson she was on a wavelength with some star out in the Milky Way. Mrs. Simpson hired Mrs. Baxter to be her companion, and she lived with us until Mrs. Simpson died a couple of years ago."

A nice bequest relieved Ophelia of concern for mundane earthly expenses, allowing her to move into Nightingale Courts and devote herself to crystal communcations without charge.

The chauffeur's opinion of Ophelia Baxter: "A Looney Tune, but a nice lady and real sweet to Mrs. Simpson. Made her feel a lot better about the voices. She convinced Mrs. Simpson that when the voices said mean things, it was just a code. Ophelia translated the voices' messages, made them real cheerful, so Mrs. Simpson was a lot happier those last couple of years."

Which was, Annie decided, not socially harmful. Still, was it really all right for Laurel to hobnob with someone who actually believed all this New Age hogwash? (Annie wasn't sure whether Laurel was actually a devotee of the occult or merely indulging herself in the most entertaining—and delicately rebellious—facet of the late twentieth century. There was a glint of amusement in Laurel's spacey blue eyes that didn't quite jibe with the utter seriousness of the true believers. In fact, Annie felt unhappily certain that you could *never* be sure of *anything* with Laurel.)

Ophelia was an active member of the Audubon Society and during the last Christmas bird count (the 24th Annual) had infuriated the leader of her group by making bird whistles to a ruby-throated hummingbird which she insisted was her great-great-grandmother, Lavinia Fitch of

Philadelphia. Ophelia was a volunteer at the island's animal refuge, where she communed with the cats, all of whom, according to her, had in past lives been humans. (No one believed her assertion that the large tortoise shell with luxuriant whiskers was formerly Teddy Roosevelt, but he was adopted by an island fan of T.R.'s, Eugene Ferramond, who reported, almost in awe, that Teddy, the cat, was especially fond of fried chicken at *breakfast*, a trait he shared in common with the twenty-sixth president.)

Annie sniffed at that. What cat wouldn't like fried chicken for breakfast?

But Ophelia's efforts at the animal refuge emphasized her fondness for cats. And her own cat had been poisoned, Ophelia believed, by Jesse Penrick.

Annie wriggled uncomfortably and wondered where Max's mother was at this moment. Lord, it was hours ago that she and Ophelia had taken out the speedboat. Where were they? Still out? And why didn't Max have sense enough to be worried, too? She looked toward the front windows. Rain streamed against the plate glass. But if Max wasn't concerned, it wasn't her place to sound an alarm.

"Annie, want some more coffee?" Barbie asked.

Coffee. Her stomach rumbled. Abruptly, Annie realized she was famished. She glanced at her watch. Three o'clock. No wonder. She'd missed lunch.

"We missed lunch," Annie exclaimed.

Barbie looked at her in disbelief. "Miss lunch? We *never* miss lunch. Max had just finished eating when you called from Beaufort. Do you mean you haven't had a bite?" Barbie was a thirtyish blonde with an *ample* figure, who spent her spare time at Confidential Commissions clipping recipes from *Southern Living* and listening to George Jones, Hank Williams Jr., and Randy Travis. She immediately rose to the challenge. "Don't worry. There's lots left," and she hurried into the room that held the small refrigerator, microwave, and coffee apparatus. Her voice wafted back to Annie. "Chicken scallopini with peppers and potato-broccoli vinaigrette. I can heat it up in the microwave. And would you like a glass of Chablis?"

Annie cast a bemused glance toward Max's open door. Did he eat that kind of lunch every day? It scarcely seemed American. And who cooked it? Barbie?

But it all smelled so appetizing. Max might be on to a good thing. She was just finishing when Barbie caroled, "Phone for you, Annie."

"I hate snakes—real snakes and human snakes."

There was an odd twist to this accent. Annie couldn't quite place it. Obviously, it was English mastered as a first language, and yet there was a Latin rhythm to it.

"I'm furious. Everyone is trying to thwart me. But I intend to prevail. At least, thank God, I didn't have to take an airplane to get to Beaufort!"

Annie made the connection. Captain José Maria Carvalho Santos da Silva, of Brazil, who hates airplanes, snakes, and women in pants. Henny.

"Why are you in Beaufort?"

"I'm at the morgue. Waiting for clearance to see that woman they found in the Refuge—Annie, why didn't you tell me she had red hair?"

The hideous picture flashed in Annie's mind. She drew in a breath. "Oh God, Henny, how could anyone tell?" The hair, dark from its immersion in water, had been plastered close to the battered skull. At the morgue, they must have dried it, which created other images she didn't want to pursue.

"Red hair. For God's sake, didn't you even think of Betsy?"

Gratefully, Annie supplanted her grim pictures with a memory of Betsy at a Fourth of July Low Country Cookout, her bright hair glistening in the sunlight, looking up and laughing as she talked to Alan beside the pool at the Palmetto House.

Annie felt her patience eroding. "Henny, Betsy's in California. Three thousand miles from here."

The Brazilian accent fell away. "I hope so, Annie. I hope so." A pause. "I'll soon be able to tell you."

Annie replaced the telephone with an exasperated head shake. Henny was going to regret this foray. Carrying her dishes to the kitchen area, Annie rinsed them and hurried back to her chair and the printouts.

MAVIS BEESON. Twenty-one. Married to Henry Clark Beeson of Chastain after graduating from high school.

Kevin born two years later. Neighbor in Chastain, Emily Kemp, said she heard screams from the Beeson house several times, but didn't call police. Not sure, and some people yell a lot. Saw Mavis twice with bruised face. Mavis had been gone since last summer. Henry wouldn't talk about her, but had been picked up for DWI twice. The Beeson family powerful in town, his father a local lawyer. Mavis from a divorced family, her mother a secretary at local junior high.

Annie remembered the slender blonde holding her little boy high in the air as he laughed down at her.

Maybe Emily Kemp would testify at a divorce and custody hearing. Annie underlined her name and added the printout to those she'd read.

Max's voice boomed from his office. "So what harm will it do to let us know about the contents of the attaché case?"

Annie glimpsed Max through his open door. She did love to see Max work. Although he approached any labor with the enthusiasm of a cat plunging into water, it really did show him off at his best. As he hunched over the desk, he was marvelously attractive, dark blue eyes flashing, jaw firm, voice steady. He was too wholesome-looking with his thick blond hair, bright eyes, and regular features to be Humphrey Bogartish. Then she had it: Dick Powell in *Murder My Sweet*.

Unaware of her scrutiny, her beloved barked in a rapid staccato (Sergeant Cribb couldn't have done it any better), "We're investigating Mrs. Raines's disappearance here, too, and that's a critical piece of evidence."

Annie smiled fondly. Really, she must make it a point, subtly, to encourage Max to work. Ah, the responsibilities of a wife!

And, thinking of work—

BILLY JOHN CAMERON. Twenty-six. Bachelor. Lives at No. 5, 316 Spanish Alley Road. Eldest of seven children. Native of Beaufort. All-state wrestler, heavyweight class; fullback, high school football team; president, student council; Eagle Scout.

High school coach: "Super athlete, team leader. And a hell of a nice boy."

Two years at Armstrong State College, majoring in law enforcement. Faculty adviser: "Serious student. Steady. Dependable. Not the brightest, but he gave it all he had." Joined Broward's Rock police department 1982.

Scuba diver, triathlete, hunter.

Owner of island sporting goods store: "An all-around sportsman, tough, capable, determined."

And, Annie wondered, a murderer?

Billy was big enough, strong enough. Why had it taken him so long to respond to the call from the checkpoint guard? But then, why not? When off duty, his time was his own. He could have been out for a midnight swim or a late walk along the shuttered main street. Spanish Alley Road was a narrow, unpaved street behind the bowling alley. An old antebellum house had been divided into apartments. It would be about a mile and a half walk along a dusty road to Nightingale Courts. If Billy wanted to avoid notice, he would walk rather than drive for his late night visits to Mavis. Was he there Saturday night?

Annie swiveled. Max was still on the phone. She understood his involvement with Betsy's disappearance and the consequent tie-up of the phone line at Confidential Commissions, but it was time for her to cast out a net, too.

The rain splashed unrelentingly against the front windows of Death on Demand. Inside, the bookstore had a greenish-grey tone, and the gloom made it a fit repository for tales of crime and woe. She passed the table stacked with Scott Turow's *Presumed Innocent*—could you believe a first novel?—and hurried down the central aisle, noting titles in passing: *The Moving Finger* by Agatha Christie, *The Spy Who Barked in the Night* by Marc Lovell, and *The Woman in the Moon* by Donald Lehmkuhl. Some of Ingrid's favorites.

Annie shrugged out of her raincoat and draped it, dripping, on a chair by the table nearest the coffee bar, then turned to face an accusatory stare from flaming amber eyes.

"Agatha, love, I'm sorry."

The cat's tail twitched. Once.

"Sweetie, don't be hostile." Annie reached out to pet the silky fur. She was able to yank her hand back just in time to avoid being bitten.

Agatha turned her head away, and her tail rippled like Blackbeard's whip. She could not have evinced her unhappiness any more clearly had she announced in ringing tones, "You've gone off again and left me for hours and hours. One piddly serving of salmon, hours ago, counts for nothing. I'm bored, hungry, and absolutely furious."

Annie put down the printouts she hadn't yet read on the coffee bar, then stepped behind it and bent down to open the refrigerator. It wasn't smart, of course, to let a cat bully you, but Agatha had a very strong personality, and the only way to get past this contretemps was to offer something especially tempting.

Cream?

Bologna?

Mince pie?

More salmon?

Annie knew Max would have several choice comments about what the contents of the refrigerator revealed about the mistress of Death on Demand and her probable cholesterol count. Agatha peered over the side of the counter. Working fast, Annie apportioned a small amount of each in Agatha's bowl and put it beside her furry friend atop the counter.

Agatha was pleased. She was as passionately fond of both mincemeat pie and salmon as her namesake was of Devonshire cream. Annie devoutly hoped the combination wouldn't result in a royal case of cat indigestion.

That important matter concluded, she measured Kona coffee into the pot, turned it on, then reached for the phone on the coffee bar. As the dark, delicious drops began to fall, she dialed.

"Police."

"Billy, this is Annie Laurance. Darling." She had almost managed her new surname in the same breath.

He didn't answer. She could picture him at his desk, his

pleasant face set, his large, powerful shoulders tensed, a massive hand locked tight around the receiver.

She saw no reason to pussyfoot around. "Billy, where were you Saturday night when your beeper went off?"

A heavy, taut silence.

She waited.

"Home." The word thudded onto the line like ice calving from a glacier.

"It took you too long to come." Her voice was almost regretful.

Again a silence. Finally, harshly, he challenged her. "Prove it." The line went dead.

Annie immediately looked up a number and dialed. And was relieved that she didn't get a busy signal.

"Hello." The voice was so young and vulnerable.

"Mavis, this is Annie Laurance. Darling."

"Yes, Mrs. Darling?" Not quite so frightened now.

Annie hated what she was about to do. Until she thought about Ingrid. She made her voice genial (*the better to eat you with, my dear*). "Mavis, what time did Billy leave Saturday night?"

Silence again, this time freighted with panic. "What do you mean?" Her thin voice wavered like a plucked string.

Annie understood that panic. If Mavis admitted Billy was there, it added to the weight of suspicion against her. If she denied it, she might lose an alibi. Worst of all, if he wasn't there, it must have occurred to Mavis to wonder if it was Billy who stabbed Jesse and abducted Ingrid.

"I'm trying to find out whether anyone was up and about late and might have seen Jesse—or someone with Jesse."

"I don't know. I wasn't up late."

"But Billy usually came on Saturday night, didn't he? Where was he this last Saturday night?"

"I don't know."

"But you'd told Billy that Jesse was blackmailing you? That you were paying him five dollars a week?"

A quick drawn breath and the receiver slammed into the cradle.

Annie slowly replaced her receiver, then pulled out her notebook from the stack of printouts. Leaning comfortably against the coffee bar, she flipped open the notebook, found a fresh page past the odd map she'd copied at Jesse's, and wrote:

1. When did Billy leave Mavis's cabin Saturday night?
2. If he was there when the beeper sounded and had been all evening, both of them are alibied.
3. If he had already left when the beeper sounded, did he have time to move Jesse's unconscious body to Ingrid's cabin and grab Ingrid before he showed up in the patrol car?
4. If he had already left when the beeper sounded, would Mavis have had time to move Penrick and abduct Ingrid?
5. Could Mavis and Billy have committed the crime together?
6. If Mavis committed the murder alone, would she act so nervous and uncertain about Billy?

It would depend upon just how wily and Machiavellian she was.

In any event, if either Billy or Mavis acted singly or in conjunction, there had been very little time to dispose of Ingrid.

So why hadn't Ingrid or her body been found by the expert and careful searchers?

It argued for another principal, someone with time and a deadly scheme that included Ingrid.

Why, for that matter, was Ingrid abducted at all?

That was obvious, Holmes would have snapped at Watson. Ingrid had quarreled with the dead man. When he was murdered in her cabin and Ingrid was nowhere to be found, it wasn't too surprising that the authorities' suspicions would rest on her. It was, of course, the murderer's great good luck that Brice Willard Posey was in charge of the investigation and that Chief Saulter (who knew Ingrid) was out of the country.

But that didn't increase the limited amount of time available to either Billy or Mavis.

Annie put the notebook down and reached for the

coffeepot. She glanced over the collection of white pottery mugs with their bright red inscriptions. Each mug was decorated with the name of a book famous in mystery fiction: *Ladies in Boxes* by Gelett Burgess, *Philo Gubb: Correspondence School Detective* by Ellis Parker Butler, *Poisonous Relations* by Joanna Cannan, *Laura* by Vera Caspary, *The Riddle of the Sands* by Erskine Childers, *The Gun in Daniel Webster's Bust* by Margaret Scherf, *Miss Pym Disposes* by Josephine Tey, and *The Penguin Pool Murder* by Stuart Palmer. Finally, with a wry smile, she lifted down *Suspects All* by Marco Page and filled it, the better to think with. Agatha, genial now, daintily licked a paw and observed.

The telephone rang, and Agatha shot from the coffee bar, streaking toward the fern and rattan chair enclave.

An English accent this time.

"Is this Roakes Common 3206?"

So Henny expected Annie to play Cousin Toby to Tessa Crichton. Anne Morice's feisty heroine frequently depended upon her agreeable cousin to serve as a bouncing board for ideas during an investigation.

"Toby here," Annie replied. Experience had taught her that cooperation would shorten the call and get her back to her papers.

"I can't *believe* I'm wrong." Yes, it had to be cocky Tessa. "It seemed so obvious that the body had to be Betsy's, when it turned out not to be Ingrid. And red-haired!" The last exclamation was accusatory.

Annie forebore to point out yet once again that Betsy was in San Francisco. No point in making Henny feel even worse.

"But there's no doubt about it. I mean, I saw her with my own eyes."

Annie shivered.

"Not that her best friend would have known her, if it had been Betsy. From her face. But it wasn't, because Betsy delivered Ruth by caesarean and this woman'd never borne a child. So apparently there's no connection. No connection at all. A wasted trip. Be back on the island as soon as possible."

Settled again at the table, Annie lifted up the next printout from her stack.

ALAN ELLSWORTH NICHOLS. Twenty-five. Bachelor. Native Flint, Michigan. Only child. Parents divorced when he was five, reared by mother, a secretary at an Oldsmobile dealership. Ran away from home at fifteen. Worked as a busboy in Dallas. Became friendly with café owner, Mrs. Bridget Wright. Completed GED for high school diploma. Two years at community college. Left Dallas for Florida. Worked at various beach resorts as lifeguard, arrived at Broward's Rock in 1985. Worked at Jolly Roger Beach Club, became manager in spring 1986. Became friendly with Elizabeth Raines, owner of the Piping Plover Gallery, joined gallery staff in fall 1986.

Mrs. Nichols: "Do you know where Alan is? Oh, I wish he would call me. No one ever really understood him. He's a sweet boy."

Mrs. Bridget Wright: "Alan Nichols? Sorry, I don't remember a waiter of that name. Oh, the young man I helped in school. I . . . was disappointed in him. I'd thought he intended to work up to manager. But young people are so fickle, aren't they?"

Cissy Womack, waitress: "Oh, Alan! He had the old lady wrapped around his finger. My God, she thought he was in love with her! No fool like an old fool. But he paid the piper for every penny, dancing with her, whispering in her ear—and he was too cute to waste himself on a wrinkled up old woman."

There were assorted comments from beach boys up and down the coast, some envious, some critical. Annie thought Max had gone a little overboard, but she did raise an eyebrow at the last tidbit.

Reba Casey, next door neighbor to Betsy Raines: "I don't care what my neighbors do, as long as they keep their dogs up and maintain their property. Betsy took good care of her home. Of course, we shared a common fence by our pools, so Jimmy and I couldn't help overhearing more than we wanted to, sometimes. But I didn't see any harm in it. After all, the boy is single and Betsy's widowed. Why not?"

No wonder Alan wore his finest to the airport.

But it didn't have a thing to do with Jesse Penrick. And even if Jesse at one time or another had spotted Betsy and Alan at his cabin, why should they care? As Reba Casey said, Why not?

Annie dropped Alan's bio and picked up the next.

DUANE ALBERT WEBB. Sixty-one. Native Biloxi, Mississippi. U.S. Army, 1943–46. Honorable discharge as master sergeant. Wounded at Battle of the Bulge. Purple Heart. Bronze Star with two oak-leaf clusters. B.A. in English, University of Mississippi, 1950. M. to Mary Catharine Carew, June 12, 1950. D., Sheila, b. 1953. Reporter, *Nashville Tennessean*, 1950–54; Dallas Bureau Associated Press, 1954–60; City Editor, *Chastain Courier*, 1960–81.

She skimmed the rest of it. Nothing new. The car wreck. His wife dead. His daughter dead. His conviction. Four years for manslaughter. Served one year. His retirement to Broward's Rock.

Bob Tibbey, publisher, Chastain Courier: "Super guy, if he was your friend. Tongue like a battering ram. Hates phonies, stuffed shirts, self-important people. A big softie underneath. Demanding boss, but his reporters respected him. He worked harder than anyone I've ever known. Too damn bad about the accident. He always drank a lot, but it never caught up with him. Till then."

Hal O'Neill, city hall reporter, Chastain Courier: "He could spot a hole in a story quicker than anybody I ever knew. And there was only one way to do it—the right way. Loved to play poker and get drunk. We were all sorry as hell."

Duane Webb. Super smart. Super critical. A fiery city editor with an arrogant, brash, give-'em-hell attitude. He'd always been half mad. Now that anger was turned on himself. And there was more than enough to spare for creeps like Jesse Penrick. But would Duane hurt Ingrid, who had been kind to him?

How angry—and how twisted by anger—was he?

Agatha leapt back atop the coffee bar and waited expectantly. Obediently, Annie stroked the silky fur.

Agatha turned twice in a tight circle, then settled on the stack of printouts, her throat quivering with a rumbly purr.

Annie absently scratched behind an ear and eased the stack from beneath Agatha to retrieve the last printout. The cat's ears flattened, but she decided not to protest.

ADELE MORNAY PRESCOTT. Fifty-eight. Native of Charleston. Only daughter of a long-time Charleston family, whose wealth was destroyed in the Civil War. Grew up in genteel poverty, but with great emphasis on background and class. Attended Sweet Briar. In 1951, m. John Grant Prescott, a hustler from New Jersey who made a fortune in garbage disposal.

"Not too high toney," Annie observed to Agatha, who was studying one pink pad with unblinking intensity. "But money's money—and it takes a lot to buy mansions."

That's what Adele and John had done, taking over Hounds Hill, a lovely antebellum mansion on the Cooper River. For eighteen years, Adele had reigned over the refurbishment of the lovely home and enjoyed social prominence.

Annie wondered who had married whom for what. Adele for money, John Prescott for social advancement?

When and why had the marriage soured, or had it never been a love match at all?

Moses Quentin, butler at Hounds Hill: "Mrs. Adele, she always had her own way, and all she ever thought about was antiques and buying them. She traveled everywhere, looking."

Susan Prescott, the second wife: "I never knew her, but everyone said she was so cold. And the older she got, the less she ever thought about how she looked. She spent all her time with her social secretary, Naomi, and she never had any time for John. He won't say much about her, but I know he wanted children, and she never would. He's just crazy about the kids. John III is seven now and Marie is three."

Beryl Ford, homeowner, Broward's Rock Island: "Adele is a jewel. I never have to worry when I go off to Cannes for a few months. She'll move in and take care of my things just like they were her own. Even though she looks like a yard worker, I don't know of anyone else I'd trust my house to."

The phone rang.

"Death on Demand."

"Annie, bad news about Betsy."

Oh, poor Max. Henny must have worried him, too. "Oh, Max, it's *not* Betsy. The woman'd never had any children and Betsy'd had a caesarean."

The silence on his end was blank. "What woman?"

"The body in the Wildlife Refuge."

"What's that got to do with Betsy?"

They sorted it out finally, but Max was still a little bemused. "Betsy's missing in San Francisco," he said finally. "And that's why I called. It looks like it has to do with the money. Her attaché case, in her hotel room. It's empty."

Two hundred twenty thousand dollars missing, as well as Betsy.

"Do they think she was robbed by a client?" Annie asked.

"A client, somebody she met in a bar, who knows? There are a lot of people in San Francisco, and so far they haven't connected her to anybody. Not a soul. The only person who remembers seeing her is the hotel maid." Max rustled some papers. "Yeah, here it is. Estrelita Muñoz was cleaning the west wing on Thursday. 'A lady came out of 1113, carrying an overnight bag. I wouldn't have remembered but she didn't see a room service tray right next to her room and she kind of tripped. I hurried to see if she was okay, and she just laughed and said she always had her head in the sky and she needed to pay more attention. I did her room next and it was real neat, the suitcases unpacked, the clothes hanging in the closet. That case everybody's asked about was on the desk, but it was closed. All I did was dust there and set it toward the back. I don't think anybody went in that room again, because the bed wasn't used when I opened it the next day. I told the desk, but she had a reservation through the week, so nobody did anything.'"

So Betsy Raines walked down a hotel hallway on Thursday and was not seen again. Had she walked into the mists of time along with Jimmy Hoffa?

Max sighed. "I called Ruth Jenson, told her. It wasn't any fun."

"I'm sorry, Max. But you've done everything you can. Did you call Billy?"

"Yes." A pause. "He sounded very uptight."

"I'm not surprised." She recounted her conversations with Billy and Mavis.

Max agreed that the young couple had plenty of reason to be nervous, and obviously they had to be high on any list of suspects. "Actually, Billy seemed glad to talk about something besides Jesse and Ingrid. He said he'd get right on the phone to the San Francisco cops. I'm afraid it really looks bad. He thinks her daughter's right; something's happened to Betsy."

Everybody seemed ready to focus their energies on Betsy, Annie realized after she hung up. So who was going to keep on worrying about Ingrid? Grimly, she turned back to her papers. Adele's printout lay beside her open notebook. Her glance moved across that odd map of Jesse's—then it froze. She reached out, touched an address, then scrambled for her phone book.

Beryl Ford lived at 926 Blue-Winged Warbler Way.

Annie scarcely breathed as she scanned her copy of Jesse's map. Yes, 926 Blue-Winged Warbler Way was listed. It was not circled.

She tapped her fingers thoughtfully against the wooden bar, then dialed the Ford number.

A maid answered.

Annie affected a British accent. "This is Maureen Smithers, secretary to her Ladyship Alexandra Ventnors, calling from London. May I speak to Mrs. Ford, please, on behalf of her ladyship."

Beryl Ford must have flown to the telephone. It took only a moment to remind her of a titled party she'd met on a yacht during her most recent visit to Cannes. (And, of course, how could Beryl be expected to remember everyone's name? But she certainly did recall her ladyship.)

From there, Annie trying hard to recall Lady Antonia Fraser's accent, it was smooth sailing.

"Her ladyship is considering the purchase of a home near yours on Broward's Rock, a residence at 924 Blue-Winged Warbler Way, and her ladyship would appreciate it so much if you could provide us with some particulars."

Beryl Ford was only too happy to recall everything she possibly could about the house, its vantage point on the sixteenth green, the dramatic entry with a cascading waterfall, and the stunning robbery that occurred two years ago.

"Of course, we hardly ever have break-ins here. It occurred when the Clintons were out of town. I *always* have a house sitter. It's just common sense. And when will Lady Alexandra be in the States?"

"Within a month or so. And you recommend hiring a house sitter. Oh, a Mrs. Prescott. And have other home-owners used her?"

Annie scrawled down four addresses.

216 Sandspur Lane
901 Spanish Bayonet
58 Sea Urchin Place
17 Ghost Crab Lane

And, after many protestations of extreme appreciation and a promise that Lady Alexandra would shortly be communicating with Mrs. Ford, Annie was able to sign off.

Parched, she gulped down the rest of her coffee, then dialed again.

Billy was downright agreeable, when her request appeared to have nothing whatsoever to do with Jesse, Ingrid, Mavis, or himself. This time she wrote down the addresses of eight homes that had been burglarized within the past five years and the dates of the robberies:

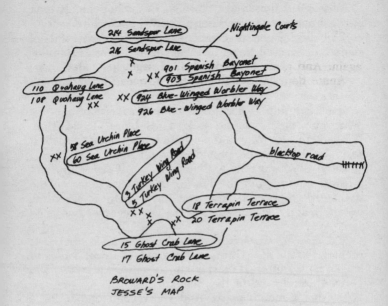

214 Sandspur Lane, May 6, 1982
903 Spanish Bayonet, September 13, 1983
60 Sea Urchin Place, November 9, 1984
110 Quahog Lane, February 8, 1985
3 Turkey Wing Road, June 8, 1985
18 Terrapin Terrace, January 2, 1986
924 Blue-Winged Warbler Way, October 3, 1986
15 Ghost Crab Lane, May 10, 1987

Annie picked up the map.

How extremely interesting that robberies occurred on the blocks where Adele had house sat.

To round it off, Annie made a few more calls. Soon her list was complete. Adele had stayed at a residence—on every block where a robbery later occurred.

No wonder Adele Prescott had so many, many lovely antiques—and paid Jesse such nice sums every month.

Had Jesse pressed for more money than Adele was willing to give?

Wait till Max saw this! Annie grabbed up her papers, slipped into her raincoat, and headed for the front door.

She was almost to Confidential Commissions when a deep bull-toned horn sounded in the harbor. And sounded again. And again, a clarion call of urgency.

Annie darted through the rain toward the harbor.

FIFTEEN

Max's crimson speedboat sliced through the choppy water. The horn now blared unceasingly.

Max caught up with Annie as she plunged down the stone steps to the docks.

"Something must have happened," Annie gasped. "Why else would she blow the horn?"

But Laurel, her wet hair sleek against her aristocratic head, appeared unhurt, and, as a matter of fact, joyously in command behind the wheel. She lifted one hand to wave, then cut the boat precipitously toward them.

Annie covered her eyes. A murmur of concern swept the watchers gathering above at the harbor's edge.

Max grabbed her elbow. "Regatta class," he said. "Never worry about Laurel."

As Laurel climbed out of the cockpit, Annie decided to take Max's advice. Although his mother was drenched, hair plastered to her head, her oatmeal-colored robe clinging, she looked stunning. Her beautiful eyes glistened like a Valkyrie en route to Valhalla. But she began to gesture, and she was clearly calling for help. Turning, she pointed toward the boat. Annie looked past Laurel and a wobbly, green-faced Ophelia at a blanket-wrapped figure slumped in the cockpit.

Billy Cameron stood beside the closed door to room 215 in Broward's Rock Municipal Hospital. "She's in protective custody. That's what Posey said to do, and that's what I'm doing."

Max was as tough as John J. Malone (but, of course, much better looking). "Ingrid has a right to talk to a lawyer."

"Fine. You go get a lawyer for her. But she's not going to talk to anybody else—and that means you people." Billy's glance swept the motley crew clotting the hallway.

"You aren't even trying to find out who abducted her," Annie said furiously.

Henny joined in, hands on her hips (Hildegarde Withers?). "Disgraceful. A miscarriage of justice. I want you to know, we aren't going to rest until Jesse Penrick's murderer *and* Ingrid's kidnapper—obviously one and the same insidious person—is apprehended."

Alan, who had joined the group at the harborside and followed them to the hospital, said pacifically, "At least Ingrid's okay. At least *she's* all right."

Ophelia, her arms crossed tightly over her ample abdomen, sneezed explosively.

"Gesundheit," Laurel blessed.

Annie stalked up to Billy. "I *have* to talk to Posey. I have all *kinds* of information about this case. He doesn't know the *half* of it."

Billy shrugged. "As far as Posey's concerned, this one's solved. He's busy investigating that new murder."

The door to room 215 opened, and Dr. Samuels stepped out. A barrage of questions met him.

Annie stood on tiptoe, flapping her hand. Dr. Samuels was a good customer, especially fond of obscure divine detectives such as Father Bredder, Sister Lucy, Soeur Angele, and the Reverend Joseph Colchester. "Doctor, is Ingrid all right?"

"Sure, sure." A big, burly, informal man (star fullback, The Citadel, Class of '56), Samuels delivered blunt opinions in a forceful, no-nonsense bark. "Tired. Woozy. Confused. Be fine tomorrow."

"What did she say happened?" Henny demanded.

"Wait a minute, wait a minute," Billy objected. "Any information the doctor has should be given to the police."

Samuels's bristly eyebrows drew down in a dark frown.

"My God, Billy, haven't you ever heard of doctor-patient confidentiality?"

Billy flushed.

"Fact of the matter," the doctor continued brusquely, "I didn't ask. Woman needs rest. We'll see how she feels in the morning."

"She'll be fine," a golden voice announced pleasantly.

Samuels eyed Laurel irritably, then with growing appreciation. (But, as Norma Gold would say . . .) Her wet gown was drying to her in a very flattering fashion.

"Fine and dandy," he boomed in agreement, "but for right now, she needs rest. Visitors prohibited." He started down the hall, but looked back twice at Laurel, who smiled winsomely.

Annie's eyes narrowed in thought, then she edged closer to Ingrid's door. Without warning, she leaned forward and shouted, "Ingrid, keep quiet till we get a lawyer! Don't worry, we'll take care of everything!"

Billy Cameron jumped like he'd been stung with a cattle prod. "Annie, stop that! If you don't, I'll throw her in jail right now." He glared at the hostile circle. "You people get out of here."

A nurse hurried toward them. "What's going on here? You'll have to be— Oh, hello, Mrs. Brawley, I didn't see you."

At her sudden change of tone, Annie remembered that Henny was not only director of Volunteer Services, she was on the hospital board.

"Hello, Iris," Henny replied. "I know, we mustn't disturb the patients. I'll take our group into the boardroom for a meeting." Gesturing for the others to follow, she led them to a private lounge in the east wing. In astonishingly short order, she had everyone disposed around a conference table and dinner ordered from the hospital cafeteria.

Max looked across the table at his mother. "Laurel, how did you and Ophelia find Ingrid?"

Henny held up a commanding hand. "Not until after dinner, Max. Then we'll attack our problem in logical order."

Dinner, when it came, was welcome, even if a little unimaginative—boiled whitefish, buttered carrots, spinach, and tapioca pudding. Alan eyed his plate unenthusiastically. Ophelia picked at her food.

As an orderly removed the plates and served fresh coffee (which couldn't compare to that at Death on Demand), Henny cleared her throat.

"One of our major tasks has been accomplished. Ingrid has been restored to us, thanks to Laurel and Ophelia." She nodded at them appreciatively. "However, our work is far from finished. Ingrid faces a murder charge!"

There was an aura of stateliness about Henny, a demeanor of calm and authority. Something about the droop of her eyelids reminded Annie— Oh yes, yes, of course. Commander George Gideon of Scotland Yard, without doubt.

"There is no need to be concerned," Laurel soothed. "Dear Ingrid will be fine. Ophelia says her aura is excellent—almost golden, which is the *very* best color— and all will be well." Her complacent smile enfolded them. "How can we question destiny, when it has been so richly fulfilled? Just as Ophelia predicted."

They all looked at Ophelia, a shapeless blob still shivering as she sipped at her coffee. The turbaned psychic managed a wan smile. "Moogwa assured me that we should find safe harbor, but I never dreamed it would be such a *bumpy* ride."

"Ophelia's never raced," Laurel observed in a tone of mild surprise.

"Moogwa?" Annie knew better than to ask, but she couldn't resist.

Laurel, of course, was delighted to explain. "My dear, the most *remarkable* celestial visitor. Not here physically, of course, but he speaks to us through Ophelia. She is such a wonderful channel. Moogwa—he lives on Alpha Centauri—is always *so* positive, absolutely an inspiration. He led us to Ingrid, just as we knew he would."

Alan whispered to Annie, "What the hell's she talking about?"

Henny forgot the heavy-lidded calm of Commander Gideon and rolled her snappy black eyes briefly heavenward. "Led you to her? Flares? A dotted line on the sound? Protoplasm marking the spot?"

Laurel wasn't fazed. Her patrician face patient, she smiled kindly. "Henny, my dear, it was nothing quite that direct. A more subtle guidance. But I understand your puzzlement. I know how *hard* it is to dismiss earth's shackles. I, too, was once bound to the commonplace, a prisoner of convention, my soul stifled."

Max was shaking his head and his dark blue eyes messaged, *Not on your life*, to Annie. She nodded.

Ophelia looked reproachfully at Henny, sniffled, and said, "Divine clues"—she paused to sneeze soppily—"must be interpreted."

"What divine clues?" Annie asked pragmatically.

Ophelia pressed her hands to her turban, which further reduced its shape. Already soggy, it resembled an ill-used soufflé. Laurel more gracefully waggled one hand in a vague gesture.

Henny wriggled. "That's fine. Don't worry about explaining divine guidance to us. I can understand how difficult that might be. Just tell us what you did."

Ophelia sneezed again. Laurel clasped her hands (the polish on her perfect nails glowed a Corinthian rose) in an attitude of sublime meditation.

Max gnawed on his lip to repress an indulgent smile, then said briskly, "From the time you took the speedboat, Ma. What happened?"

Ophelia clasped a hand to her substantial tummy and squeezed her eyes shut.

"Had our mission not been so serious," Laurel said demurely, "it would have been an *exciting* outing. I'd forgotten how a boat *thumps* when you drive directly into the waves."

Max's eyes widened. So much, Annie thought, for regatta class.

"Really, it was almost as delightful as skiing the Matterhorn in a whiteout," Laurel reported with a cheerful trill of laughter.

Ophelia shook her head miserably in remembrance.

"In any event, Moogwa had made it clear that dear Ingrid was a captive."

Henny rolled her eyes again. "Obviously, she was either a captive or dead," she muttered in disgust.

"I *kept* telling everyone she was alive," Ophelia complained pettishly.

Laurel patted her plump shoulder. "You did indeed, my dear. But they of little faith—"

"You took the boat out," Max prodded.

"We knew Ingrid was on water," Laurel said simply.

There was a moment's silence. Four pairs of eyes were on Laurel. (Ophelia was blowing her nose, lids clamped shut.)

"On water?" Annie asked finally.

Laurel nodded eagerly. "It was quite clear, from Moogwa's point of view. He told us"—here her voice dropped to a sepulchral monotone—"'Neither land nor sky/Up and down, by and by; Safely sheltered from the waves/In wise Phoenician ways.'"

Laurel looked at them brightly.

Alan tilted his head again toward Annie. "Is she crazy?" His whisper hung in the silence.

Laurel leaned across the table to pat his hand. "Of course, you have to have *experience*. It was quite clear, really. Think about it. Those dear Phoenicians, such *wonderful* sailors, they always put into a bay or inlet when a storm threatened. They never tried to ride storms out at sea, if they had *any* choice."

Ophelia massaged her temples. "I *kept* seeing skulls. Which would be a discouraging portent, but Moogwa emanated tides of warmth, reassuring me about Ingrid."

"Skull Creek?" Henny ventured.

Laurel beamed in approbation. "My dear, you may become one of *us*! Had you only been with us this morning! Because we did have a *little* difficulty in deciphering Moogwa, though it should have been obvious. But we went first to Skull Plantation—and that's on Broughton Creek—then we tried Skeleton Lagoon and I'm afraid we took the wrong channel and we were lost for a long time, but, finally, our search was crowned with success. We found Ingrid, adrift in a rowboat, far up Skull Creek."

Henny was too appalled at her inclusion in Laurel's select group to respond.

But Max frowned. "In a rowboat, Mother?"

"Do you mean she wasn't tied up?" Annie demanded.

Ophelia sneezed resoundingly. "Jesse's rowboat," she sniffled.

With Max's prodding and Henny's direct questions, Laurel managed to keep almost to the point, with only a few sojourns into other byways. (The necessity of listening to celestial speakers with an innocent heart, the mystical properties of crystal, and the kinship of mankind to dolphins . . .)

When Laurel had finished, Max leaned forward. "Mother, let's see if I've got it right. Ingrid was in Jesse's rowboat. She wasn't tied up. She had only one oar."

"My dear, what a succinct summing up." Laurel smiled admiringly at her worried son, and Annie wondered if she understood that Ingrid could be convicted of murder if a jury heard this.

"Mother," he appealed, "*what* did Ingrid say?"

Laurel's eyes widened. "Oh, my dear, Ophelia and I have long known that one must always let others share their thoughts in their own good time, as a flower unfolds when it is ready. But I must admit that in the delirium of our discovery, we so far forgot ourselves as to ask in great excitement what had transpired."

She folded her hands. Her smile was seraphic.

"So?" Henny demanded. "So? So?"

"Patience, as the great Moogwa reminds us, is the hallmark of civilization."

Enough. Annie exploded. "My God, what happened to Ingrid? Who took her? What in heaven's name was she doing in Jesse's boat?"

Laurel looked at her reproachfully. "Annie, my sweet, Ingrid I'm sure will share with us, when she is ready. But when she broke into tears at our questions, we knew the time was not yet. So, of course, we *urged* her to remain silent."

"Oh, God," Annie cried, "we have to talk to Ingrid!"

Annie wished she had on tennis shoes. Her white leather flats, though quite stylish, had a tendency to slip, even when jammed into the decorative open fretwork that a budget-conscious board had selected when modernizing the back of the hospital. And she knew that any well-dressed cat burglar would find her peach shirtwaist dress laughable. At least the rain had stopped, although, thankfully, the night was still overcast. She was grateful, too, that the fretwork wasn't as slippery as the chateau tiles Cary Grant traversed in *To Catch a Thief*. At that moment, however, an edge crumbled beneath her foot. She began to slip, flailed wildly, grabbed at a drainpipe and dangled awkwardly in space. Life, she thought miserably, is never like the movies.

"Hold on," Max hissed from behind the flowering oleander at the corner of the building.

Annie was in no position to answer, but she wondered what the hell he thought she was doing! Her heart thudding, she fastened onto a drainpipe like a leech, then again began her ascent, testing each foothold as she went. At the second floor, she stepped onto a narrow ledge and edged toward Ingrid's window, the fourth from the corner.

She hoped Max was keeping watch. Should anyone approach, he was to imitate the wavering, tremulous, descending moan of a screech owl.

What she would do at that point, they had not really discussed.

Henny, meanwhile, was poised to swoop up the hall and engage Billy, now comfortably ensconced in a chair in front of Ingrid's door, in animated conversation. This plan had been devised in a hurried consultation by Annie, Max, and Henny, after Laurel and Ophelia departed, cheerfully certain that all would be well and that mundane, earthly efforts on Ingrid's behalf were no longer necessary. Alan had tried to hang around, but Max obviously felt a trio of conspirators was quite enough and succeeded in sending him home.

Inching along the ledge, Annie counted windows. Reaching Ingrid's without further travail, she peered inside.

The room was not quite totally dark. A glow from near the baseboard between the bed and bath indicated a night light. But there wasn't enough illumination for Ingrid to be able to see her, so, the trickiest effort came next. She must open the window, get inside, and attract Ingrid's attention, yet avoid alerting Billy out in the hall.

On cue, and Annie admired her sense of timing, Henny's brisk voice rose angrily in the hall. Giving Billy hell, all right.

Annie gave the window a hard shove, swung her legs over the sill, dropped to the floor, and hurried forward, whispering, "Ingrid, it's me, Annie. Ingrid, don't be frightened."

The bedside light switched on. Ingrid groggily struggled to sit up.

Annie reached the bed in two steps and gathered her friend in a tight embrace. A successive wave of shudders shook Ingrid's thin body.

"It's okay, Ingrid. It really is. Don't be frightened. I won't let anything happen to you."

Ingrid's voice was muffled against Annie's shoulder. "So awful. It's been so awful."

Annie gave her another reassuring hug, then loosened her embrace to reach across the bed and snap off the light. "We'd better keep it dark. You're not supposed to talk to anybody." Then she took Ingrid's thin hands and gripped them in her own.

"Why can't I talk to you?" Ingrid's voice rose, sending Annie's heart thudding again. "Why is Billy out in the hall? Why do I have to have a lawyer? Oh, Annie, I don't understand what's going on."

Annie hesitated. Was Ingrid in any condition to be told that she faced a murder charge?

But Ingrid was chattering feverishly, "Somebody killed Jesse. In my living room. I found him when I got home. I called you. I didn't know what else to do with Chief Saulter out of town. I called and then I heard a noise behind me. Oh God, Annie, it was so . . . awful. I started to turn and there was something all in white, just a big shapeless blur of white, and the smell of pines—so strong—that's all I remember . . . until—I don't know how long it was—I woke up. My head hurt and I was tied up, and it was all dark." Her voice shook piteously.

"Do you have any idea where you were?"

"A boathouse. I was lying in the rowboat. Once I

thought I heard people calling, a long way away. I shouted and shouted. But no one came."

"How did you get loose?"

Ingrid's hands tensed. Annie felt them stiffen in her grasp.

"Laurel said they found you in the rowboat, out on Skull Creek. How did you get loose?"

She didn't answer for so long, and when she did, Annie could hear the change in her voice, the care with which she picked her words.

"Last night, very late, a motorboat came. It tied up outside. I heard a padlock being opened. Someone came in and beamed a flashlight straight in my eyes and whispered for me not to struggle, that I didn't have to be afraid. My feet and hands were tied behind me. The—the person cut me free. I was still lying in the bottom of the boat. Then the motorboat pulled it out of the boathouse. I was terrified. I thought of jumping over the side, but I was so afraid of snakes and I didn't know where I was or how far I would have to swim and I was stiff from having lain there so long. There wasn't any moon. The motorboat pulled the rowboat quite a distance and then, suddenly, my boat was still in the water, and the motorboat was going away. I waited until I was sure it was gone, then I called for help. When the sun came up, I saw I was on a creek a long way from anywhere. But there was only one oar, so I couldn't go very fast. I was trying to go downstream, then the rain started, and it was so cold. It was a long time before Laurel and Ophelia came."

"Ingrid, who did this? Who was it?"

Such a careful choice of words. Such tense, sweaty hands.

"I couldn't see the person."

Annie knew Ingrid so well. So very well. She was hiding something.

Posey would say her story was all a lie, that she was picking and choosing her words because none of it had happened, that she had fled in Jesse's rowboat and lost her way in the interconnecting and confusing backwaters of the island.

"Did you ever get a look at this person?"

"No. Never."

"But you were told you needn't be frightened? Was it a man or a woman, Ingrid?"

Ingrid's hands trembled.

"I don't know. It was just a whisper, that's all—"

"Ingrid?" The hoarse call came from across the room from the opening connecting door. A deep, husky whisper, but somehow familiar to Annie—

"Ingrid? Are you there?"

Ingrid gave a frantic moan and then she began to scream, her voice keening higher and higher through the stillness of the hospital.

SIXTEEN

All hell broke loose.

The door from the hall burst open.

Light flooded in.

Billy shouted and leveled his pistol.

Henny dove for the bed, brandishing her furled umbrella.

Ingrid subsided into sobs.

And Annie and Duane Webb ended up with their palms pressed against the south wall of Ingrid's room in the classic posture of apprehended felons.

"Don't move a muscle," Billy warned.

The head nurse and the floor supervisor arrived simultaneously, demanding to know what was going on, for God's sake!

Billy glared at his prisoners. "Incommunicado, that's what she's supposed to be. I'm half a mind to put all three of you in jail."

The head nurse advanced on him aggressively. "This patient isn't to be disturbed. Doctor's orders. Out of here. All of you. This minute."

She didn't give a damn how many guns, umbrellas, or intruders were involved.

Annie envied her simplicity of approach.

As they were shooed out of the room, Annie looked over her shoulder into Ingrid's pitifully imploring eyes, then the door shut with a bang. It opened immediately, and the supervisor poked her head briefly out. "And put that thing up before you shoot yourself in the foot," she snapped at Billy, before slamming the door with utter finality.

Billy flushed, but he shoved the pistol into his holster. Breathing heavily, he vented his frustration on Annie and Duane.

"What were you two doing in there? And why did Mrs. Jones scream?"

Duane Webb wasn't intimidated. "She screamed because she's got sense enough to be scared when people creep into her room. She knows there's a murderer out there somewhere, even if you fools are too stubborn to admit it."

Annie watched him with fascination. Talk about taking an aggressive position!

Duane shoved his thick-lensed glasses higher on his nose, and his moon-shaped face settled into a bulldog glare. "I figured she wasn't safe. And I've proved it!"

"But why did she scream?" Billy demanded.

"She's scared," Duane reiterated.

Billy looked at Annie.

She very carefully didn't glance at Duane. She had a damn good idea why Ingrid screamed, but she couldn't ignore the plea in those dazed and exhausted eyes. Not yet, at least. Not until she thought about it more. But she didn't want to take chances with Ingrid's safety.

"Mr. Webb's right." It was Annie's turn to pick her words carefully. "Ingrid may be in danger. The murderer may think she has some idea as to his identity—and, obviously, the security here is nil."

"We can take care of that!" Henny exclaimed.

Moonlight bathed the back side of the hospital in a mellow glow. Annie wriggled, trying to convince her hip that those rocks beneath her sleeping bag weren't relevant. It *was* peaceful, but she couldn't sleep. Snores sounded near her, from some of Henny and Madeleine's cohorts. Forty-three had answered the call for sentry duty, and Madeleine had enthusiastically ringed the hospital with volunteers. Henny came up with extra sleeping bags for

Annie and Max. Because, of course, they would want to be a part of the team.

"Of course," Max said stalwartly. "Absolutely."

He was, as might be expected, deployed in the Men's Line, which guarded the front of the hospital.

Annie missed him, but, actually, she needed time to think.

Ingrid's story was a disaster. Posey would never in a million years believe in a white formless attacker. It would be just like poor Sam Sheppard with his claims of a bushy-haired intruder. Years passed before a jury listened to his claims and freed him. Annie could picture the bright red, headline-covered jacket of Jack Harrison Pollack's *Dr. Sam an American tragedy*. And, even worse than the athletic osteopath, Ingrid had not one unlikely story to tell, she had two. Posey would certainly scoff at the likelihood of any murderer taking the trouble and effort to hide, then free her. And Ingrid's stilted description of her abductor's return would elicit nothing but suspicion.

Annie turned restlessly, and the rocks poked into her abdomen.

But Annie had an advantage. She knew Ingrid was telling the truth—if not all of it. So Annie had to figure out why a murderer would go to so much effort. What made it necessary? Why . . .

Sleep overtook her, and with it came skewed images, a rowboat bobbing in a lagoon, a bloated woman's body, a chubby finger pointing at a pile of ashes, Ingrid's eyes, a scarlet A blazoned on plate glass. . . .

Early Tuesday morning

The spartina grass glistened like gold in the early morning sun and rippled like prairie wheat in the soft warmth of the on-shore breeze. A white ibis moved majestically in the shallow water, breakfasting on crayfish and fiddler crabs. A yellow-billed egret nosed into the smelly muck, searching for a tasty snack, anything from a minnow to a young cottonmouth.

Nightingale Courts.

After breakfast, when Max departed for Confidential Commissions and the continuing search for Betsy Raines, Annie had intended to settle quietly in the coffee shop at the hospital and study her notebook. But she didn't even stay long enough for her second cup of coffee. Instead, she drove across the somnolent island, irresistibly drawn here.

She stood in the sunlight by the honeysuckle-laden entrance arch.

Any resident of Nightingale Courts could have murdered Jesse:

Ophelia Baxter—All her ESP hadn't saved her cat from a hideous death.

Duane Webb—Jesse's cruelty enraged him. And Jesse, true to form, hadn't missed an opportunity to remind Duane of his wedding anniversary.

Adele Prescott—She loved her beautiful possessions and would hate a prison cell.

Mavis Beeson—She was willing to go to any length to save her son. (And non-resident Billy Cameron bristled with fury when Mavis was threatened.)

Tom Smith—He disappeared when the law came too near.

Annie surveyed the seven cottages. Funny how much it looked as it had on Saturday morning when she'd rushed here to find Ingrid. The tent that had housed the searchers was gone, and only an occasional scrap of paper plate or cigarette stub indicated any recent occupancy of the courtyard. The wooden piers glistened in the sunlight. They were empty of fishermen this morning. Across the inlet, flowering yucca flaunted drooping blossoms and squashlike fruit in a last burst of summer glory.

Jesse's cabin still had its closed, empty look. Ophelia's curtains were open. Her magnificent Persian sat on the porch steps. Unblinking emerald eyes followed Annie until she was well past. The yellow tape around Ingrid's cabin sagged a little, pulled down by the breezes. Newspapers collected on her front porch. This morning's paper rested on Duane's stoop. Annie wondered whether he was home and resting, or if he had stayed at the hospital. Was she pleased at the deployment of Henny's troops, or furious? Did he even suspect just how distinctively he whispered?

Adele Prescott's front door opened. For once, Adele wore a dress, a Kelly-green jersey, and green alligator mid-height heels. Her dark hair was coiled in a coronet braid today, emphasizing her blunt cheekbones, high-bridged nose, and square chin. She saw Annie and paused on her porch, an overnight case swinging in her hand. The color drained from her heavy face. Her dark eyes turned as cold and lifeless as pools of dirty ice. Then, jerking her gaze away, she hurried, head down, to her car and slammed into it. The car jolted to life and sped away, leaving a curl of dust in its wake.

Annie looked after it thoughtfully. Adele was the mastermind behind a series of robberies, and she'd paid Jesse for his silence.

But had she killed him?

As for Mavis and her little boy, apparently they still slept this morning. Annie moved past their cabin. She knew everything she could hope to learn from Mavis. The only unanswered question was whether she'd opted for murder to stop extortion.

The front door to Cabin 7 was still ajar. Annie knocked as she had yesterday, and, once again, there was no answer.

She'd expected none.

Tom Smith was still lying low. But was he avoiding exposure as an anti-war fugitive or as a murderer?

Restlessly, Annie swung about and paced back toward her car. But she paused with her hand on the door. Nightingale Courts and its environs held her. This was Jesse's habitat. Here he had lived. Here he had prowled. She shaded her eyes against the brilliant sunlight and looked across the inlet. Jesse rode his bicycle, rowed in his boat, and walked.

Annie turned decisively and strode down the dusty grey road.

She welcomed the shade of the sentinel-tall pond pines. They towered seventy-five to a hundred feet in height with long, straight trunks and distinctive silvery umbrella crowns. The scent of sunbaked pitch drifted everywhere.

As she came around the bend in the road, she smiled at the carroty-haired young man working on a tire in the open garage at Jerry's Gas 'N Go. He grinned in return. He had flirty brown eyes that admired Annie in a very grown-up way.

She fished in her memory. Henny had talked to a gas boy at Jerry's. His name was—

"J.D.?" she inquired.

"Yeah. What can I do for you?" He squirted water on the tire and turned it, looking for telltale bubbles.

"I'm trying to find out more about Jesse Penrick, the man who—"

"Sure. I know. Got a sword in his gut. Served him right." The water bubbled. His fingers were quick and sure as he poked in the sealant, twisted, then pulled out the tool.

"Why do you say that?"

His protruding ears flamed. "Sorry, miss." His eyes touched her wedding band, looked infinitesimally disappointed. "Er—ma'am." He returned the tool to its place. "A couple weeks ago somebody dumped a box of kittens in back." His head tilted toward the inlet. "I was gonna take 'em home with me, after work. My mom would've yelled, but she likes cats. Anyway, about nine o'clock Jesse came sneakin' by here. He was always out at night. Anyway, when I went to get the box, the kittens were dead. Somebody broke their necks, all four of 'em. Fluffy yellow kittens." Muscles bunched in his jaw. "So I hope somebody twisted that sword in his gut, that's what I hope."

He pulled up the tire, bounced it on the cracked cement floor of the open garage. Sunlight spilled inside, but it took a long moment for an ugly vision to vanish.

"Did you often see Jesse?"

"I didn't pay too much attention, but yeah, I've worked here a couple years and I probably saw him two, three times a week, sneakin' by."

"Where was he going?"

"Who knows? Someplace not too far, probably, when he walked. Sometimes he went by on his bike."

Annie followed as J.D. rolled the tire to a jacked-up Olds. He squatted down to work the tire on the axle.

"Did he spend a lot of time in the Bird Preserve?"

He shot her a brief look of disgust over his shoulder. "Lady, he wasn't no bird watcher." He turned back to the wheel, shook it in place, then fitted on the nuts. "I've worked here three years and never seen him go near the place, 'cept to walk by."

"But he went in there Saturday." She looked down the road at the white gate that marked the entrance.

"Yep. Hurried in there like he was on his way to a fire sale, then came out a few minutes later with a package." He finished tightening the nuts, then swiveled to face her. Curiosity burned in his eyes. "And I swear he didn't have anything in his hands when he went in."

"But he had a package when he came out."

"Yeah, well, it was little. Package makes it sound big. It was maybe like four inches long, a couple inches high. Wrapped in brown paper. And he was grinnin' at it like a hog in a wallow."

"Did you see anyone else go in the Preserve about the same time?"

He picked up a rubber mallet and pounded the hubcap in place. "I don't know for sure." He stood and worked the jack to lower the car. "I was kind of curious about Jesse, so I sort of kept an eye out. That pretty blond girl who lives at the Courts, she walked by, pushin' her kid in a stroller. And the guy who grins all the time, the one who lives in the Vincent cabin, he jogged by. And maybe there was a couple of cars. But they were all on the road. I didn't see anybody else go in the Preserve."

The road past Jerry's curved in tandem with the marsh, but the semi-tropical forest hid the water from view. On both sides of the dusty ribbon rose live oaks, frond-topped palmettos, southern red cedars, and slash pines. Sword-sharp yucca, wild bamboo, and poison-ivy thrived. It was a good five hundred yards before the road angled to the right to the first cottage and Annie could again see the water.

She shaded her eyes and looked across the inlet at the piers and the pink cottages of Nightingale Courts. As the crow flew or the cottonmouth swam, it wasn't far. On foot, it seemed a long way. Jesse Penrick had sometimes walked this way, sometimes putting across the inlet in his motorboat, moving, as was his custom, under cover of night.

Annie looked at the ramshackle cottage close at hand. Overgrown shrubs pressed against the cabin. The front door screen sagged on its hinges. She circled the cabin,

careful to avoid piles of leaves or debris. She had no wish to
disturb the late summer retreat of a rattlesnake or cottonmouth.

There was no indication anyone had been near this place
in months, perhaps years.

She returned to the road and followed it to the second
cabin. It was in good repair, and the yard was well kept. A
webbed hammock hung on the front porch, a bicycle was
casually propped against a palmetto, an empty bait box was
left open to air. The mailbox read in faded brown letters
VINCENT, but Alan had inked his name on a strip of
adhesive.

She knocked at the front door, but, of course, there
wasn't any answer. Alan would be at the gallery, keeping
everything running and wondering, no doubt, if his job
would soon end, and worrying, with more than an employee's concern, what had happened to his boss.

Annie paused at the foot of the steps to look toward the
inlet. She was tempted to borrow Alan's motorboat and
scoot across the water, but, sighing, she turned to go the
long way around.

She was dripping by the time she reached the Courts,
but pleased with her outing. She felt now that she had a
good grasp of the geography and a better sense of Jesse's
environs.

She headed for the middle pier and had it all to herself
this morning. At its end, she dropped down and pulled her
notebook out of her purse. She gave one last survey to her
surroundings, the pink cabins, the glittering corrugated
roof of Jerry's Gas 'N Go, the two cabins across the water.
Then, shading her eyes, she flipped through the pages. The
tide was coming in, the water sucking and swirling around
shell-encrusted legs of the piers. Two dolphins sported out
in the sound, jumping and curving, the sun glistening on
steel-colored skin.

By the time she finished her careful review of all she'd
seen and heard these past two days, the sun was high in the
sky. Annie tapped thoughtfully with her pen on a fresh
sheet, then, swiftly, she made a final list:

1. Ingrid and Jesse quarreled early Saturday morning.
2. Jesse's corpse barefoot.

3. Jesse's boat taken.
4. Adele saw Jesse in the Gas 'N Go phone booth Thursday night.
5. Shirley May Foley found the remnants of a fire behind the Gas 'N Go Sunday morning.
6. Jesse visited Shangrila Travel Agency Saturday morning, got brochures on the *Queen Elizabeth II*. Looked in the window of the Piping Plover Gallery and dropped by the Oldsmobile agency.
7. A wedding ring hung from Jesse's dog tags.
8. Jesse went into the Bird Preserve about four P.M. Saturday, came out a little later carrying a small package wrapped in brown paper.
9. Ophelia saw Jesse late Thursday afternoon, sitting and smoking his pipe at the end of the middle pier. He was still there after dark.
10. Adele saw Jesse in his boat late Wednesday night, and he had an ugly, satisfied smile on his face.
11. The blackmail file at Jesse's cabin, with its information on Duane, Adele, Mavis, and Tom. Jesse's cabin had been searched (as had his pants pockets).
12. Unidentified telephone call to Jesse at Parotti's bar Saturday night. It made him angry and he left immediately.
13. Betsy Raines not on return flight from San Francisco on Monday. Last seen there Thursday. Attaché case empty of $220,000.
14. Despite its red hair, body of middle-aged woman in Savannah National Wildlife Refuge definitely not that of Betsy Raines. No caesarean scar.
15. Jesse priced new motorboats on Friday.
16. Ingrid smelled pine just before she was attacked.
17. Ingrid screamed when Duane whispered her name.

Annie leaned back against a prickly piling heavy with the scent of creosote. Although it was just mid-morning, she knew it was going to be a hot one, much like last Thursday, when the thermometer recorded a toasty ninety-three degrees in late afternoon.

And this was where Jesse Penrick had sat.

Waiting for what? Looking for what?

Jesse was a night prowler but on Thursday he'd settled on this pier for hours in the late, hot afternoon.

A night prowler, abroad with nocturnal creatures, owls, raccoons, and cotton rats, skates, dogfish, and ghost crabs, night hawks, foxes, and wild boar.

But Thursday afternoon, despite the blazing heat, the night prowler settled in the sun for a panoramic view of Nightingale Courts, the inlet, Jerry's Gas 'N Go, and the opposite bank.

A panoramic view—

Annie jumped to her feet. She walked so quickly she was panting by the time she reached the back of Jesse's cabin. She gave a swift look around, used Ingrid's key and slipped inside.

The garbage was even smellier this morning, with the heat and the continuing passage of time. She found a stack of old newspapers in the broom closet and put several on the floor, then carefully tipped over the pail and let the garbage slide out.

Coffee grounds. Crusts of moldy rye bread. Banana peels. Last week's *Gazette*. A discarded undershirt. An empty shaving-cream can. A buttermilk carton. Three empty frozen-food packages. An empty fifth of Jim Beam. An unappetizing mess of rotting apples.

But it was what she didn't find that made all the difference.

Annie knew now who had killed Jesse Penrick.

Oh, yes, now she knew. But was there any way—ever—to unmask this calculating killer?

SEVENTEEN

"Furthermore," Annie snarled, "if you don't show up, I'll invite every news reporter from here to Atlanta, and when the killer's announced, they'll know who found him—and it won't be you!"

She slammed the receiver into its cradle.

"Dear little hedgehog," Max murmured.

"What did you say?" she snapped, still breathing heavily.

"Nothing, love," he said sweetly. "Just admiring your combativeness. You know, Annie, maybe we should send you to law school. You make most D.A.'s look like cream cakes."

"Puffs," she corrected.

"Whatever." He poured just-brewed coffee into two mugs. He'd chosen *One Foot in the Grave* for himself and *Killer in the Crowd* for Annie.

The phone shrilled.

Annie snatched it up. "Death on Demand. Yes, just like I told you, I've called everybody and asked them to be here at four. And I—" Twice, she tried unsuccessfully to interrupt, then said firmly, "No, I'm not going to tell you who did it. But I promise you, Mr. Circuit Solicitor, I know—and I even know how you can prove it."

"Oh, you've forgotten the cream." Ingrid struggled to rise.

Annie pushed her down firmly. Social niceties weren't

important this afternoon. "You are here subject to good behavior—and good behavior means not stirring out of your chair."

And there subject to Posey's surly announcement that if Annie didn't have the goods, Ingrid would go straight from Death on Demand to jail. Without stopping.

Annie, of course, hadn't told Ingrid that. Even so, Ingrid was so pale! "Ingrid, honey, maybe you shouldn't be out of bed."

Ingrid lifted her chin determinedly. "I want to be here." She looked miserably at Annie. "I have to know."

Annie hated that pinched look of unhappiness. She bent and gave Ingrid a swift kiss on her cheek, and the bell tinkled at the front door as the first of Annie's special guests arrived.

Annie stood beside the coffee bar, her hand resting lightly on a sheaf of papers—the computer printouts, her sketches, her copies of the information in Jesse's folder, her notes, and her final list.

But she didn't need them.

She surveyed the silent assemblage. It was, perhaps, one of the oddest gatherings in the history of Death on Demand.

Circuit Solicitor Posey stood with his back to the Private Investigator–Police Procedural bookcase, his arms crossed, his snoutish face locked in a scowl. Billy Cameron stood stiffly at his right. Billy determinedly did not look toward the back table where Mavis sat. Mavis's slender fingers nervously pleated a paper napkin. Despite the cheapness of her blue rayon suit, she was as robustly pretty as a beleaguered heroine floridly pictured in an illustration to one of A. M. Barnard's steamy tales in the 1870s (and therein lies a tale for admirers of Louisa May Alcott).

Ingrid sat stiffly between Henny and Duane at a middle table. She'd given Duane one anguished look when he joined them, then huddled in her chair, her eyes downcast. He leaned close and murmured, but she shook her head determinedly. Every so often, he looked at her in concern, then glowered at Posey. Duane looked unaccustomedly dapper, freshly shaved and in a crisp white shirt and brown slacks. Henny tapped a pen impatiently and stared down at a legal pad. She was a vision of executive elegance this afternoon in a subtly patterned suit with a long cutaway jacket over a short, slim skirt. A sterling band, accented by black onyx insets, circled her throat. Her earrings matched. Henny looked up and their glances locked for an instant in mutual understanding.

Alan Nichols smiled at Annie from the table nearest the coffee bar. His blue blazer was a perfect fit. The scent of shaving lotion tickled her nose.

Laurel and Ophelia, both still attired in oatmeal-colored robes, occupied the other middle table. A third chair contained the largest woven carryall Annie had ever seen. Occasionally, Laurel repositioned it, ever nearer to her. Laurel's golden hair was drawn back in a bun this afternoon, and she was the image of Grace Kelly in *To Catch a Thief*, which was odious at her age. She flashed a brilliant smile at Annie, exuding good cheer almost as visibly as a painted medieval saint with appended golden rays radiates holiness. Ophelia, as usual, suffered by comparison. Today's orange turban, however, matched the splotches of rouge on her cheeks.

At a rear table, Adele sat ramrod straight, her face somber, her dark eyes intent on Annie.

Posey cleared his throat and opened his mouth.

Annie hastily rustled her papers. "I appreciate everyone coming this afternoon. As I told each of you on the telephone, I felt that if we had a conference, if we pooled our knowledge, we could solve Jesse Penrick's murder." A slight smile touched her lips. "I've been thinking of a book by Agatha Christie. Not the story itself, but the title, *A Murder Is Announced*. What I didn't tell you on the telephone was that this afternoon a murderer will be announced."

Ophelia gave a tiny gasp. Laurel gazed with bright interest at her nails, turning them back and forth to catch the light, obviously not terribly interested in her surroundings, then she flashed an *encouraging* smile at Annie. (Annie decided that she must, later, delve into her own immediate emotional response: a fierce desire to strangle her mother-in-law.) Mavis darted a frightened glance at Billy. Adele's expression didn't change. Henny nodded approvingly and somehow managed to make her narrow bony face look plump, bland, and Oriental. (Charlie Chan?) Ingrid pressed trembling fingers to her lips. Duane reached out to touch her and she jerked away. Alan murmured, "Give 'em hell," and lounged back in his chair.

"Ms. Laurance—"

"Mrs. Darling," Max said firmly.

Annie ignored them both. "Why did Jesse Penrick die on Saturday night, the nineteenth of September?"

She surveyed her audience.

"Why not last Christmas, when he played a vicious trick on Mr. Webb? Why not a year ago, or two? Why not next week? Why last Saturday night? That timing is important. Just as important are the circumstances of his murder." As Posey moved restively, she said firmly, "Let me remind you of what we know: Jesse received a telephone call at Parotti's Bar and Bait Shop about eleven o'clock the night of his death. The call made him angry, and he immediately left. Shortly after midnight, in response to a plea for help from Ingrid Jones, my husband and I found Jesse's body in her cabin. What happened between eleven o'clock and midnight?"

Posey broke in pompously, "The critical time period, Ms. Laurance—"

"Mrs. Darling." Max was firm.

Posey ignored him. "—is from the moment Mrs. Jones arrived home until she made her calculated telephone call to you." He stabbed a pudgy finger at Ingrid. "She quarreled with Jesse Penrick Saturday morning. No doubt he accosted her as she returned from the wedding festivities and the quarrel resumed. Mrs. Jones, goaded by his actions, reached up for the sword above her mantel and thrust it into a defenseless man's chest." His assertion ended as a bellow.

Duane Webb jumped to his feet.

Before he could launch into a defense, Annie interceded. "That, of course, is what you were supposed to think. But it leaves a few loose ends, doesn't it? Why were Jesse's shoes and socks removed? Why were pine needles stuck to his clothes? How did he receive the contusion on the back of his head? These questions have answers." She waved Duane back to his seat. "Instead of a murder resulting from a quarrel, I suggest a murder that was well-planned and cunningly crafted. We are not dealing here with a killer striking out in the heat of emotion. We are dealing with a careful, calculating, and cruel murderer.

"Here is what happened Saturday night:

"The killer, using a disguised voice, called Jesse at Parotti's. I feel sure the murderer imitated a voice Jesse would recognize and not fear. Perhaps that of Adele Prescott."

Adele's head jerked up and her eyes blazed, but she said nothing.

Annie nodded at her listeners. "Yes, I'm sure that Jesse thought he recognized his caller, and it was someone he didn't fear. The speaker, sounding like Adele or perhaps Ophelia, told Jesse that he'd better hurry home, it looked like someone had been in his cabin.

"That brought him immediately. Why? Because Jesse had something of value in his cabin, and he didn't want to lose it. So Jesse jumped on his bike and raced home. He found his cabin dark, but he ran up the steps and inside. The intruder, waiting there, hit him from behind and knocked him out, then, quickly, searched the cabin.

"And here's where the plans went awry, because the search didn't yield its expected result. But time was racing on and the intruder had to hurry. Jesse had to be put in Ingrid's cabin before she returned from our wedding reception. The intruder carried Jesse from his cabin to Ingrid's, but had to put Jesse down on the ground until the back door could be opened. That's when the pine needles adhered to Jesse's clothing. Once inside Ingrid's, the intruder put Jesse on the living room floor, and, knowing Ingrid would be home shortly, stabbed Jesse with her sword. It was then that the murderer pulled out Jesse's pockets in a final search and even removed his sneakers and socks. But the object wasn't found.

"Turning off the lights, the murderer waited in the kitchen for Ingrid's arrival. She came in, saw Jesse and ran to the phone. Before she could complete her call, the murderer came up behind her, struck her, and carried her away, unconscious.

"The murderer had a motorboat waiting and had already hooked up Jesse's rowboat to it. The murderer went in the motorboat to the pier behind Jerry's Gas 'N Go, tied up, ran to the cement area behind Jerry's and set afire some papers taken from Jesse's. The murderer then returned to the boat and left the inlet, going far up Skull Creek to a boathouse whose owners were out of town. Tying Ingrid up, the murderer left her in Jesse's rowboat and returned to the inlet."

"Balderdash!" Posey trumpeted. "My dear young woman"—and the irony dripped from his voice—"how could you possibly believe such complicated nonsense?"

"It gets even more complicated," she said agreeably. "The murderer deliberately chose Ingrid's cabin because of her quarrel on Saturday morning with Jesse. But the murderer was far from through with Ingrid. She was not only to be a suspect, she was to be a suspect with an absurd story. So, on Sunday night, the murderer returned to the boathouse where she was held prisoner, untied her, and set her free in a rowboat." Now Annie's face was stern. "More than that, the murderer spoke to her—although in a whisper—and told her she needn't be frightened."

Posey's eyebrows were oblique flags of disbelief. "Indeed!"

"Absolutely." Annie looked at Ingrid, who was shaking her head in distress.

"Ingrid." Her voice was gentle, encouraging. "Trust me now. Who spoke to you? Who whispered?"

"Annie, I don't— Oh, Annie, please!"

Even Posey was affected by the anguish in her tone, and he looked at her thoughtfully.

"It's all right, Ingrid. I promise. Who spoke to you?"

"It was a whisper—just a whisper—but—" She looked at the man beside her. "Duane, why did you talk to me? Why?"

There was an instant of stunned silence.

Duane Webb's heavy face sagged with shock.

Posey gave an exasperated snort. "I'm running out of patience. You've rigged this to try and convince me that

Mrs. Jones is innocent. Well, I'm nobody's fool, and I know a concocted story when I hear one."

"Concocted," Annie said sternly, "by the murderer."

"Absurd, absurd," the circuit solicitor trumpeted. "Why would anyone go to so much trouble to embroil an innocent person in a crime?"

"Why, indeed? It was that question which set me onto the right trail. Why should anyone go to so much trouble to kill an old man? Why not knock him over the head and leave his body in his own living room? Why not? Because Jesse *snooped*—and the murderer was desperate to focus attention away from that fact." Her gaze swept the room. "I decided the answer had to lie in Jesse's character. In part, I was right. I discovered that Jesse was not only vicious and vindictive, he was a blackmailer."

She certainly had everyone's attention now.

"He was blackmailing Mavis Beeson, Adele Prescott, and Tom Smith. He tried to blackmail Duane. And I discovered something more. Jesse liked to taunt his victims. He loved that extra twist of the knife. In the case of Duane Webb, he derived no money, but he caused him misery with reminders of the car accident and the loss of his family. Despite Mavis's payment, he went ahead and painted a scarlet A on her mailbox. So Jesse wanted to have his cake and throw it in his victims' faces, too.

"But what I found out by myself wasn't enough. It was Henny who insisted that anything out of the ordinary in Jesse's final days might be important. Between us, we nosed out a number of unusual actions on Jesse's part:

"One. Jesse sat at the end of the middle pier in the heat late Thursday afternoon and into the evening.

"Two. Jesse used the telephone at the Gas 'N Go Thursday night.

"Three. On Friday, Jesse priced new motorboats.

"Four. On Saturday, Jesse picked up travel brochures on *the Queen Elizabeth Two*, looked in the window of the Piping Plover Gallery, dropped by the Oldsmobile agency, and went into the Bird Preserve and came out with a package."

Alan shoved a hand through his curly chestnut hair. "Annie, I hate to say it, but it doesn't add up to anything."

Annie straightened her papers decisively. "Oh, but it does. It adds up to money. A very great deal of money."

"Jesse didn't have any money," Adele snapped. She gripped her handbag and started to rise.

"Sit down."

Adele responded to Annie's steely tone and sank back into the chair, the beginnings of fear in her dark eyes.

"Didn't he?" Annie glanced at the watching faces, and one of them now was wary. "Oh, I think perhaps he had his eye on a potful of money, and the first installment was in the small package he picked up in the Bird Preserve. In fact, I'm sure of it, because I spent a messy twenty minutes going through Jesse's trash, and the funny thing is, there was no brown paper there, nothing that could be the remains of that package. If the package were unimportant, Jesse would've just tossed that paper away, and I would have found it. And it's interesting to note that there are no travel brochures in his cabin. Where are they? The murderer buried them along with the brown paper on Saturday night. Why? Because it was vital that no one think of Jesse in terms of money. Big money."

Posey's cheeks puffed. "Mrs. Darling, do you mean to say you had the effrontery to—"

"Don't say another word, Annie," Max warned, hurrying toward her.

Annie flashed him a sunny smile. "Actually, Mr. Posey's going to buy us a steak dinner, when I'm through."

"Mrs. Darling—"

Duane Webb barked, "Nobody at Nightingale Courts has any money. And Jesse's little game was played close to home."

Annie nodded in agreement. "That's exactly what everyone would think from the blackmail folders in Jesse's cabin."

Max clapped his hands to his head. Posey sucked in a deep breath.

Before he could attack, Annie moved swiftly on. "Yes, there are a lot of motives at Nightingale Courts." She looked toward the back of the coffee area. "Mavis Beeson was paying Jesse to keep quiet about her relationship with a young man, not her husband." Annie was careful not to look toward Billy. "But this wasn't the usual story of a wife intent upon hiding a love affair. No. Mavis's fear is much deeper and stronger than that. She lives in mortal fear of an abusive husband, who has threatened to harm their son."

Mavis looked fearfully at Posey.

Laurel rose, scooped up her bag, and swept toward the table. She patted Mavis's tense shoulder reassuringly. Her throaty murmur carried clearly. "My dear child, do be of good cheer. Annie is merely circuitous. Amanda Cross, you know. You have *nothing* to be concerned about."

Had Annie possessed a handy bludgeon, Laurel, too, would have been relieved—permanently—from the necessity of concern about anything whatsoever.

Annie continued crisply. "But Mavis is not the only resident of Nightingale Courts who had good reason to kill Jesse Penrick. Adele Prescott feared him, because Jesse, with his usual clever eye for skullduggery, had noticed an interesting pattern. Whenever Adele guarded a house for absent owners, another house on that block would soon be robbed."

Posey's blunt head swung toward the back of the coffee area.

Adele pushed back her chair. "I don't have to listen to this! You can't prove anything. Do you hear me? You can't *prove* it."

"Sit down."

Adele's face crimsoned, but, slowly, she sank back into the chair.

"So that's two of the residents," Annie continued. "Mavis and Adele. Then there's Duane."

Ingrid gasped softly.

"Duane despised Jesse. Jesse struck back by reminding him of the deaths of his wife and daughter. Saturday was the anniversary of Duane's wedding—Jesse gave him an anniversary card."

Duane's deep voice carried clearly. "The sorry, sorry son of a bitch."

Ingrid covered her eyes with a shaking hand.

Posey stared hard at Duane.

"And then there's Ophelia," Annie mused. "She would like for everyone to think she's dithery and listens to beings from other worlds. But she has ties to this world, too. Like many lonely people, she becomes very attached to a pet. Jesse poisoned her cat, and so she hated him."

Ophelia pressed her arms tightly across her chest. "Evil, evil." Her voice was low and hoarse; her eyes tightly shut. "Evil here. Among us. The concentrated beam of self burns and destroys like sun through a prism. Evil."

Laurel wafted back to their table. "Now, now, dear, rest easy. All is well. I am in control."

Annie didn't take time to dispute it. "The other resident of Nightingale Courts isn't here today," she said briskly. Did she want to set the law after Tom Smith? He'd fashioned his own prison, hadn't he? A solitary world confined to tiny objects of a distant past that held no pain for him. "Tom Smith is hiding from his past, and I'm sure he won't return to Broward's Rock until Jesse Penrick's murderer is arrested.

"But Duane made a very clever point. As he observed, there is no big money available from any resident of Nightingale Courts. So where could Jesse have expected to obtain the kind of money that would pay for a trip on the *Queen Elizabeth Two* or a new car?"

Heads shook. No one answered.

"I have an idea," Annie said quietly. "Let's ask Alan."

EIGHTEEN

Alan froze for just an instant, then his infectious smile lighted up his blue eyes, though his hands on the table clenched hard. "Oh, hey now, Annie, that's reaching. Really reaching. Hell, I don't have a dime. I'll show you my tax return."

"I'd rather see the key to the safety deposit box you rented recently."

His smile faded.

"I don't know where it is, but the police will find it. And there'll be almost $220,000 in it, minus however much you put in that package for Jesse. I'll bet you haven't had time to get that money to the bank. It'll be hidden in your cabin."

He edged his chair back from the table.

"You're not going anywhere," she said quietly. "Because once the police start to look, you're finished. There'll be traces, of course. Maybe a strand of Betsy's hair in your cabin—or the trunk of her car?"

He shook his head. "Oh, you're off base. You're trying to railroad me, to save Ingrid. It won't work."

Posey stalked to the front of the room. "Mrs. Darling, that body in the Refuge is *not* Mrs. Raines. Just because she was a redhead, you and Mrs. Brawley jumped to a lot of conclusions. But that's what comes of amateurs mixing into police work."

"Have you identified that body?"

"Sure have." He was expansive. "Good solid police work." He pulled a small notebook from his pocket, cleared his throat, and read, "Deceased identified by fingerprints—left index, middle, and little fingers—as Miss Lucinda Burrows, speech teacher in Savannah."

"Has the time of death been estimated?"

Posey wriggled his nose. "Autopsy report suggests death occurred approximately three days before body discovered on Monday by Refuge ranger."

"And when was Miss Burrows last seen?"

"Mrs. Darling, what possible interest can you have in this poor woman? I assure you this identification is rock solid."

"Nonetheless," she said mildly, "I'd like to know. When was she last seen in Savannah?"

Posey did enjoy the sound of his own voice. "She called in sick Wednesday morning, but her landlady said she left early, about seven, all dressed up, and carrying an overnight bag. Sounds like she was going off with a man, though the people at school say she was a high-type lady and never hung around singles bars." He thumbed through his notebook. "One of her best friends said, 'Lucinda was a little bit silly and giddy sometimes, but I'm sure she wouldn't go out with a stranger. She didn't like singles bars, said they were dangerous. We're all absolutely stunned. And how she ever got to the Wildlife Refuge, we can't imagine!'"

He snapped the notebook shut. "So, this poor lady left her apartment Wednesday morning and likely was with a man until she was strangled, probably around Thursday evening, and her body dumped in the Refuge." He smiled patronizingly at Annie. "And she doesn't have anything to do with Mrs. Raines, who's out in California, and may be shacked up with a man herself."

"No," Annie said wearily. "I wish it were so, but no. You see, Alan killed Betsy, probably very early Wednesday morning, the day she was to fly to San Francisco. He hid her body in his cabin, then took her car. Perhaps he wore a red wig and a picture hat, so that anyone looking at the car would think they'd seen her. Anyway, he took the ferry to the mainland and drove, minus the wig, to Lucinda's apartment house and picked her up. He gave her Betsy's tickets and her luggage, which would have been all packed, and the attaché case—empty, of course—and Lucinda flew to California and checked into the St. Francis."

Alan jumped up. "That's crazy. Really crazy! I didn't know this—what'd you say her name was?—this Burrows woman, and even if I did, why would she go through with this charade?"

"You knew her. Maybe not for long. You picked her up somewhere. You look so all-American, so wholesome." The disgust in her voice was scathing. "You probably pitched her a big story, convinced her you were CIA, maybe, and she was going to be a courier. She didn't know Betsy was dead. She thought her job was to take the luggage, check into the hotel, leave the suitcases and purse behind—and I'll bet Alan even had the airport claim check for the car in Betsy's purse—"

Max was nodding.

"—and fly back the next day. Thursday. You picked her up at the airport Thursday night, strangled her, and dumped her body in the Refuge, leaving her nude just to confuse the issue."

"No way. Listen, how could I get back to the island from the airport on Wednesday if I drove Betsy's car there and left it?"

"Limousines leave the airport three times a day for the Palmetto House. When we check, I'll bet we find that some guy in a beach hat and shades took a limo in Wednesday morning."

Alan took a step backward.

"You came back to the island and worked all day. It was probably Wednesday night that you dumped Betsy's weighted body in the sound. I'll bet Jesse was watching. You were halfway done and probably very pleased with yourself. Then Thursday night, you picked up Lucinda, killed her, and came back to the island.

"But you weren't home free, Alan. Jesse called you Thursday night—and he had Betsy's wedding ring. He must have found her body in your cabin early Wednesday, maybe after you'd left in her car to go to Savannah. Anyway, he called, and he could prove he'd seen her dead body as long as he had that ring."

"Mrs. Raines's wedding ring?" Posey demanded, and he turned to look at Alan.

"Yes. Betsy's wedding ring. To keep it safe, Jesse slipped it onto the chain that held his dog tags. That's what Alan searched for so furiously, even taking off Jesse's shoes and socks. Alan searched Jesse's cabin as well as he could in the time he had. He'd hurried over to Nightingale Courts from our wedding reception. But it never occurred to him that Jesse would wear anything around his neck. And that high-neck sweater Jesse wore effectively hid the dog tags. You can imagine how Alan started to sweat when the news came out about Jesse having a wedding ring on his chain, and how relieved he must have been when the press reported the initials inside the ring as E.P. But a jeweler can look at that more closely, and I'll bet the store that the initials are E.R.—Elizabeth Raines. Betsy Raines."

"Crazy," Alan shouted, but sweat filmed his face.

"You're all through, Alan, because now that the police know where to look, they'll find proof: Lucinda's finger-prints in Betsy's car and in the hotel room in San Francisco, traces of Lucinda in your car. Surely she struggled hard enough that a single hair—just one—is in your car or some fiber under her fingernails. You're all through—and you deserve to be. Making love to Betsy, then killing her. Fooling that poor Burrows woman, then killing her. Imitating Duane's voice when you freed Ingrid. That was a little fancy, Alan. Do you want to do any voices for us? Maybe Betsy? I'll bet you can do her great."

His chair fell with a clatter as he turned and tried to run.

A lariat whistled cleanly through the air, settled over his arms, jerked him backward. He slammed to the floor.

Every eye in the room followed the taut line which bound him to Laurel's slender hands.

Smiling serenely, Annie's mother-in-law said just a trifle quickly, "Henny, dear, do stamp on his hand and kick that knife away."

Posey dispatched Billy to the island police station with a handcuffed Alan, with instructions to call the sheriff's office for transportation to the county jail.

That done, he approached Annie, his face like a thundercloud. "Breaking and entering, that's just for starters. Keeping information from the properly constituted authorities. I've a good mind—"

"I know the press will be so excited that you've solved this very complex and unusual crime," Annie said smoothly.

His mouth a large round O, he looked at her for a long moment, then slowly nodded. "I *did* do an outstanding job of investigation."

Ingrid sniffed and pointedly directed her question at Annie. "How did you know? How did you ever know?"

Annie had no desire to be in the next cell to Alan. She took a deep breath. "As Circuit Solicitor Posey undoubtedly has recorded in his own investigation, Jesse Penrick did several things in the days before his murder that observers said were out of character for him. First, he sat on the middle pier in the heat late Thursday afternoon. If he'd wanted to watch for anyone in Nightingale Courts, he would have had a better—and cooler—view from his living room. So his attention was focused on the inlet, and across it on Alan's cabin. Second, he made a phone call Thursday night. How much easier just to talk in person to someone living in the Courts? Third, he went into the Bird Preserve Saturday afternoon. Again, why such a convoluted approach if he was to receive something from someone in Nightingale Courts?

"I decided then that Jesse was focused on something other than the Courts, that a great deal of money was involved, and I started thinking about Alan, who lived on the other side of the inlet and who liked to make love to older women, and who liked expensive clothes and, I'd bet, good wines and fine hotels and lots of other things he couldn't afford. Alan knew Betsy Raines was carrying a substantial amount of money in her attaché case. Henny kept insisting all the crime on the island had to be linked, so I started to wonder if maybe Betsy never left the island. From there, it was easy."

"Just the way I'd figured it out," Posey intoned.

"Evil," Ophelia intoned. "Betsy is dead, her hair wavering in the water."

The pause was uncomfortable.

Laurel nodded brightly. "Such *direct* thinking, Annie. Very, very good. But, of course, we knew, almost from the first. He smiled with the sweetness of a serpent. So, I came to the bookstore prepared."

"A lariat?" Duane muttered.

Max answered almost absentmindedly. "Community theater. *Annie Get Your Gun*. Laurel was smashing. She's done bottle tricks at parties ever since."

"And it was his shaving lotion I smelled, just before he knocked me out!" Ingrid exclaimed.

"I'd like to wring his goddamned neck," Duane said gruffly.

Ingrid's face turned to him and tears filled her eyes. "Oh, Duane, I'm so sorry. I don't know how I could—"

"Fellow was a crackerjack impersonator. Heard him often enough at Parotti's. Goddam, woman, why'd you keep your mouth shut for me? Till Annie bullied it out of you. Damfool thing to do." A smile tugged at his heavy face. "But a nice damfool thing." Then, briskly, he nodded at Annie. "Pretty damn good work, kid. I have to hand it to you." He pushed back his chair, then paused and looked up at the paintings. "And somebody's got good taste in mysteries."

Ingrid blushed. "Do you recognize the titles?"

"Sure. Any fool would. *The Chinese Bell Murders* by Robert van Gulik, *The Virgin in the Ice* by Ellis Peters, *Crocodile on the Sandbank* by Elizabeth Peters, *Murder on the Yellow Brick Road* by Stuart Kaminsky, and *The Key to Rebecca* by Ken Follett."

"Somebody does have good taste," Annie said softly, and she put Ingrid's hand in Duane's.

Light from the rose-shaded lamp in Annie's bedroom cast a cheerful glow over the bed, its cover invitingly turned down. At last, they would have their official honeymoon night. Everything was taken care of, Ingrid safe and free, Mavis equipped with a lawyer and funds and twenty-four-hour security, Laurel safely enroute to Connecticut. (Could Laurel be safe anywhere? But that was another question of a philosophical depth Annie did not wish to plumb this night.) But, so far as they knew, all was well that ended well, and tomorrow, they would leave for a two-week mystery tour in England. The news had delighted Annie. "Oh Max, how wonderful. A honeymoon with murder!"

"Actually," he'd replied, "I think we've had enough murder lately. What I had in mind was a honeymoon with love."

He opened his arms and she stepped toward him. "Mrs. Darling—"

The telephone rang.

Max swung around, glaring with a most un-Max-like frown.

Annie started to move past him. To answer the phone, of course.

But Max sprang ahead of her. The ring ended in mid-shrill. Max turned to face her, the ripped-out cord dangling from his hand, a beatific smile upon his face.

ABOUT THE AUTHOR

CAROLYN G. HART is the author of nine award-winning "Death on Demand" mysteries featuring Annie Laurance Darling, including *Something Wicked*, for which she won an Agatha and Anthony, *Honeymoon with Murder*, which won an Anthony, and *A Little Class on Murder*, which won a Macavity. She lives in Oklahoma City with her husband, Phil.

If you enjoyed Carolyn G. Hart's Henrie O mystery, SCANDAL IN FAIR HAVEN, you will want to read Carolyn's latest mystery, MINT JULEP MURDER. Look for it at your local bookseller's!

Here is a special look at MINT JULEP MURDER.

MINT JULEP MURDER

A Death on Demand Mystery
by
CAROLYN G. HART

Annie Laurance Darling almost sideswiped a cleaner's van when she neglected to yield at the Sea Pines traffic circle. Although she didn't know how anybody could be expected to master the intricate give-and-take of the circle, in her view as complex as the instructions for assembling a computer. In a word, the damn traffic circle wasn't user-friendly. Despite its evident problems, however, island residents tenaciously refused to approve a change to stoplights. Annie gritted her teeth and lifted her hands briefly from the wheel in a mea culpa apology to the indignant driver of the cleaner's van. If bumper-to-bumper cars weren't bad enough, the island's stubborn retention of the two traffic circles at the beginning and end of Pope Avenue hopelessly aggravated the problem.

But she managed to make the swing around and

peel off onto Pope without smacking into another vehicle, even taking time to notice the ducks who inhabited the small pond and the sign cautioning traffic to watch for crossing ducks. She glanced at her watch and picked up speed.

She would be making this trip a lot today, each time with an author. She tried to see the landscape with a stranger's eye and smiled with almost proprietorial pride at the dense pockets of huge pines, the always appealing compact palmettos, the blooming oleanders in the grassy median, the carefully homogenized commercial buildings in shades of beige, tan, and lime.

She would have enjoyed taking her charges to Broward's Rock with its quiet lanes and equally gorgeous beach, but Hilton Head, though bustling, was just as lovely. May was a perfect month on any of the Sea Islands. The air was balmy, the temperature in the seventies, and no humidity. Hilton Head's fourteen miles of beaches were never really crowded, even at the height of the tourist season.

Annie pulled into the Buccaneer's parking lot. The Festival Committee couldn't have assigned her charges to a nicer hotel. The Festival events were occurring at open-air, tented booths on the public entrance to Coligny Beach, just a short stroll from the Buccaneer. Authors were also quartered at the beachfront Holiday Inn and at several other luxurious beachfront hotels.

The Buccaneer was one of Annie's favorite hotels. Small, elegant, and charming, it was built like an

Italian villa with dusky mauve stuccoed walls and arched windows.

She hurried up the oyster shell path between fragrant banana shrubs. Brilliantly flowering hibiscus flamed in clay pots by the side entrance.

She had a hand on the door when the six-foot-tall pittosporum bush quivered. Henny Brawley darted out into the path. "Annie, I'm so glad to see you."

Broward's Rock's most accomplished reader of mystery fiction wore a scarlet linen suit. A slender gold necklace supported an oblong ceramic likeness of Agatha Christie. Henny's gray hair was swept back in soft waves. Her expression of surprise mingled with delight would have done justice to Jessica Fletcher upon finding a corpse. Annie wondered how long Henny had lurked behind the bush, waiting.

"How'd you know I'd come in by the side door?"

Henny's eyes narrowed, then she capitulated. "You had to park," she said tersely. "Look, I wanted to give you this." She thrust a two-by-three-inch piece of cardboard into Annie's hand. "I know this will hit the bestseller list. I'm thinking a *little* book, with a single quote on each page. You know, like *Life's Little Instruction Book* or *Everything I Know I Learned from My Cat*. A book doesn't have to be big to succeed, just big in scope!" She nodded in undisguised self-congratulation. "*The Quotable Sleuth* can't miss, Annie. You can leave a message for me at the desk. Room 403." She smiled brightly and turned away, paused, called back, "I plan to use Miss Marple on page one: 'The great thing to avoid is having in any way a trustful mind.'

"Then at the bottom of the page, it will say: Jane Marple, *A Pocket Full of Rye*. Isn't that wonderful? Annie, I'm so excited!"

With a wave of her hand, Henny disappeared behind the pittosporum bush.

Annie almost called out to tell Henny about a terrific collection, *The Mystery Lovers' Book of Quotations* by Jane Horning. Then, with a decided head-shake, she dropped the piece of cardboard into her purse. No reason to deflate Death on Demand's indefatigable reader. Henny's book would have its own flavor. Still, Annie had other things to do than focus on her best customer's search for a publisher. Now all Annie needed to top off her morning would be for Miss Dora to be waiting inside.

A long, cool hallway with meeting rooms—Snowy Egret, White Ibis, Great Blue Heron, Brown Pelican—led to the central lobby and a rectangular reflecting pool. Whitewashed walls gave the lobby a bright, fresh aura. Brilliant scarlet bougainvillea bloomed in yellow terra-cotta urns.

Annie went directly to the desk. The assistant manager greeted her cheerfully. Jeff Garrett's carrot-hued hair sprigged in all directions. Freckles spattered his snub nose. His wide mouth spread in an infectious grin that Annie returned despite her preoccupation. She felt she and Jeff had forged a bond, she'd been there so often in recent days.

"Everything's just as you ordered, Annie. Fruit baskets and a magnum of champagne in each room. And, let's see, a manicurist will be up to Ms. Sinclair's room at four, the six-foot pine board's in place beneath Mrs. Kirby's mattress, the foot massage appliance is in Mr. Crabtree's suite." Jeff paused, leaned forward, and his voice dropped. "Got a call this morning with a special request from Mr. Blake. I made a special trip off-island to pick up three 'adult' videos for his suite."

Annie merely nodded, but she felt a twinge of surprise. Alan Blake's charming, boyish persona didn't square with the X-rated video request. But as Miss Dora was wont to remark: You can't always tell a package from its cover. In any event, Annie was glad Blake hadn't asked her to get the videos. There was a limit to how helpful she intended to be.

Jeff's eyes widened. "Do you know how much those kind of movies cost? Wow. If my wife finds out I've been in that place, I'm in deep trouble"—he glanced down at a list—"and I've got the keys ready for you." He pulled out a manila envelope from a drawer. "You'll find the room numbers inside with the keys. And do you want the key to your suite?"

Annie took both the envelope and her own key and thanked him. She opened the larger envelope. Five folders with oblong cardboard electronic keys were enclosed. She handed the folder for Room 506 to Garrett. "Emma Clyde will pick her key up at the desk." At least, Emma should—if she would. Annie added calling Emma to her mental list of responsibilities. She tucked the other four folders back into the envelope. "I understand Kenneth Hazlitt is staying here. Has he checked in?"

Jeff stepped to a computer, punched in the name. "Yes. Could I call for you?"

She felt a tiny spurt of irritation. For heaven's sake, she was hardly a security risk. Jeff knew who she was. He had just handed her the oblong cardboard room keys for five expected guests. To be fair to Jeff, that was different. The Festival was paying for the accommodations for the honorees. And it was contrary to hotel policy to provide inquirers with the room numbers of guests. So okay, Jeff was just following the rules.

"Yes, please."

Jeff nodded toward an alcove. "The house phones are over there, Annie."

"Thanks." She crossed to the alcove, picked up a receiver.

The desk rang the room.

"Hello." The deep drawl was instantly attractive.

"May I speak to Mr. Hazlitt, please?"

"Which one?"

"Mr. Kenneth Hazlitt."

"Ken's not in. This is Willie. Can I help you?"

Damn. Annie looked again at her watch. "I need to speak with Mr. Hazlitt. Do you know when he will return?"

"Who knows? If he's found a good party, it may

be a while. But we've got our own little party this afternoon, and a book open house all day tomorrow. You can count on catching him one time or the other. Ken never misses a party, especially not his own."

"Do you know anything about the book he's writing?" She had reached that level of desperation.

"Not much," Willie replied cheerfully. "But I can paw through the stuff we brought. See if I find anything. I think maybe there're some flyers he's going to have at the booth. Kind of a teaser, you know? For the open house. Are you press?"

Annie would have claimed membership in the Mafia if she thought it would help. She gave it some consideration (she credited a vicious second-grade teacher with helping her shed any compunction always to tell the truth), but in this instance, she didn't see any advantage to be gained. "No. I'm a bookseller, and I'm serving as an author liaison." It sounded official even if it didn't have a thing to do with Mr. Kenneth Hazlitt's literary aspirations. "Could I have a flyer?"

"Sure. Come on up. Room 500."

Annie was halfway across the lobby when she remembered Emma. She scooted back to the alcove, found a pay phone, and dialed Emma's number. The answering machine picked up. Of course. But Annie knew damn well Broward's Rock's most famous author was in her office because Emma's routine was invariable—a half-hour walk on the beach in front of her palatial home, then three hours at her computer.

Neither war nor storms (excepting electrical failures) nor holidays nor celebrations nor illness (unless major surgery) varied Emma's writing schedule.

Annie enunciated loudly and clearly. "Emma, the Medallions are strictly on the up-and-up. I've got the word straight—"

Emma picked up her phone. "From whom?"

"Blue Benedict. She swears that Hazlitt guy had nothing to do with your selection. So you'll come, won't you?"

The silence was frosty—and thoughtful. Emma's voice was as cool and sharp as a dueling sword. "If that's true, it makes Kenneth's novel even more interesting."

And she hung up.

Annie glared at the phone. The public might adore dear Marigold Rembrandt (". . . America's sweetest and canniest sleuth," *The New York Times*. ". . . delights readers with her warmth and charisma," *Chicago Sun-Times*. ". . . won the hearts of readers from coast to coast," the *Los Angeles Times*), but her creator had about as much charm for Annie as the seven-foot alligator that lived in the pond behind Annie's home. Annie knew dangerous beasts when she saw them.

Annie slammed the receiver into its cradle, jolting her fingers. "Ouch."

All the way up in the elevator, Annie tried to figure it out. Why did it make Hazlitt's novel more interesting? Or was Emma being supercilious?

And did Annie really give a damn?

Well, yes. She was responsible for the care and feeding of the honorees and their mental well-being throughout the Festival. So, yes. But she didn't understand what Emma meant. . . .

The elevator doors opened, and Annie confronted her own image in a huge mirror with a gilt baroque frame.

She had that instant of surprise that always came when seeing her reflection. Sandy hair. Gray eyes. Slim, athletic figure.

Annie paused.

Laurel always urged Annie to relax, to imbibe more deeply from Life's Fountain of Joy.

Annie thought the message was clear. She frowned. Dammit, did she really look harried and intense?

She forced her shoulders to relax. Actually, she looked stylishly resortish, her smooth cotton top crisply white, her light blue chambray skirt long enough to swirl. Annie smoothed her hair and tried a casual smile. Okay.

The door to Room 500 opened immediately.

Annie looked into amused green eyes that widened with perceptible pleasure as they surveyed her.

"*Do* come in, said the lonely guy to the good-looking girl." His voice was a pleasant baritone, and he used it to matinee-idol perfection. He thrust out his hand. "Hi, I'm Willie Hazlitt, and my crystal ball tells me you're the author liaison who just called. I had no idea author liaisons were beautiful. What a delightful surprise."

Willie's hand was warm, his grin seductive.

Annie smiled, but with definite reserve. She knew all about the Willie Hazlitts of the world. Good-looking, charming, playful. And not to be trusted with either the household silver or a woman's reputation.

"Hello, Mr. Hazlitt. I appreciate your help." The room behind him was nice. Lots of white wicker and brightly striped pillows and a seashell motif in the sand-shaded wallpaper. If all the suites were this attractive, her authors should at least be pleased with their accommodations.

"Anything I can do, anything at all. And my name's Willie." He looked at her expectantly.

"Annie Darling. Now, this flyer—"

"Sure, sure, Annie." He led the way into the living area. "Let me take a look in these boxes."

Willie Hazlitt made it look easy to heft four big cartons onto a table near the wet bar. He was about six feet tall, with broad shoulders and muscular arms. He was also so spectacularly handsome— thick, smooth black hair, regular features, a smile that combined charm with a hint of wickedness— that not even his vivid sport shirt—emerald-beaked, crimson-feathered toucans against a bright fuschia background—could compete with his looks. And it would take a man inordinately confident of both his appearance and his masculinity to wear that particular shirt.

He kept up a nonstop chatter as he poked

through the boxes. ". . . more than you ever wanted to know about the fall list from Mint Julep Press: *Red Hot Tips from Hot Rod Hal, Blue Grass in My Old Kentucky Home, Press the Pedal to the Metal* —huh, now that sounds like fun, the memoirs of a long-haul trucker—*Sea Island Reverie*—oh, poems. I thought it might be a primer on how to have your very own little grass shack, which I could relate to, ma'am"—here he favored Annie with a bright, not too suggestive glance—"*Root Hog or Die,* which I do *not* relate to. Well, not this box, I guess. Let's see." He pushed the first box away, pulled the second one close. "Nope. This one's got party stuff in it, nuts— the house-brand peanuts from a discount store—you can count on Ken to cut corners wherever, oh yeah," Annie heard a remnant of a southern drawl, but she guessed Willie had spent some years elsewhere, "and paper plates, that kind of stuff. Now here's a box that's taped shut. That's special for the open house. Can't get into those yet. But I know there's a bunch of other flyers. Unless he's already taken them to the booth. He's really on a high about his book." A shrug. "My brother publishes books—I mean, we do. You'd think it would just be another day at the office. But no, Ken's beside himself."

Willie delved into the last box and, triumphantly, yanked up a stack of sheets so electrically pink that Annie blinked.

"Here we go." He handed one to Annie.

Annie took the sheet.

Annie took a deep breath. Oh, Lordy.

"Would you like extra copies?" Willie asked helpfully.

"Five."

Before pulling the brochures from the box, she saw him glance at her wedding ring.

Annie took the flyers. "Thanks so much."

"Oh, we've got hundreds. We'll have a stack of them here this afternoon at the cocktail party."

"Who's coming to the cocktail party?"

"Ken sent out invitations to booksellers. But you're definitely invited. Five o'clock. Here in the suite. And feel free, take some extra copies of the flyer."

Willie smiled happily, obviously unaware his offering was as welcome as the Bud Light truck at a Baptist church social.

Annie accepted another handful. Should she give flyers to her authors as they arrived? Or should she await a propitious moment?

She turned toward the door.

Willie didn't exactly block her way, but he was right there, an eager hand on her elbow. "How about a drink tonight?"

"I'm not sure," she replied vaguely, "but thanks."

"Anytime. Just give me a ring."

He leaned against the doorjamb and watched as she walked toward the elevators.

As Annie punched the button, she gave him a final, noncommittal smile. Willie probably preferred married women. She stepped into the elevator, the pink sheets in her hand, and wished that she had nothing else to do that day but fend off Willie's advances. That she could do. Duck soup. Instead, she had a horrid premonition that her Gang of Five might make mincemeat out of her. She opened her purse and absently dredged up a partially squashed mint.

No, stress didn't make her hungry, fill her mind with images of food.

Of course not.